PRAISE FOR WITHOUT GRACE

Searching, soulful... **Without Grace** is a heartfelt exploration of that small town in all of us, our bittersweet Place of Angels.

—Arthur Kent, journalist, documentary filmmaker, and author of Warlord Reborn

Like Scout Finch and Mattie Ross and Ellen Foster before her, Vicky, the young heroine of **Without Grace**, has grit and will and insight, a wry eye for the world around her, and a deeply engaging way of finding there a place of her own.

—Michael Malone, author of Handling Sin

Without Grace is not indeed without grace. Told through the consciousness of a young girl coming of age, it is a masterfully crafted tale of love, devotion, hope, and the search for personal identity. A monument to the power of the human spirit to make sense out of a mundane reality that can take fortuitously what it gives, this one will surely make you think compassionately about what really matters in life!

—Elliot D. Cohen, Ph.D., author of What would Aristotle do? Self-Control through the Power of Reason (Prometheus, 2003)

Without Grace is the story of a girl's search for her mother, a subject that cannot help but make the reader, and this reader, wonder what is going to happen next.

—Rona Jaffe, author of The Best of Everything

Without Grace *drew me in with its tale of the complicated threads that hold a family together and when cut can send them spinning apart. It's a beautiful story of how determination can stand up to almost anything and is the declaration of a gifted new writer in Carol Hoenig.*

—Martha Randolph Carr, author of *Wired* and *The Sitting Sisters*

*If you begin reading Carol Hoenig's **Without Grace** at the start of the work day, you might as well call and tell your boss that you are engaged in a work that transcends the day. A meal, it is as smooth as lobster bisque, a grand main course, and what a dessert! What more can we want in a book? Get it and plan to take the day off.*

—Malachy McCourt, author of A MONK SWIMMING

Without Grace *is a story of tragic loss and subsequent self discovery. Vicky Finley's tale is haunting and unforgettable, as Hoenig's narrative deftly draws us into the drama of her character's life.*

—Susan Shapiro Barash, author of
THE NEW WIFE: The Evolving Role of the American Wife

WITHOUT GRACE

WITHOUT GRACE

A Novel

Carol Hoenig

iUniverse Star
New York Lincoln Shanghai

WITHOUT GRACE

Copyright © 2005, 2006, 2007 by Carol Hoenig

All rights reserved. No part of this book may be used or reproduced by any means, graphic, electronic, or mechanical, including photocopying, recording, taping or by any information storage retrieval system without the written permission of the publisher except in the case of brief quotations embodied in critical articles and reviews.

iUniverse Star
an iUniverse, Inc. imprint

iUniverse books may be ordered through booksellers or by contacting:

iUniverse
2021 Pine Lake Road, Suite 100
Lincoln, NE 68512
www.iuniverse.com
1-800-Authors (1-800-288-4677)

This is a work of fiction. All of the characters, names, incidents, organizations, and dialogue in this novel are either the products of the author's imagination or are used fictitiously.

ISBN-13: 978-1-58348-036-6 (pbk)
ISBN-13: 978-0-595-81440-4 (ebk)
ISBN-10: 1-58348-036-6 (pbk)
ISBN-10: 0-595-81440-9 (ebk)

Printed in the United States of America

To Jason, Corrie and Natasha, all who know first hand what it's like to live with a writer.

Acknowledgment

If you encouraged my endeavors, if you support my passion, if you believed in my writing, then know that this heartfelt thank you is for you.

CHAPTER 1

❦

The first time I began to understand that the words *gone* and *dead* have different meanings I was about six years old. The year was 1961. It was a cold winter day in February, which wasn't unusual for Churubusco, a speck of a town in Upstate New York. I was immersed in making hearts out of construction paper along with the rest of the kindergarten class when Mr. Baxter, the elementary school principal, summoned Mrs. Gadway into the hallway. Mrs. Gadway had taught us at the very beginning of the school year that principal ended with the word "pal" and that we should always think of Mr. Baxter as our pal. But by the serious way he motioned for her, he seemed more a threat. We all stopped our cutting, gluing, and glittering and watched wide eyed. I wondered what kind of trouble kindly Mrs. Gadway could possibly have gotten into to be taken out in the hallway.

"Bet Brenda's in trouble," Mike said. "She's using crayons to color her fingernails."

My gaze went to Brenda Hannigan, the skinny little girl with a mess of frizzy red hair. She dropped the crayon, pulled a tissue from her pocket, spat on it, and began working furiously to wipe off the red crayon from her fingernails. She'd finished only three fingers when the door opened; however, it was my name spoken.

"May I see you out in the hallway?" Mrs. Gadway said.

I looked at Brenda before standing, hoping Mrs. Gadway would see the colored fingernails and change her mind about calling me out.

"Come on, Vicky."

My classmates watched in silence as I left the room. Mr. Baxter was nowhere in sight. In the hallway, Mrs. Gadway bent down to talk to me face to face. She brought me close to her. I could smell her breath and tried to back away, but she pulled me closer.

"Your daddy called the school, honey. He's coming to pick you and your brother up."

"Can I finish my Valentine?" It was a surprise for Kevin. I hadn't yet drawn the birds on it; glitter would be their feathers.

"I'll tell you what. Why don't you bring it home with you and you can finish it there? You see, your grandma is...is gone."

"Where'd she go?"

Before I even saw Kevin, I heard the thumping of his feet as he came running toward me. He was coming from the wing of the junior high school.

"No running in the halls, young man." Mrs. Gadway stood to show her authority.

"Don't tell her!" he yelled, wiping his drippy nose with the sleeve of his opened coat. "She's my sister. I'll tell her." He reached me and pulled me next to him.

"Where'd Grandma go?" I said.

Glaring at Mrs. Gadway, he said, "You told her?"

"This should be handled by an adult."

"I'm her brother."

"Do not raise your voice with me, Kevin Finley."

I watched the power struggle, knowing I had something to do with it.

"Vicky," she said, "why don't you go get your things?"

"Yeah, Dad's on his way," Kevin said. "I'll help you."

Amid whispers, I gathered my things, eyeing the bottle of glitter. Kevin collected my papers, scooping up the Valentine and putting it in my schoolbag. So much for surprises.

"Got your lunchbox?" he said, helping me slip on my boots, coat, hat and gloves.

I nodded.

"You have to go to the main office to wait for your father," Mrs. Gadway said. She bent down again and took my face in her hands, gazing into my eyes. "Honey, I'm so sorry. Okay?"

Another nod, but I wasn't sure why she was apologizing. When I shuffled by Brenda, I saw that she had repainted her fingernails fire-engine red.

Daddy said very little in the car as I sat alone in the back seat. Kevin asked how Grandpa was doing.

"Shell shocked."

I didn't know what that meant.

I called up to the front, "Is she coming back?"

No one answered, so I asked again. Kevin turned and looked at me. I see that his eyes are filled with tears. "No, she's not."

I suddenly had worries: Who was going to put out my clothes in the morning? Who was going to run a comb through my hair to search for knots? Who was going to tell me to brush my teeth?

These had become big concerns the night before I was to start the first day of school. Until then, I had selected my own pants and shirt for days filled with playing with paper dolls, watching cartoons, and swinging on the tire hanging from the maple tree in the front yard. As for the brushing of my hair and teeth, I accomplished both with little effort and no follow up from Grandma. Kindergarten was to change all that.

The night before I was to start school, Grandma came into my bedroom with a bag from Woolworths and took out a couple of dresses, one plain, the other frilly—three pairs of pants—all the same style but in different colors—and three matching polo shirts. Striped. I hated stripes. She then took out a package of white underpants and put them in my drawer, except for one pair, which she placed on the end of my bed along with the frilly dress.

"Now, these are your school clothes," she said. "I won't have you looking like little Orphan Annie to give people more to talk about. Come on, let's get you in the tub."

Kindergarten also meant cleanliness, I soon realized. Grandma scrubbed my neck and behind my ears, the skin on her arms wobbly, her sagging breasts grazing my face. "I'm too old for this," she muttered.

Wincing, I said, "I don't wanna go to school."

"Well, it's not about what little girls want." Grandma rinsed the washcloth and handed it to me. "Wash good down there." She pointed to the gap between my legs.

Long after she had sent me to bed, I tiptoed into Kevin's room. He was propped on his elbow, an opened book lying next to him.

"What's wrong?" he said.

"I don't wanna go to school."

"Sure you do. You'll have fun. We'll be on the bus together."

"I hate that dress."

He scrunched up his mouth. "Grandma's pretty much got her heart set on it."

"Are you scared?"

"Nah," he said, "but seventh grade's gonna be a lot harder."

Just then, Grandma yelled from the bottom of the stairs, "What's that chattering I hear? Vicky, go to bed."

Kevin called back, "She's just worried, Grandma. I'm talking to her for a minute."

To no one in particular and loud enough to be heard, she said, "If your mother was here then maybe she could deal with this nonsense. I go out and buy her daughter clothes—"

Kevin got up and shut his door. He rolled his eyes and went back to his bed. He patted it and said, "You can sleep in here tonight." He took one of his pillows then pulled a sleeping bag from under the bed and shook it out. "I'll sleep down here."

I crawled under the covers. The only other time Kevin had ever let me sleep in his bed was during a thunderstorm. Was school as scary as repeated streaks of lightning cutting through a blackened sky, followed by wall-shaking claps of thunder?

"I hope my teacher's nice," I mumbled. Kevin didn't answer, and I looked over the side of the bed to see that he was deep into his book. "I can't wait to read."

He glanced up at me. "Want me to read it out loud?"

"Not too loud, so Grandma won't get mad."

He smiled and then began, and before I knew it, he was waking me up for school the following morning. Soon, Kevin and I were waiting in front of the house. The bus eventually turned the corner. I used to watch from the porch window as it pulled up to our farmhouse and took my brother away for the day, then wait endless hours until it brought him back. Now it was my turn to be carried into that same world.

The bus came to a squawking stop and gave a loud sigh, the doors opening. Kevin helped me up the steps and guided me to a seat. He sat beside me. I noticed there were other boys his age who shot him sidelong glances and snickered. He didn't seem to notice. I also noticed a scattering of redheads in various sizes. I tugged on Kevin's sleeve.

"What's wrong with their hair?" I whispered, never having seen so much shocking red hair on a single head before. And now there were several in my midst alone.

"They're the Hannigans," he said. "They live in that big farmhouse off Whalen Road."

I nodded, having little idea where Whalen Road was. Peering at me over the seat was the smallest of the Hannigans. We stared at each other without speaking, and later that morning I found we were in the same classroom.

My fears about Mrs. Gadway were put to rest immediately after I met her. She told me my dress was very pretty but that she would send a note home to my mother telling her I should come to school in play clothes.

"I don't have a mother," I said, causing a couple of the children to look at me as if I had said something in a different language.

"Well, then, I'll send the note to your father. You do have a father, don't you?"

I nodded.

School wasn't so bad, and it had the biggest playground I'd ever seen. I was eager to climb the monkey bars, but when I did, swinging upside down, my dress went over my head, causing all the kids to tease me. Brenda started the commotion by singing, "I see London, I see France, I see Vicky's underpants."

Grandma read the note. It was the first thing I handed her from my school-bag, even though Mrs. Gadway had told me to give it to my father. She breathed hard and tossed the note in the garbage. "So, besides being told how to dress, what else did you learn today?"

I stared at the crumpled letter resting on top of the garbage, wondering how I could get it without Grandma seeing me. "I learned a new song."

"Really?" she said, pouring water in a pan then carrying it to the stove, indicating it was going to be macaroni-and-cheese night. "Let's hear it then."

"Five little monkeys jumpin' on the bed. One fell off and bumped his head. Mommy called the doctor and the doctor said, 'No more monkeys jumpin' on the bed.'"

I was about to go to four little monkeys, but Grandma stopped me. "*Mommy* calls the doctor, my eye. Where was Mommy when you needed your diaper changed? Where was Mommy when you needed your nose wiped? Where was Mommy when you'd wake up in the middle of the night cryin' hysterical from a bad dream?" She pulled a box of elbow macaroni from the cabinet, going on about how her son should have never married *that* girl. "You tell Mrs. Gadway your mommy is gone."

Like Kevin had done the night before, I shut her off by slipping away to the living room, where I turned on the television and watched Batman and Robin fight evil. Later, when she was drying me from my bath that night, she started singing the song, except she sang, "*Grandma* called the doctor."

Apparently, when my grandmother keeled over on that cold February day and the ambulance arrived, it was too late to call any doctor. By this time, I'd adjusted to kindergarten. Now I had to adjust being in a household down to four little monkeys.

Turns out Grandma wasn't gone at all. There she was lying in that strange but comfortable-looking box. Kevin held my hand and walked me up to it, instructing me to kneel next to her. Kevin knows things about religion, so I followed his lead as he made the sign of the cross. Under my breath, I said, "One, two, three, four" then bowed my head. I pretended to pray but didn't know what to say. Besides, I kept trying to see if her eyes were going to open. I looked over my shoulder to see if anyone was watching and saw Dad standing in a corner with a small gathering of people. He motioned for me to come to him, and I did. He lifted me, cradling me in his arms. "We'll be okay," he said, not once but several times. I looked around the room and spotted Grandpa sitting in the front row. I hardly recognized him in his suit.

"Grandpa's sad," I said.

"Why don't you go make him smile," Dad said, putting me back on my feet.

I went to Grandpa and rested my hand on his knee. He looked down at me and without any effort on my part, gave me a crinkly-faced smile.

"There's my angel," he said, taking off his glasses and wiping the lenses. He pulled me up onto his lap and I stayed there, resting against his sunken chest while groups of people came in, their voices hushed as they told us how sorry they were. Grandpa kept a tight grip on me while saying, "Never got to tell her goodbye." My father remained standing in the corner, shaking hands and talking to each person who went to him. Kevin kept looking at the doorway every few minutes, as if he expected someone important to walk in.

Most people who came in I didn't recognize, until the flock of redheads appeared. Brenda Hannigan was steered in my direction by her robust-looking mother, then prodded to speak.

"Sorry your grandma died," Brenda said.

"That's okay," I said, noticing a hint of red in her cuticles.

We both began to giggle, though I wasn't sure why. Mrs. Hannigan expressed her condolences to Grandpa then led Brenda away. Two of the Hannigan boys were scuffling their feet and fidgeting with their suits as they stood near Kevin, but his eyes kept darting toward the doorway.

At the cemetery, the priest said some prayers, tossed some water on the closed box, and then left us to say our goodbyes. Grandma was gone. *Gone.* This was how my mother's disappearance had been explained to me. I began noticing the many gravestones surrounding us. Kevin said that Grandma would also have one soon.

"See," he said, pointing to one nearby. "It's going to have her name on it, just like"—he crouched down to get a better look. "—like Ross Soucia."

I went next to him and reached out, touching the letters. "What does this say?"

"He was born on July 6, 1908, and he died on November 19, 1952."

'Oh," I said, reminded of the prayer all the old people had said during mass. Something about beginnings and ends. It got me to thinking, and I said, "Where's Mommy's stone?"

It was a question that turned Grandpa and my father's red, moist eyes in my direction. Kevin cleared his throat, stood, and walked back over to Grandma's box.

"What you talkin' about?" my father said.

"Where's Mommy's stone?" I stood tall, realizing it was probably the first time I had asked a question about the woman I couldn't testify actually having existed. There was no memory of her for me.

"We're here for Grandma," my father said. "She's the one we're mourning."

Instead of standing in the cold any longer, my father walked over to me and grabbed my hand to lead me out of the cemetery. We trudged through the few inches of snow toward the car, no one speaking.

I climbed into the back seat along with Kevin and scrambled up to my knees so I could gaze out the back window as we drove away. I began to think about this woman, wondering what she'd looked like. Then I began to miss her, to miss a woman I had never known, more than I missed my grandmother.

CHAPTER 2

The relatives, most of whom I'd never seen before and would never see again, left to go back to the daily routine of their lives. The only thing they left behind was their stale smell or the overwhelming aroma of the cheap perfume they used to cover up their staleness. Grandma was still around, as far as I was concerned. I'd make sure not to run down the stairs in fear of her shouting at me to "quiet down." I'd keep the volume on the television low so not to disturb her. It didn't matter what she was doing; I always managed to disturb her. The freezer was filled with home-baked bread that I'd watched her knead. Her dirty handkerchiefs were still balled up and stuck between the cushions of the couch. Yes, Grandma was still very present.

It was my mother whom I needed to know about.

When he wasn't too tired from working all day and seemed to be willing to talk to me, I'd ask my father about her, but all he'd say was that she was gone.

"Did she die like grandma?" I'd ask.

"Vicky," he'd say, warning me with his tone, "that's enough. She's gone, and you'll be better off if you just forget about her."

I wanted to ask Grandpa, but he was having a hard time forgetting about Grandma. All he seemed to do anymore was shuffle a little slower while getting ready to go out to the barn, his cheerful whistling stifled. When he ate his supper, he would chew his food the same way a cow chewed its cud, leaving me to wonder if he was ever going to swallow. Kevin said that he was still sad Grandma was dead and that I should be sad, too.

I wasn't sad, though, about Grandma. I didn't have time, because my thoughts were always on the woman no one wanted to talk about. Even Kevin, who had always liked teaching me things, whispered that we weren't allowed to talk about her, which made me all the more curious.

"Maybe she was a witch," Brenda said, sitting across from me at lunch time, chomping on her peanut butter sandwich. I was attempting to eat a ham sandwich, the ham so thick I could barely sink my teeth into it. My father would make the sandwiches for all of us the night before, and I suppose the men found them easy to swallow, but I was forced to clamp down on the sandwich, the bread and meat too much for my small mouth and baby teeth, until I had to give up.

"Or maybe she had cancer. *My* grandma died of cancer," Brenda said.

I smashed the sandwich in my napkin, leaving it on my tray. "Maybe," I said, resting my chin in my cupped hands. Everybody I knew had a mother. Except me.

Mrs. Gadway had told us that it was the first day of spring. We made pictures of flowers and trees replenished with vibrant green leaves. The school bus was filled with chatter, which Brenda and I added to by singing "I've Been Working on the Railroad" until the bus came to a stop. I watched the entire lot of redheads climb down the steps, greeted by Mrs. Hannigan. She ruffled Brenda's brother's hair as they all made their way up the long driveway toward the farmhouse. The bus door closed and we roared away. Kevin had to stay after school for an FFA meeting—whatever that was—so I was left alone with my thoughts.

The bus was still abuzz with chatter, but I gazed out the window as we rolled along. Each day I waited and watched until we came up to where the cemetery was. The bus would stop at the corner and let some kids off, giving me time to try to see the gravestones, time to will my mother's spirit to show itself somehow. So, when the bus approached the cemetery, and having no brother to stop me, I simply followed the kids down the steps. I didn't look back at the driver, hoping he wouldn't spy me. The kids crossed to the other side of the road and I ran away from the direction the bus was heading as it rumbled away. I stood there for a moment, swallowing hard, and then raced into the midst of the gravestones, not knowing at all what I was looking for.

I dragged my schoolbag along the damp ground and passed the headstones one by one. Each day, when we passed the cemetery, I would ask Kevin if Grandma's stone was there yet, and each day he would say it wasn't. But then I began to remember what other kids on the bus would say about ghosts coming up out of the ground at night, and I stood frozen. Everything had an eerie stillness to it. I began to feel more alone than I could recall. Just then, I wanted my mother more than I ever had before. I would have even settled for my cranky grandmother.

I began to cry. Then I slumped down onto the ground, immediately feeling the dampness seep in through my corduroy pants, and cried some more.

When I opened my eyes, the sun had disappeared. The statues and stones loomed large all around me. Out on the road, two cars and a truck thundered by. I stood there shivering uncontrollably. I wanted to be home, but knew I wasn't allowed to go near the road. Headlights came from where I should have been going all those hours ago, and more headlights came from where I'd been. The cars slowed then came to a stop. I heard voices shouting back to each other.

"A pink jacket and red lunchbox," yelled one of the voices.

My lunchbox was red and tucked safely in my schoolbag. I huddled in my pink jacket.

"Damn bus driver says he has no idea where she got off!"

Just then, I saw flashing lights approach and realized it was a policeman. He pulled up behind the car, stopping directly in front of the cemetery. He got out of his car, the lights still flashing. He walked over and stood between the two stopped cars. I couldn't hear what he said, but I realized that I might be in trouble and would go to jail. I began to bawl.

An hour or so later, I was in my flannel pajamas and eating chicken-noodle soup while my father held me on his lap, rocking me back and forth, swiping tears from his eyes. My escapade had not only gotten me some harsh words, but, more importantly, it had gotten me information I could hardly believe: my mother wasn't gone the same way Grandma was. She wasn't in a box, buried deep in the ground, but was out in the world somewhere. Just where, no one knew for sure, but she was breathing and walking.

My father told me all this because he wanted me to finally stop my foolishness. He figured my curiosity would at last be satisfied. However, I now understood why Kevin kept staring at that doorway in the funeral home: He was waiting for her return, something I would learn to do.

CHAPTER 3

❦

Her name was Grace Finley. *Is* Grace Finley. Kevin told me on the night that I caused mayhem, having let me sleep in his bed again without the excuse of school jitters or threatening thunderstorms.

"Grace Finley," I whispered. "That's a pretty name." I leaned over the side of Kevin's bed and looked down at him.

"She was pretty. Beautiful." Kevin was tucked in his sleeping bag, lying on his back, his arms akimbo under his head. There was a faraway look in his eyes. "She made Dad cry."

"She did?" I'd only seen my father cry real tears once, which had been on the night when the policeman brought me back home. He'd snatched me out of the officer's arms and hugged me so tight that I thought my breath was being stolen. Grandma always boasted that her son had been a state champion wrestler in high school, and I could still feel the strength in his arms.

"Yup. When she left."

It was the last memory Kevin had of our mother. It was one filled with silence. He didn't recall any fights between Mom and Dad; there was no screaming, no tossing of dishes or hand against flesh. She had brushed her lips against Kevin's forehead, one hand gripping a suitcase, the other her guitar case. Dad was in the garage tinkering with some old jalopy, a part-time hobby then that now filled his empty hours.

Kevin's voice cracked as he went on, "I begged her to stay, yelled at Dad to make her stay. But he said…he said he couldn't, something about how you can't stop someone from wanting to chase their dream. He was under the hood of the car, pretending to be fixing a gasket or something, but I could see his shoulders shaking, his hand brushing tears off his face."

"Where was I?"

Kevin shrugged. "Probably in your crib, I guess."

"Did she kiss me, too?" I touched my forehead, wanting to feel the moistness of a mother's lips.

"I don't know. You were probably asleep."

"What did Grandma do?"

"Grandma and Grandpa were still living in the little house."

I'd been in the little house a few times. It was on the other side of the field, visible from our kitchen window. Grandma would take me for a walk there on occasion to get something else from what had been her home to bring back to our house and make it a permanent fixture. Soon, she and Grandpa were permanent fixtures.

Kevin turned off the light.

"You're not gonna read?"

His "no" came out sniffly, and I didn't ask any more questions. Not that night, anyway.

I began to think that maybe Mrs. Gadway was Grace Finley in disguise. I'd study her for any telltale signs and would hint at the possibility to see her reaction. I'd tell her how Kevin and I needed a mother. She'd smile and pull me into her and tell me maybe someday my mother would come back. Okay, so Mrs. Gadway was not my mother. Besides, my mother's breath would smell like cotton candy.

With Grandma gone, the house began to become cluttered, suppers nothing more than a slapdash sandwich. My father's boss tried to help by giving us a puppy that was some mix of collie and retriever and a dash of every other breed. He said it would take our minds off "things." We named the mutt Conroy and before long it was as if he'd always been around. As nice as it was to have a companion, it didn't change the fact that our house was rarely cleaned and our meals consisted of nothing more than bologna and cheese on bread, no longer home baked but store bought.

Eventually, the Rosary Society voted to help our family get through the next few months. I thought of the ladies as the "good deed society," because each week they came to give the house a good cleaning and to do a load of laundry. It didn't matter if it was Mrs. Humphrey, Mrs. LeClair, Mrs. Hannigan, or Miss Smith; I would always let them know that soon enough they would not have to bring food or clean the house, because my Mommy would be coming back.

"Oh, I don't think so," Evelyn Smith said, looking at her reflection in the mirror over the kitchen sink. She didn't seem happy with what she surveyed and pulled a tube of Avon lipstick from her pocketbook. I knew it was Avon, because that's what she had tried to sell to Grandma. Grandma always waved Miss Smith away, telling her she looked like a clown with all that junk on her face.

"Your Mommy left a long time ago, honey," Miss Smith said. "She would've come back by now." After her lips were a bright red, she dropped the tube in her pocketbook and snapped it shut. "Now, what's your daddy's favorite meal?"

I shrugged.

"He will be home for supper, right?"

Another shrug.

She sighed. "Well, I guess I'll stick to my specialty."

Before long, while meatloaf was baking, Miss Smith dusted and vacuumed, paying particular attention to my father's bedroom and little attention to the rest of the house. When he didn't show up for supper that night and Miss Smith found out from Grandpa that Daddy rarely came home before nine o'clock, she sputtered, gathered her things, and dashed out the door without saying goodbye.

I was young but still smart enough to tell Miss Smith's opinion about my mother's return was more from her own intended agenda and less on any actual fact.

"My Mommy's coming back," I announced yet again.

"Is that right?" Mrs. Humphrey would say, her expression doubtful, as she pinned wet laundry to the clothesline.

"Yup," I said with certainty. "I wrote her a letter." It was springtime, a season of new beginnings, a season of worn-out sheets flapping in the wind.

"Where'd you send it?" Now it was Mrs. LeClair who gave me a dubious response while placing a pot of chicken stew to simmer on the stove.

"To Grace Finley. That's her name. And I put a lot of stamps on it, in case she's far away." I wasn't very good at spelling yet, but I knew I had spelled her name correctly because Kevin had showed me how. Kevin would then take the letter to the mailbox as I watched from the living room window. He'd look back at me and wave as he'd open up the mailbox and raise the flag.

When I shared this with Mrs. Hannigan, she gazed down on me with her powerful blue eyes and said, "Well, till then, we'll help out as best we can. Now, why don't you and Brenda go out and play?" Then she turned on the vacuum.

Mrs. Hannigan came on Saturdays and always brought Brenda along.

"Your Mommy's never coming back," Brenda said, swinging on the tire hanging from the maple tree in the front yard.

"Yes she is!" I shouted.

"No. My mommy said she's selfish."

"She's not." I was less vehement this time.

"Yes, the Hannigans are psychics and we know stuff."

I didn't know what a psychic was, but it sounded important. I decided to change the subject. "Want to play dress up?" I said, while thinking I would ask Kevin later if what she had said was true.

As the months passed, the casseroles and pot roasts began to become less and less. It never occurred to me that while the household chores were being taken care of, so was I, and that whatever lady was helping wouldn't leave until one of the Finley men came home. More and more, Kevin was left to keep me under his charge.

In the early mornings, while he was helping Grandpa milk the cows, I'd be safe asleep in bed, but in the late afternoons my doings were of more concern. Kevin had it figured out, though.

He'd turn on *Tom and Jerry* or *Lassie*, depending on the reception we got from the black-and-white television, place a plate with three cookies and a glass of milk on the rickety end table, and instruct Conroy to sit at my feet.

I discovered I'd had more freedom before, when I was being watched by one of the ladies—even Miss Smith, who always pumped me for information about my father. "Why can't the ladies come here anymore?" I asked one day.

"They're helping out the Ryans now," Kevin said. "Mrs. Ryan is very sick, and she has all those kids who need help."

"Can I play with Brenda again?"

"Yes, but not today. Now, what do you do if you need me?" he said.

"Put a flashlight in the window."

"Which window?"

I sighed. "The garage window, so you can see it from the barn."

Satisfied, he'd race to the barn to join Grandpa in the evening routine of milking the thirty or so cows we had.

This went on for some time, until one day I got tired of *Lassie*—believing Conroy could do everything the collie did, perhaps more—and decided to turn the channels. I climbed off the couch, went to the TV, and turned the dial. Two boring men appeared on the screen talking about something equally boring.

Another click and there were teenagers dancing to a song about someone named Bernadette. Conroy looked up at me with what I took to be impatience, so I gave the dial another turn. A woman standing in a kitchen was preparing a meal.

"A good meal is what draws a family to the table," the woman said, her voice sounding both shrill and strange.

That made perfect sense to me, and I went back to the couch to watch. Since the ladies weren't cooking for us anymore, the Finleys were not sitting down at the table together as much. We were back to slapdash sandwiches and canned soups. Well, I'd watched the ladies bake enough cakes and prepare enough stews to know how to do the same, and I decided I'd have a surprise for my family that night. Off to the kitchen I went.

"What…are…you…doing?" Kevin said, walking into the kitchen. His mouth was dropped open as he surveyed the five eggs and bit of eggshell, along with a bag each of sugar and flour, poured into the largest mixing bowl I could find.

"I'm cooking supper." I pointed to the plate with the variety of cheeses, fanned out and garnished with salt and paprika, a dish of which I was particularly proud. Conroy didn't budge from my feet, waiting for whatever morsel fell to the floor.

"What's that smell?" Kevin whirled around and ran to the oven just as smoke began roiling out. When he opened the door, plastic, mixed with eggs and cheese, was dripping off the racks. "Vicky, you know you're not supposed to touch the stove!"

He snapped the oven off and opened the kitchen door, attempting to wave out the offensive smoke and fumes. Conroy took the opportunity and ran outside.

"I wanted to surprise you."

"I told you to stay put." His face was deep red. "Why didn't you listen?"

I realized then that I might have done something wrong. Low and meek, I said, "But I was cooking supper."

Just then, Dad walked in, carrying his lunch pail and wearing a look of exhaustion. Most days he did double shifts, but this day he came home early. His expression changed when he saw both the kitchen and me covered in flour. "What the hell…?"

His voice suddenly soft, Kevin said, "She was just trying to help, Dad. She didn't know better." He took the mixing bowl and dumped what was to be supper in the garbage.

Dad's face was scrunched up and he began choking, his eyes tearing. "Christ, she could've burned this place down."

"She could've hurt herself," Kevin stressed.

Dad set his lunch pail on the kitchen table and came over to me. He began squeezing my arms, shaking me. "Vicky, what were you thinking?"

"I can cook," I said, my bottom lip quivering. "I'm almost eight years old."

He dropped onto one of the chairs. "We can't live like this," he said. "It's too much for everybody."

Kevin began to panic. "It's okay, Dad. I'll come in and check up on her more often. We're going to make it work."

Later, when Grandpa was in the house, there was some sort of powwow. I remained on the sidelines but within earshot.

"The farm's been in this family for years, Dad," Kevin said. "How can you just want to give it up?"

It wasn't the first time I'd overheard a conversation about how difficult it was to run the farm, but I wasn't sure what it had to do with me.

"I don't just want to give it up," Dad said, "but sometimes you have to know when enough is enough."

I peeked around the corner from the hallway to get a better look. Grandpa's hands were resting on his lap, his fingers curled involuntarily. Dad looked defeated and Kevin worried.

"They offered me the supervisor position," Dad said. "That'll be extra income. We keep a few cows for ourselves and sell the hay, we'll be better off 'en before. Besides, we nearly lost everything tonight."

They all glanced in my direction, and I backed up just far enough that I could hear without being seen.

"Why?" Kevin's voice began to shake. "Why you doing this? If you sell, she'll win. You want her to win?"

I was sure he meant me, but I wasn't sure what I might win.

Dad's tone was sharp, suppressing. "You don't know what the hell you're talkin' about. It has nothing to do with that." There was a long pause, and then he said, "Can't do much about anything right now, anyway. Just don't know what we'll do with your sister."

"I'll bring her out to the barn with me," Kevin said.

"The barn's no place for Vicky," Grandpa said.

I reappeared. "I'll go."

"Just give it some time," Kevin said. "Let me prove I can do it."

So, after that, I was taken out to the barn and instructed to stick close to Kevin while he hooked milk machines to the cows' teats, cleaned the gutters, and pitched hay. I'd be given jobs, like putting feed in the trough and opening the stanchions when it was time to let the cows out to graze. While going from one chore to the next, Kevin would regale me with stories about how someday he was going to have a barn twice as big, with a hundred or so cows. "And horses," he said. "What's a farm without horses?"

The Finley farm used to have horses, until Grandpa felt he could no longer care for them. Kevin never liked me to see him cry, but he had failed when Molly and Flossy had been sold.

The smell of burnt plastic finally faded from the kitchen, but my desire to cook hadn't diminished. I didn't dare bring it up to Kevin, even though I'd sit and scour over an old Betty Crocker cookbook that had been Grandma's while Kevin read *Your Farming Community*, a book he'd checked out of the school library. He was now in ninth grade, but instead of playing hockey on Benny's Lake with the Hannigans and other boys, who chatted on and on about their victories and losses each day on the bus, he sat at home taking notes about raising prize-winning cattle.

One afternoon, I cleared my throat and said, "What did Mom like to cook?"

He shrugged, keeping his eyes on the opened page.

"You don't remember?"

He shut his book and said, "Any recipes for chocolate cake in there?"

I sat at the other end of the kitchen table, letting the question go unanswered for a moment. I then looked up and nodded, scrambling to find the page. Before I knew it, he had me stirring and adding measured ingredients while he turned the oven on, then off once the cake was done. While the cake cooled, we whipped up frosting. When I presented it to the Finley men that night, I gazed, watching as the men ate something that I'd baked, Dad asking for seconds and licking the crumbs off his plate.

Later, I carried the cookbook off to bed with me and circled pictures of sumptuous lemon meringue pie and rack of lamb.

One season rolled into the next, and finally, once I turned ten, I was trusted to be on my own for short periods of time. Sometimes I would tag along with Grandpa and Kevin while they went out in the fields to hay, but often I would lag behind, causing Kevin to break his rhythm while tossing the bales on the wagon as he prodded me along. So most days I stayed at the house or went to play with Brenda at her house. Those days were my favorites, running around with the gaggle of redheads, all cheering and laughing, sharing secrets that no adult should hear, but I was always anxious to get home to see what had come in the mail.

There was no longer any rule forbidding me to go to the end of the driveway to get the mail, so on the days I stayed home I'd sit on the front steps waiting for the familiar mail truck. So far, I hadn't gotten any replies, but I didn't stop writing letters, covering the envelopes with hearts and kisses, thinking that would certainly get her attention. Each time I put another letter in the mailbox, I hoped it would be the one. I imagined what my mother's response would be and how Kevin would read it to me and how we'd in turn read it to Dad, who would forgive her and he'd call her up using the phone number she'd given in the letter and he'd beg her to come home.

And she would.

So, when an unopened letter I'd sent to her floated free from flyers and other mail that was useless to me, I slumped to the floor and cried. When I first began writing her, I barely knew how to read; now the words stamped on the envelope were very clear: Address Unknown.

I cried for a while then remembered the box that Brenda and I had found shoved all the way in the back of the upstairs hall closet. At the time, we had thought they were just old photos, when what we were really looking for were clothes to play dress up in. Taking a flashlight with me, I went upstairs to that closet.

"Do you have any idea how long I've been looking for you?" Kevin was standing outside the closet, peering in. "If I hadn't seen the shine of the flashlight, I'd still be looking!" True, he was going through adolescence, but his voice sounded as though it had become hoarse from screaming. I sat up, rubbing my eyes, sleep having caught me unaware.

He climbed over stockpiled boxes, some old coats, and an inoperable Electrolux to reach me. "What're you doing?"

Pictures were scattered all around me. I showed Kevin the box I'd discovered. It was filled with old black-and-white photos. I shined the flashlight on them for him. He settled down next to me. "Anything interesting?"

"I was looking for pictures of her." I'd trained the flashlight on each photograph, searching for her, hoping that if she wasn't in the foreground, she would at least be somewhere in the background.

"There aren't any. Grandma threw them out."

"I just want to see what she looks like."

"Come on," he said, tugging me from the pile of coats and boxes into the light of the hallway, so bright it hurt my eyes. He led me to his room, closed the door, and locked it. He pressed his finger to his lips, and I stood very still, watching him. With a grunt, he lifted his mattress and pulled out a marble notebook. He patted his bed, instructing me to sit beside him. He flipped the notebook open to the middle and gingerly slipped out a three-by-five Polaroid, holding it for me. The image took my breath away. Sitting on a stone wall, with the spray of waterfalls in the background, was the most beautiful woman I had ever seen. She was wearing a pair of red slacks and a white sleeveless turtleneck, her breasts filling it out. Her legs were crossed at the ankle, her head tossed slightly back, as if she'd been caught laughing—a wonderful way to be trapped in time.

Finally, when I was able to speak, I whispered in awe, "It's her?"

He nodded.

"Why didn't you show me before?"

He shrugged. "I was hoping you'd just forget about her."

"Where'd you get it?"

"When Grandma was throwing out pictures, I hid it from her."

"There's no more?"

He shook his head. "This is it."

"I hate Grandma."

"Vicky."

"Well, I do. Maybe she's the one who made Mommy leave."

"Grandpa says she was antsy."

"Mrs. Hannigan says Mommy is selfish," I said.

"Mrs. Hannigan is a nosy body."

I looked at the photo again. The woman was too pretty to be selfish. I wasn't too sure what the word meant, anyway, but I knew it was something a mother shouldn't be.

"You can come in and look at it whenever you want to, but you have to hold it by the sides, okay?"

"Can we take turns? I mean, keeping it under our beds."

He didn't answer right away, and it wasn't until I promised to be very careful with it that he said, "Okay, but you have to be *very* careful with it."

"Tell me again about when she left. How she kissed you up there." I touched his forehead.

He repeated the story, but then added a new detail. "I remember now," he said. "She did go into your room—I was watching her—and she kissed you right there." He touched my left cheek.

Gasping, I said, "Really?"

After some hesitation, he said, "Really."

That night I fell asleep with the photograph under my mattress, slipped between the pages of my *Curious George* book. I got up several times to check on it before I drifted off.

CHAPTER 4

❀

Each spring meant me trailing along with Kevin through the woods, buds overhead just beginning to sprout. I wouldn't have noticed those buds if Kevin hadn't pointed them out to me. We'd gotten through another winter, one that had kept us inside, protected from the cold and ice. Now, we had buckets swinging at our sides, spigots for the maple trees to tap for syrup, and our camaraderie. While the conversation took many dips and turns, Kevin would stop and plug the spout into the maple tree and I'd hand him the bucket to catch the sap. Not that it poured out right away or anything, but I'd be there. Once we were finished, it was a sure bet that Kevin would want to linger beneath a blue sky where the air smelled of new growth. Sure enough, we wended our way back to where the boulder jutted out of Benny's Lake and climbed atop it. We gazed up at the Great White Pine, tall above other pines, maples, and spruce, which would be grand in their own right if they weren't in the shadow of such gigantic splendor, and sprawled on the boulder. Eventually, our thoughts were given a voice.

"Can you imagine anyone ever wanting to leave this place?" Kevin said to me.

I shrugged and picked up a stick. I leaned over and began swirling it in the water, watching the ripples go wider and wider. "Brenda hates it here."

He expelled a sound of disbelief. "What about you?"

"I like it." Of course, I had nothing to compare it to, and I did plan to leave someday to go looking for her.

"Can you keep a secret?" he said.

I sat up, hoping for some wonderful news.

"I've seen Benny."

My shoulders slumped. "Who's Benny?"

"This is his lake, Vicky."

"Oh, yeah. I forgot. Where does he live?"

"He doesn't. He died a long, long time ago."

I studied him.

"It's weird," he said. "I just know it's him. Sometimes he's standing by the Great White Pine."

"You see a ghost?"

"I never think of him as a ghost. Just Benny."

"You're scarin' me, Kevin." I looked over where the tree stood, not knowing what I would do if I saw a ghost. "What does he say?"

"Nothing. Everything."

That first day of kindergarten, when we were taking the bus home, I had heard the kids call Kevin a nerd. He'd acted as though it didn't bother him and simply opened up a book and read. He didn't just pretend to read, but he actually devoured the words, lost in another world. Brenda calls him weird.

Nerd. Weird. Kevin was my brother, and I defended him against each disparaging remark, but I wasn't sure whether I could believe in phantoms who showed themselves when mothers did not.

"I wonder why she really left," I said. It was how I had to discuss my mother: a question here, another there, one that longed for another piece of the puzzle.

"She said she needed to breathe," Kevin said, sliding off the boulder.

"Was she sick?" I said, following him, feeling my heart pound with the thought. His stride was long and resolute, and I knew Kevin was finished talking about her, at least for the time being.

Time did not stop when Grandma died. Grandpa began to get back to himself, even whistling through his chores. Dad kept up his routine of working at the cheese plant then tinkering with broken-down vehicles at night. And Kevin and I did what we were expected to do.

The following spring, after Kevin had shot up a foot or so and after our ritual of tapping for syrup, we forfeited spending time on the boulder and gazing at the Great White Pine to wander over to Mr. Miller's. I didn't want to go with him, but Kevin was intent on asking our neighbor about a rumor he'd heard and I was at Kevin's mercy, having to trail along. On our way, I talked about a maple sugar candy recipe I wanted to try. I'd found it while leafing through a new cookbook I'd gotten my hands on. While Brenda would leaf through *Seventeen, Glamour,* and other fashion magazines, I would search for new recipes anywhere I could get them. Brenda circled makeup tips and I prepared grocery lists. So, while Kevin and I swished through tall grass to get to Mr. Miller's, I talked about the tricky process of making the candy.

"First, I'll have to boil the sap down, of course," I said. "And I'll keep a close watch on the stove."

"Hmm," Kevin said, walking with purpose.

"I was thinking maybe I could sell it for the bake sale at school." Mr. Miller's barn came into view and Kevin's quick strides forced me into a run.

There was a John Deere tractor sitting idle in the barnyard, and a dog ran out to greet us with a ferocious bark. I stayed behind Kevin for protection, but he kept his pace and held out his palm for the dog. The barks evolved into sniffs.

"Kevin." Mr. Miller thumped down the steps to his rickety front porch, his rotund belly hanging over his worn-out jeans. He nodded, barely acknowledging me. "What's going on?"

"Heard a rumor, Mr. Miller," Kevin said.

"That so?"

"You're thinking of selling this place?"

"My old lady just made some Kool-Aid. Care for a glass?"

Kevin and I both said thank you but no. Then Kevin, his eyes locked on Mr. Miller, added, "Is it true?"

Mr. Miller pushed back his hunting cap and rubbed his belly. "Farming ain't what it used to be. You're either big business or you just don't make it."

"That's what makes it so challenging," Kevin said. "We can't give up."

"See that tractor over there?" he said. "Can't get the sonofabitch to run and I can't afford to have someone fix it. Without it, there's no farming to be done."

"What'll you do?" Kevin said.

"Can't say for sure."

Kevin wandered over to the tractor. "Does it turn over?"

For the next couple of hours Mr. Miller and Kevin tinkered, coached, and practically summoned the cantankerous machine's spirit, but to no avail. The engine did not give a hint of life. "It's no use," Mr. Miller finally said.

"Why you giving up?" Kevin said. "You need to get it running."

Mr. Miller stopped and gave Kevin a strange look. "Shouldn't you be out playing basketball or doing something with your buddies?"

Kevin didn't seem to hear him, looking as though he was trying to figure out the problem. It occurred to me then that I didn't recall Kevin ever having any buddies. He couldn't be bothered with anything that had little to do with farming.

The mutt was licking my face and I'd drained two glasses of cherry Kool-Aid by the time Kevin said, "I'll see if my dad can come over and give a look at it. He's got a knack for engines."

While Walter Cronkite reported on civil unrest in the South, the constant threat of war, and earthquakes shaking up foundations thousands of miles away in countries I'd never heard of, Churubusco was going through its own struggles. It seemed the closest farm to make it big was in Vermont, about a hundred miles away from our profitless region. Kevin refused to give up, though, and he expected all of our neighbors to be as determined as he was. I tried to imagine fields flourishing with corn rows that went on for miles and cow-filled pastures on every farm instead of barrenness, but it was proving more and more difficult. Most farmers, like Dad, had to make ends meet by finding other jobs. Mr. Puryea, whose farm had been one of the more successful in 'Busco, was one of the first to be hired by a paper mill, which was a good hour's drive away. One farmer after the next approached Mr. Puryea to see what he could do about getting them into the factory.

"They're being foolish," Kevin said one night during supper. "Instead of investing in what they have already, they're going to lose everything."

I didn't say anything, but the facts spoke for themselves: Mike Puryea, who was my age, no longer came to school with holes in his jeans and sneakers. Cindy Barcomb now had braces. And since Dad's promotion, we no longer had to wait between wide gaps of empty-shelf time before filling the refrigerator.

Not everyone was relinquishing, though. There were farmers who continued in the struggle. However, it was when one particular farm finally decided to call it a day that Kevin went into high gear.

Twelve was the magic number for me. That was the age at which I was allowed to use the stove unattended, and now that Dad was supervisor of the cheese plant, his hours were less erratic and he was always home for supper, suppers for which I was now responsible. This particular night, I'd made beef stew—or heated it up, rather, leaving the empty cans on the counter.

"Let me get that for you," Dad said, saving me from having to lift the steaming pot from the stove. He poured the counterfeit conglomeration into the big bowl and carried it to the table, where I had laid out the expected plate of cheeses and basket of bread. Even though I was only twelve, I knew the difference between canned and the real deal, and I apologized for it as everyone sat down.

The times I had been invited to Brenda's for a meal, I discovered that supper at the Hannigans was nothing more than competition among the brood of seven kids, who all shouted at once, hoping their words would land on someone's caring ears. Usually it was Mr. or Mrs. Hannigan who responded, even if only with the briefest of smiles. Their feast was not the utilitarian food served but more in the way I thought a family should function. Conversely, conversation at the Finley table often consisted of one-word responses to the same tired questions while Grandpa's false teeth clattered with each bite he took. But things were about to change.

Dad cleared his throat then said, "Got an offer for the cattle."

Kevin looked up, stopping as he was about to put a folded-up piece of bread into his mouth. "Hope you told whoever it was, no."

Dad and Grandpa exchanged glances. Grandpa said, "It's time, son, before we lose everything."

"What're you talking about?" Kevin said, dropping the bread on top of his stew. "Lose everything?"

"I can't do it no more," Grandpa said, his tone sorrowful.

I wasn't sure how Kevin could have missed that Grandpa was taking a little longer gathering himself up to head out to the barn. Or the way he always rubbed his fingers, trying to uncurl them.

Kevin tossed his hands in the air. "I'm not asking you to. I'll take it over."

"Who'll do it when you're off at college?" Dad countered. Kevin had been offered a full scholarship at Paul Smith's, a university that majored in forestry and conservation.

"I won't go," he said.

"Son, you don't want to be a farmer," Grandpa said.

"Yes, I do. But I want us to stop straddling the fence. What were you offered for the cows? I'll match it."

"How the hell you going to do that?" Dad said, his mouth stuffed with bread and cheese.

"I'll take out a loan."

"No bank is going to loan a seventeen-year-old a thing, especially once they find out what you want to do with it."

"I'm almost eighteen, and I have plans for this place," he said. "I can do it. It can be done."

"Not by yourself," Dad said. "And your grandfather is not able—"

"I'll help," I said, but no one seemed to have heard me.

"I'll hire some hands," Kevin said. "I'll cultivate every damn field we have."

Dad sighed. "But that scholarship is nothing you can sneeze at, Kevin."

"If losing the scholarship means gaining a chance to make this farm work again, then I'll take the farm."

"You just don't understand the work involved, Kevin," Grandpa said, his voice strained, his eyes welling up with tears.

Dad shoved in a mouthful of beef stew, swallowed, and then said, "What the hell is this I'm eating?"

I said, "I didn't have any fresh vegetables, and I didn't know how to—"

He shoved his bowl aside, splattering the mess on the table. He took a chunk of cheddar cheese from the plate, wrapped it in a slice of bread, and shoved the whole thing in his mouth.

I knew it was a tasteless meal, but I was sure the ingredient missing was less from what was on the table than who should be at it. Then, for the first time I can recall, I looked in my father's face and said, "You're the reason she left. You did things like that to her, didn't you?"

The three Finley men stared at me, our meal coming to a halt. Dad's eyes settled on me, his breathing heavy.

Grandpa said, "Leave her be, son. She didn't mean it."

But I did.

"Vicky," Kevin said, "say you're sorry."

I picked up my fork and jabbed at a small piece of what was I suppose was beef and shoved it in my mouth. But I couldn't swallow.

In a flash, Dad stood, his chair slamming to the floor.

"Vicky," Kevin said, "come on, say you're sorry."

I had no intention to do so, and Dad must have known, because he didn't wait, but raged out of the house.

After a few tense moments, Grandpa said, "Maybe we'd better not mention her again."

I stared at my bowl, at the mushy carrots and potatoes and bits of meat. No one spoke for a few minutes, until Kevin said, "I can do it, Grandpa. I can make this farm work."

"You just really don't know what you're up against," Grandpa said.

After some more time stretched by and it was apparent Grandpa and Kevin were finished eating, I began clearing the table.

Kevin said, "Just you wait, Vicky. Next year we'll have a garden filled with fresh vegetables for stew and the best beef from our very own cows." He was virtually glowing with anticipation, but I swore I was never going to make beef stew again.

CHAPTER 5

I always thought it was appropriate that little girls were made of sugar and spice, perfect ingredients to a special recipe, but as the years went by and I grew to become a young woman, I discovered being the only girl in a house full of men was a complicated matter. I had what I needed by way of school supplies and clothes, and my family saw to it that I went to the dentist and doctor on a yearly basis. However, as I grew older, I came to rely more on Brenda and her advice, handed down to her by her older sister Jane, and less on Kevin and his limited knowledge about the female species. Jane had supplied valuable information to a couple of young girls on the cusp of becoming teenagers, and it was Jane who had told Brenda, who then told me, that I was not dying of some dreaded disease. The blood on my panties was normal. Brenda hadn't experienced it yet, but she behaved as though she had.

"It's going to happen every month," she said. "You'll have to get used to using tampons. Pads are too bulky. Those machines in the bathroom have what you need, long as you have a nickel."

"What can I do to stop it?" I imagined bleeding for the rest of my life and I wanted to cry. We were walking side by side down the hallway, heading to social studies. It was our first year in the junior high wing.

"One thing, really," Brenda said. "Get pregnant."

The bell rang, and we ran into the classroom in time to hear Mr. Lagnier say we were going to have a pop quiz. While I was matching explorers to the lands they had discovered, I kept wondering what Brenda had meant. These were the times I missed having a mother more than ever. Once the test was over, I immediately raised my hand and asked if I could go to the bathroom. Growing up was becoming complicated.

The older I got, I'd find out there was always more to learn. And Brenda, who was a wealth of information, took it upon herself to teach me. We'd finished seventh grade and were looking forward to eighth. Well, Brenda was looking more toward graduation, so she could move far away, where there would be "night life and culture."

It was a hot summer day and we were in my bedroom passing time. I longed to be at her house, one filled with friendly sounds and the distant buzz of the sawmill her father ran. Meanwhile, she longed to be at my house, away from her mother's harping and the taunts of her brothers. She usually won, which was why we were in my bedroom.

We were sprawled across my bed, surrounded by four walls covered with a mix of posters of cuddly kittens and Herman's Hermits. I was on my back, my pitched ceiling directly over me. Brenda was polishing her toenails a bright red and going on about boys. Seems the moment she became a teenager, which wasn't all that long ago, it was all she could talk about.

"Then," she said, "they get a hard-on, which can be really embarrassing for them. That's what Glen had when Sheila walked by him in that skimpy bathing suit the other day at the lake. Remember all the guys teasing him?"

"But then, why do they put them on, if it embarrasses them?" I said.

Brenda stopped polishing and looked up at me. "Put what on?"

"The hard. Why do they put it on, if they don't want us to see it?"

She immediately fell back, knocking the bottle of polish over. I grabbed it in time, but she didn't notice since she was laughing so boisterously. She must have found it really funny because she was usually self-conscious about exposing her crooked teeth. Finally, she sat back up and wiped her eyes. "A hard-on isn't something guys wear. It just happens to them." She motioned to the space between her legs. "*It* gets big and hard when they want to have sex."

It took me a moment to digest what she was telling me, and Brenda kept laughing and teasing me. "Look at you, vermilion as a beet."

Brenda had taken it upon herself to become better educated, telling everyone that she had become "autodidactic" so she could escape the ignorance of the small rural town in which she had had the misfortune of being raised. Classmates usually made fun of her word choice, as did her five brothers, but she reminded them that she was going to have the last laugh when they were still stuck in hell town while she was living in a luxurious high-rise in some magnificent city. Her dictionary had been dog eared dozens of times over, and I didn't want to ask what vermilion meant, fearing she'd laugh at me again.

This was about the time she began not only memorizing vocabulary words but to sneak peeks at dirty magazines as well. I was afraid she was referring to something else sexual.

"Man, Vicky, guys are always hitting on you. The way you're built. Seniors! Not knowing anything could be dangerous. It gets hard so that way they can have intercourse with you. You know, *sex*."

One in a long line of Hannigans, Brenda was the queen of hand-me-downs: hand-me-down bikes, hand-me-down clothes, and hand-me-down information.

"Guys really do that?" I said, feeling the warmth in my face, not quite sure if she was toying with me.

She nodded with authority. "You just got to be circum...circumspect. Jane said Debbie got in trouble because she thought Danny was going to take it out before anything happened."

Brenda must have read my mind, because she mellowed and said, "It must be terrible not having an older sister or mother to explain all this to you. I wonder what she looks like."

"Who?" I said.

"Your mother. I mean, was she fat? Ugly?"

I didn't have many secrets I could share with Brenda, but right then I felt I had the biggest. I climbed off my bed and lifted the edge of my mattress, feeling around until I found my diary, where I had transferred the photo quite some time ago, the *Curious George* book long gone.

"What're you doing?" Brenda said.

Leaving the diary under the mattress, out of Brenda's nosy sight, I clutched the three-by-five Polaroid to my bosom. "Promise you won't tell anybody."

"Tell 'em what?" Brenda craned her neck to try and get a peek.

"What I'm going to show you."

"What is it?"

"Promise me!"

Brenda threw her hand in the air. "I promise."

"And if I'm lying..." I prompted.

Rolling her eyes, Brenda said, "And if I'm lying, may Davy Jones die."

Still, I hesitated; besides Kevin, no one else knew I had the picture. I began to wonder if showing her was a mistake.

"Come on, Vicky," Brenda whined, causing me to hand it over.

She gazed at it for a moment or two, looked at me, and then looked back at the photo. "Wow."

"My mother," I whispered, wondering if it had faded some since the last time I'd looked at it. Could looking at something too much suck the life out of it?

"How come you never showed this to me before?"

I wasn't sure myself. I guess I was afraid she'd say something mean.

"She's gorgeous." She looked back at me. "Man, you look just like her. Same hair, everything."

Her comment disheartened me, confirming my suspicion that Dad saw the same thing when he looked at me. It hadn't always been that way. When I was just a child with missing teeth and scraped knees, I'd look forward to Dad coming home from work. I anticipated his warning knock on my door before he opened it to come in to say goodnight. He would tickle me then kiss me on my forehead, telling me to sleep tight. As I got older, though, the knocks became less frequent. Then they stopped altogether.

I huddled next to Brenda, and the two of us stared at the image. "She looks so stylish."

"She had some nice clothes," I said.

"How'd you know?"

I dropped to the floor, dragged out a long, flat box from beneath my bed, and lifted the lid. I pulled out a deep blue wool dress from a pile of polyester pants, flowery dresses, and practical coats for the harsh winters, and held it up to myself.

"Your mother's?"

I nodded, bringing the dress to my nose and inhaling, but discovering yet again nothing more than the aroma of mothballs.

"I thought you said your Grandma threw all her stuff out."

"Things from her bedroom closet. These were in storage. She must've left in the spring or summer. These are all winter things." I dug deeper and pulled out a black velvet dress, cut low in the back. "This is my favorite."

Brenda reached out to touch it. "It's really nice. I bet it'd fit you. Try it on."

"Oh, no," I said, folding it and placing it back in the safety of the box.

"Come on. Please." Brenda leaned over the bed and pulled the dress back out. "It'll be fun. Remember when we used to play dress up?"

"I remember when you used to use crayons to polish your nails."

She rolled her eyes then went back to begging me to try it on. Finally, I went to the bathroom and slipped out of my denim cut-offs and tank top. The bra had to come off, too; otherwise, the straps would show. Black velvet lined with silk glided over my shoulders and along the curves of my body. The bathroom mirror provided a top view only, and I hesitated in the hall before actually going back into my bedroom.

Brenda gasped. "Oh my gosh! I hate you!"

I stood in front of my full-length mirror and surveyed the reflection. It was a perfect fit. "Where do you think she went in this?" I said, caressing the velvet.

"Nowhere around here," Brenda said.

"I wish I knew where she was," I said aloud. I had never tried to send her another letter, but that didn't mean I had given up looking for her. I started to head back to the bathroom to change back into my shorts but stopped upon seeing Brenda's strange expression.

"This is incredible," she whispered.

"What is?"

"I'm getting some sort of powerful vibe."

"What are you doing?" I said, seeing her hands tremble.

"*I'm* not doing anything," Brenda said, grasping the edges of the photo as if it were a divining rod. Her eyes squeezed shut, she said, "I'm getting a visual. It's amazing."

"What is?" I sank on the bed, watching her. I'd learned what being a psychic meant since I'd first heard the word all those years ago. I never really bought into it, but maybe it wasn't so foolish after all.

"It looks like some sort of theater, and there's a huge crowd." Her eyes were still closed and she was crimping the edges of the picture. In a whisper, she said, "There she is."

I moved in closer, wishing I could use Brenda's eyes, see what she was seeing.

"She's on stage. Singing. And the crowd is going wild."

"Really?" My throat tightened. "Can you tell where she is?"

"I see a sign. It says, Place des…Place des—"

"Place des Arts?" I squealed. "That's in Montreal, isn't it?" I was in Brenda's face. "This isn't happening now. Can't be. I mean, it's daytime and—"

Brenda opened one eye, then the other, and broke out in laughter. "Gotcha!"

I caught my breath, staring at her. "You…you…"

"I'm full of shit!" She clutched herself, rolling on her side. "I had you going."

I snatched the picture. "That's not funny. Go home."

"What? You really think she's this big star? If she's so spectacular, how come we never heard of her?"

"I said go home! I'm never going to show you anything again. Ever. Now go."

"Temperamental!" She grabbed the bottle of polish and walked out. "Call you later," she yelled, cackling all the way down the stairs and out the front door.

I tried to flatten the edges of the photo before tucking it between the pages of my diary and then wiped the deluge of tears streaming down my face. *Of course she was a star; otherwise, she would have come back by now. She's just following her dream.* I dropped on my bed, hugging the black velvet I was surrounded in and cried myself to sleep.

I woke up some time later to the sound of my name being called from downstairs. I was covered in sweat.

"Where's supper?" my father shouted from the bottom of the stairs.

I lunged from the bed, feeling groggy while my mind spun. Chicken needed to be baked and potatoes peeled; that much I remembered. Since it was already past five-thirty—an unacceptable time for the Finley men to eat—I'd have to do soup and sandwiches.

"Vicky!"

I raced out of my room and down the stairs. Perhaps I could boil some macaroni and make a salad instead of soup, which wouldn't be welcome anyway on such a hot day. I ran into the kitchen, mumbling apologies and avoiding my father's gaze.

"She was asleep, Jack," Grandpa said. "I let her be."

"What're you wearing?" Dad said, his jaw tight.

I looked down and realized I was covered in black velvet, *her* black velvet.

"Where'd you get that?" He looked at me hard.

"Upstairs, in the hall closet."

"Upstairs?"

I nodded.

"Any more clothes like it in that closet?"

I shook my head. It was the truth, since the box was now in my bedroom.

"I want you to take that off and throw it out. Understand?"

"Sorry I'm late," Kevin said, rushing in. "Took longer than…" He stopped, his eyes darting from me to my father, then back to me.

"No," I said.

"I said take it off, goddammit."

"Vicky," Kevin said, "what's wrong?"

Refusing to speak, I stormed to the refrigerator and gathered several potatoes, forgetting my second menu plan. The dirt from the potatoes smudged the dress as I carried them over to the sink and dropped them down.

"Ah, to hell with it," my father said, going back outside, slamming the screen door behind him.

"I'm not taking it off. I'm not." I scrubbed the potatoes under a mad rush of running water. "He can't make me."

Grandpa had already gone after my father, but Kevin stood watching me in silence while I washed the potatoes, coated the chicken, and tossed everything in the oven.

Finally, he said, "It's a pretty fancy dress to be cooking in."

"I like it," I said, brushing the dirt from it.

"Fits you nice. Why don't you save it for something special?"

"I'll never go anywhere special."

Kevin didn't say anything else, but went to the cabinets and pulled out four plates, cups, and utensils. I did begin to feel foolish in such a fancy dress, and I headed upstairs while dinner baked. "I'm changing," I shouted out, "but only because I don't want to ruin it!"

After things had settled and supper was ready and we all had sat around the table, me back in my cut-offs, Dad never mentioned the dress. I don't know what Grandpa said to him, but whatever it was had calmed him down. Later that night, when I was in my room, there was a knock on my door.

"Come in," I said, expecting it to be Kevin, who'd want to show me some agriculture magazine. Instead, it was my father.

"I'll be going to the A & P tomorrow. Need anything?"

Barely looking at him, I shook my head.

"You sure?" He cleared his throat then said, "I know you're getting older and need...well, women things."

I felt myself blush. Again, I shook my head. I knew what he meant, but a steady supply of nickels had kept me well stocked to that point.

He sighed. "Okay then." His footsteps were light as he walked down the hallway, leaving my door opened. I got up and slammed it shut.

That night, I wrote in my diary about how cruel Brenda had been. While gazing at the Polaroid, I imagined excited fans cheering on the spectacular Grace Finley. Then it occurred to me that perhaps she was no longer alive. I placed the picture back in my diary, put it under my mattress, and fell asleep. Before long, I was awoken by another knock. This time it was Kevin.

"What time is it?" I mumbled.

"Come here," he said. "I want you to see something." He led me across the hallway and into his room. He'd taken the screen out of his window, and he made me climb through it and onto the slanted garage roof. It hadn't occurred to me not to follow.

He faced north and pointed toward the sky. I slumped down in reverence and fear at the sight: oceanic waves were rolling across the heavens.

"Earlier, you said you'll never go anywhere special" he said. "I don't see how this could be any more special."

In silence, I watched rippling reds and yellows travel across the mantle of sky. I shivered from both awe and a North Country night chill.

Kevin draped an arm across my shoulder. "They're the northern lights."

"Northern lights?"

"*Aurora borealis*, if you want to get technical."

I didn't. It was enough sitting out in the cool of the evening watching a celestial production unfold, one that seemed to be meant solely for us.

"Kevin?"

"Hmm?"

"Did you ever try looking for her?"

"Nope. Didn't see the point."

I looked at him, at his fine jaw line, at the slight stubble that grazed it, at his penetrating eyes. He'd grown to be a man, and I couldn't be sure when that had happened. I was also surprised at his answer. I was certain he'd been doing his own detective work all these years. Maybe he didn't know where to begin, just like me. I said as much.

"Nah. The way she hurt Dad, I didn't think it'd be a good idea to bring her back. She left. Wanted to leave where angels live."

"Dad thinks I'm just like her."

He squeezed me. "You're nothing like her. You'd never do anything like she did."

I wanted to believe him, but at such a young age, I wasn't sure of what I was capable.

CHAPTER 6

Once I realized Kevin wasn't searching for her, I knew it was up to me. So, when school started again in the fall, Brenda and I would ask for passes to go to the library instead of attending study hall. We'd pull out maps and scour the atlas, trying to figure out what route Grace Finley had taken when she walked out.

"Did she have a car?" Brenda whispered, leaning over the book.

"I don't know," I said.

"Maybe she left with some man."

"No," I said without hesitation. "I think she must've been sick. Kevin remembers her saying for weeks before she left that she couldn't breathe." The thought that she had gone somewhere to die alone with some fatal disease made me crazy with worry.

"Well, I'll make a list of the towns she could've gone to, but you'll have to make the calls from your house."

Andy Reynolds and Donnie Marks were sitting across the room staring at us. Brenda alerted me to the fact with a giggle.

"Come on," I said, nudging her. "Are you helping or not?"

"I think they have a crush on us," she said.

"Not interested."

While my finger was traveling the routes from Churubusco leading out to the rest of the world and Brenda was writing down the names of towns, a paper airplane floated by and landed at my feet. Brenda reached for it, but the boys across the room whispered loudly, "No, not you, Brillo head. Give it to her. Give it to Vicky."

Brenda handed me the paper and I unfolded it. A scribbled note stated, *Andy thinks you're pretty. Would you go out with him?*

I looked up and shook my head no, then went back to the map. The screech of chairs echoed throughout the library, and the red-faced boys immediately left.

"I hate my hair," Brenda said, pulling a rubber band from her schoolbag. "Yours always looks perfect." She pulled back her hair and wrapped the rubber band around it, in an attempt to tame the wild red frizz. "Guys just love your long blond tresses."

"Are you helping me with this or not?"

That night, after supper was over and I'd cleaned the dishes and put away the pots and pans, and the kitchen was clear of any man, I sat on the floor with the phone on my lap and began my task. I called one town after the next, and by the time I was in Danbury, Connecticut, I had to hurry and hang up because Dad walked in to grab a cup of coffee and a handful of oatmeal cookies I'd baked the day before.

"What you doing?" he said.

I shrugged. "Oh, just trying to figure out my math homework. Brenda was helping me."

"I'm not so bad in math. Maybe—"

I stood, placing the phone back on the counter. "That's okay," I said, clutching the list to my chest. "I think I got it now." I walked out of the kitchen, frustrated that I had managed to cross only a couple of towns off my list. Most did not have any listings for a Finley, but some had one or two. Each time I dialed the number the operator had given me, one in Latham and another in Buffalo, my mouth was dry, the beat of my heart thumping louder and louder. On the first call I was told by a Cheryl Finley that she'd married Chad. Her maiden name was Daniels. She even told me about their baby, named Mickey. The Finley in Buffalo was a Norman Finley, and he had never heard of anyone by the name of Grace Finley. Discouraged, but not at all ready to give up, I'd repeat the routine each night for weeks, until one night when Dad was sitting at the kitchen table waiting for supper and sorting through the mail. He opened up the phone bill.

"Jesus H. Christ," he sputtered. "What the hell is this?"

It hadn't occurred to me that all this time I'd been leaving a costly trail. My hands shook as I put supper on the table.

"What's going on, son?" Grandpa said.

"Phone company's trying to screw us, saying we made calls to...to New Jersey, Pennsylvania. Hell, I don't know a soul in New Jersey."

As it had proven, neither did I, since that lead had come up empty along with the dozens of others. I'd even begun calling hospitals, but they refused to give me any information.

Kevin walked in, having just milked the cows. After graduating high school, he'd moved in to what had been Grandma and Grandpa's house, but he would eat supper with us if he finished his chores in time. He tossed his cap on top of the refrigerator. Once he saw Dad's demeanor, his expression suddenly looked cautious. "What's wrong?"

Dad tossed the bill at Kevin to show him what had him so enraged. Kevin blew a low whistle.

He said, "Just call them tomorrow and tell them it's a mistake. They'll take it off."

I kept my eyes down as I made sure to place the cheese right next to Dad. For supper, I'd attempted crab cakes, but they were nothing more than dark brown plops. My first bite confirmed that I'd used too much bread crumbs and egg to make up for the scarce amount of crabmeat.

I said, "This is awful. I'm sorry. I'll make something else."

"It's fine," Kevin said.

"Don't think I ever had crabmeat," Grandpa added.

Dad didn't speak, but merely chewed while examining the phone bill, shaking his head. I couldn't imagine what he'd say once he did call the phone company and found out it wasn't a mistake after all. I toyed with the idea of throwing some clothes in a bag and asking Mrs. Hannigan if she'd adopt me.

Dad tossed the bill on the table and held up his fork with a scoop of crab cake. He said, "Why don't you stick to burgers and roast beef from now on?"

My throat tight, I nodded in agreement.

I couldn't sleep that night, wondering how I was going to get out of trouble. I still had a long list of towns I was supposed to call, but knew I couldn't go near the phone. It was well past midnight when I got up to get a drink of water. When I came out of the bathroom, I met Grandpa in the dimly lit hallway.

"Can't sleep?" he said.

I moved out of his way so that he could continue on into the bathroom, but he didn't budge.

I shrugged.

"Need to talk?"

There was little chance of Dad hearing, since his bedroom was downstairs off the kitchen. Grandpa's bedroom was upstairs, where mine was and Kevin's had been before he moved his things into the little house across the field.

"I made those calls, Grandpa." Tears filled my eyes. "I didn't know it was going to cost so much money."

He gazed at me for a moment then said, "Who were you callin'?"

"Nobody."

"Pretty high bill for callin' nobody."

I hesitated. I didn't think Grandpa would be too pleased with the answer, but of the three menacing men, he was the one I feared the least. I said, "I was trying to find my mother."

"That right? Any luck?"

I shook my head. "Now I have to stop."

"Either that or spend the rest of your life looking for someone you might never find."

Though still sniffling, I was relieved the truth was out. "Mrs. Scott asked me if I'd baby-sit for her sometimes. She says she thinks I'm old enough now. I'll help pay the bill."

"You'll have to do an awful lot of baby-sitting," he said. He hugged me and mumbled, "My little angel. You don't deserve this."

"Dad's going to hate me even more."

"He doesn't hate you. Your father loves you."

I scrunched up my nose but didn't argue.

"Listen, I'll take care of your father. You just promise not to make any more calls like that, okay?"

I nodded, but a sinking feeling came over me as I realized my search had been stifled. However, the setback would only be a temporary one, because I had no plans to stop looking.

The bill was never mentioned again, and I'm not sure what Grandpa did to take care of it. If Kevin knew the truth, he didn't let on that he did. Perhaps he was simply too busy to notice, his time filled with milking, cultivating, and tilling.

The Finley Farm had begun to look revitalized. Some of the fields of the one hundred or so acres had been rototilled and were waiting to be seeded for a large crop of corn. Others were a sea of green grass ready to be mowed down to dry then packaged into bales of hay. Dad and Grandpa pitched in when they could, since Kevin hadn't been able to hire any help so far due to a lack of funds, but he was able to rent the services of a bull, which turned out to be a source entertainment for Brenda and myself. We christened him Hercules and spent hours watching him, giggling at his valiant efforts to mount one particular distracted cow that had won his ardent attention.

"I don't think she likes it," I said, watching the cow moo and struggle to free herself from determined Hercules.

"Sure she does. She's just playing the game." Brenda said, as if she'd played "the game" herself. At fourteen, the only games with which I was familiar were Monopoly and crazy eight's.

But before long, Hercules was carted away and, to Kevin's delight, the stud's services had proved successful.

I rarely saw my brother anymore. If he didn't make it for supper, I would walk a hot plate over to him, placing it on the kitchen table with written instructions on how to reheat it. There were often notes for me taped to the refrigerator door asking if I needed anything from town, since he had to run there the next day anyway. Often I'd write down a certain ingredient for a recipe I planned to try, and he'd always get it for me.

One fall afternoon I saw him trudging through the field, his unkempt hair blowing in the breeze. I slipped a sweater on over my head and ran out to see him. He pulled me into him in a grateful hug. "How you doing?" he said.

"Better than you are. You look sick." He had dark circles under his eyes and, even though he had never had an ounce of extra fat on his body, he looked almost skeletal.

"Hey, I'm doing great." He sucked up the country air. "Better than poor Mrs. Passino. Mr. Passino died."

"Yeah, I heard. She's never going to be able to run the farm by herself."

"She'll do fine," he said. "I already went over there and told her I'd be by in the mornings to help."

"Kevin! You don't have time for all that."

"Sure I do. Who needs sleep, anyway?" He smiled then said, "This is my favorite season. Look at the leaves. It's like nature's telling us we are at our brightest and most vibrant right before we go back into the earth."

"Like Mr. Passino?" I said. I was being serious, but he laughed. I guess the image of the old man, who had been missing almost all his teeth and had only two tufts of hair springing from his bald head, wasn't Kevin's idea of vibrant.

"Things are actually looking good, Vicky," Kevin said. "We're going to be all right."

I wrapped my arms around myself, the air suddenly going cold. Winter was near, but we were used to what they brought, and I expected nothing would be different in the upcoming season.

At the intersection of Looby and Mills Roads huddled a shadow in darkness so concentrated that if I didn't know it was Brenda, I'd have been tempted to turn my bike around and scoot back home. Once I got closer, I saw that she was straddling Timothy's bike, a rare thing for her to get a hold of in a house full of brothers. Even though Jane had recently married and moved to Syracuse, she had never had a bike to hand down to Brenda. Brenda, therefore, had to fight along with her younger siblings for Timothy's rattling hand-me-down wheels. My breath puffing out all around me, I said, "You're nuts."

Her whole body shook and her question of "why" came out in two syllables.

"It's freezing, and you're dressed like it's springtime." I wasn't exaggerating. It was the middle of November, and the air was so cold it pressed in on you, making you numb. Yet, there was fashion-conscious Brenda sporting a thin blazer instead of the poly-filled, sensible coat Jane had left behind in the closet of the bedroom the sisters had once shared.

"Kiss it goodbye," she warned, hopping on the bike and pedaling away, her body shuddering so hard she could barely manage the handlebars. She wasn't wearing a hat, of course, because once she took it off, it would have made her hair even more difficult to manage. And she said the reason she wouldn't be caught wearing a sensible coat was because it made her look *dorky*. Her weak, shaky voice prodded me: "Hu…hur…ry!"

I jumped on my bike, jostling over the ice-rutted road. Me, I was bundled in a heavy wool coat, hat, and gloves. Certainly not the fashion statement Brenda made but I didn't feel the need to race to get to the warmth of the town hall either. Of course, I wasn't looking forward to what would be happening there, and I might be purposely dawdling. Eventually, I caught up to her, our heavy breathing keeping rhythm with our pedaling. High overhead was the mantle of black sky, speckled with a mass of twinkling stars.

Her nose dripping with snot and eyes tearing, she called out, "After all this, it better be on their agenda." We passed Immaculate Heart of Mary, a church older than God, as Grandpa describes it. Prying one gloved hand from the handlebar, I did a quick one, two, three, four, making the sign of the cross. Brenda must've seen me, because she shook her head and said, "Give me a break."

We'd made our first communion together in that church, the two of us making sure we sat next to each other while Sister Margaret Elizabeth taught us how to accept the body of Christ on our tongue. Some years later, we sat in the same pew as we learned how to be ready for the slight slap on the face from Father Richards, a sign the Holy Spirit had come upon us in the sacrament of confirmation. Recently, though, Brenda thought it more fashionable to be an atheist, although she was never brave enough to share this with her family. Her mom was still involved with the rosary society, and her father was in the Knights of Columbus. All of her brothers had been or still are altar boys.

"Didn't he stop by the house tonight?" she said, meaning Kevin.

"No," I said, "he didn't."

We passed *Phil Up*, the only gas station in town, owned by Phil Dumont. I noticed the pumps were off, a sure sign he'd be at the monthly meeting, which would not be like any monthly meeting before.

"It's probably all a rumor," I said, part of me hoping so.

"I doubt it."

"Dad and Grandpa said they can't imagine anyone wanting to spend any kind of money here. *They* said it's probably just a rumor."

"Scuttlebutt, huh?" she replied.

"Up to the S's now?" I said, recalling the worn out dictionary Brenda kept next to her bed. I suppose it was her Bible. We passed the sign announcing we were in the town of Churubusco and then turned left down the road.

"Holy shit," she said, letting the bike coast, "look at all the people."

Obviously, town hall was the place to be tonight. People were climbing out of their cars and trucks, taking mincing steps across the ice-slicked road while racing against the bitter cold. Snowmobiles were beginning to collect out front. And, as we pedaled closer, I saw Kevin's red Datsun pickup parked off to the side of the road. Buried beneath my layers of clothing, my heart pounded at the thought of what he might do this very night, the trouble he would stir.

People had been talking about it all week. Ruby Dupree had even followed me out of church on Sunday morning to ask if my brother—with his highfalutin ideas, as she stated it—was going to be putting nonsense in everybody's head at the meeting on Wednesday night. My reply was a shrug as I dashed away. But how could these people, our neighbors, who had known Kevin and his passion for 'Busco for the last ten years or so, accept anything less from him?

Brenda's pace quickened, and by the time I caught up to her, her bike was leaning against the lopsided two-story clapboard building. Huffing, I dropped my bike to the ground and started in, but instead of running ahead of me, Brenda grabbed my arm to stop me. She nodded toward Mr. LeMieux, who was stumbling up the walk. He looked to be trying to find his footing. There were patches of ice to watch out for, but I suspect his caution had more to do with having just come from the "ho-del" down the road. The "ho-del" pronounced like "yodel" but with an H wasn't that at all, but was the only bar in town. It had a pool table, a foosball table, and a jukebox loaded with the twangy voices of Loretta Lynn and Kitty Wells and the baritone sounds of Johnny Cash, who was always able to add to the drunken stupor in the room by rallying the crowd to sing "Ring Of Fire." I'd been there a total of three times—twice to use the bathroom during our yearly fireman's field day and one other time after Brenda's grandmother's funeral. It had been the place the Hannigans had chosen to gather after the interment to console one another—if console meant sucking down one beer after the next. Because the jukebox has not been updated in years, I had learned every stanza to Cash's song.

We trudged up the creaky steps behind Mr. LeMieux, who was trailing an aroma of beer. Brenda took out a ball of tissue from her pocket and dabbed at her drippy red nose with trembling, chapped hands.

"No gloves?" I shrieked.

She rolled the tissue back up and shoved it in the pocket of her blazer. "I don't have any that match."

"You're gonna get pneumonia."

"I'll take the risk, MOM."

Mr. LeMieux opened the heavy metal door and the sudden smell of cow dung met us. Brenda slipped by a knot of farmers and headed toward the front, no doubt wanting the best seat in the house. I didn't follow, scoping out the room instead, looking for Kevin.

"Hi, Vicky. Came to see your brother make an ass of himself?" Leaning against the wall was Brad Hunt, a lit cigarette hanging from his lip. Brenda thought he was cute, but she thought all guys beyond adolescence were cute. A couple of his buddies eyed me with boyish eagerness while Brad took his time looking me over with his beady brown eyes. I could feel those penetrating orbs on me even as I walked away, scooting around a cluster of people.

Cold air rose from the collection of bodies, while voices rumbled and whispered, all speculating the outcome. Snippets of conversation reached me:

"He's starting to be nothin' but a rabble rouser."

"This could be the most money this town's ever seen, and I say to hell with everything else."

"But Kevin is such a nice boy. I'm sure he's sincere."

"He's a strange one—always been."

There was a man I did not recognize and he was jotting notes on an opened notepad.

Brenda appeared. "He's up there, but so are my parents." She weaved her way through the crowd, heading toward the back of the room, but I went to find my brother.

And there he was, in a sea of hunting jackets and overalls, his tall, wiry body standing at attention, his hands deep in the pockets of his jeans, his pea coat open wide.

"Hey," I said, nudging him.

"Hey."

I needed something more from him. "Uh, Conroy messed with a porcupine and it took me hours to get the quills—"

"Excuse me," the man with the notepad interrupted. "Would you be Kevin Finley?"

"Who are you?" Kevin said.

"I'm with the *Plattsburgh Press*, covering this story. Would you mind answering a few questions?"

I made my way to the back of the room where Brenda stood. She said, "He's so weird."

"No he's not. He's being interviewed."

"Uh, oh," she said.

"What?"

"Your dad's looking this way, and he looks pissed—peeved."

I looked over, my wave feeble and unreturned, my face instantly warming. Grandpa was sitting next to my father, attempting the same admonishing look. What did they expect? All they had been talking about lately was this meeting. It had been the night's sole topic during supper. Did they think I'd cook the pot roast, peel the potatoes, then clean up the whole boring mess so that I could hide in my bedroom and study while everyone else in 'Busco promised to be at this meeting?

The quick knock of the gavel caused the people milling about to find any available chair or space against the wall they could find. Everyone's eyes seemed to make their way to Kevin. He wore a pumped-up expression. I edged closer to a rime-covered window, where a cold draft was seeping in.

While the minutes were read, Brenda kept nudging me. "This is going to be intense," she whispered. "I can tell. There's so much energy in the room."

Whenever I thought Brenda's telepathic side had been buried beneath her teenage angst, somehow she would find a way to resurrect it. However, it didn't take a psychic to feel there was something in the air beyond the smell of cow dung.

Evelyn Smith's voice droned on without inflection as she went into detail about the previous month's meeting, but no one seemed to be paying attention with prior concerns. I scanned the faces of the weathered farmers and tired housewives, all filled with anticipation, while I searched for that one unfamiliar face. Or would it be familiar to me? What would she look like all these years later? Just a single Polaroid isn't a lot to go on, but something told me that if I did see her, I'd know who she was in a second. Maybe she would be huddled in some corner or skulking behind hefty Mr. Begore, hoping no one spotted her. Especially my father. It was easy to imagine him spitting in her face then walking on with confidence, certain that his family was following him. However, if she had heard about this meeting, about the trouble her son was starting to stir, wouldn't that be enough to draw her into the circle once again, to take the risk of being spit on?

"Okay, we can open the floor to new business," Evelyn Smith declared. The room immediately turned its attention in Kevin's direction. Sure enough, he raised his hand to be recognized.

I stopped breathing. Or it felt like it.

Once he was acknowledged, he strode toward the front of the room. His Adam's apple quivered as he cleared his throat. "It's come to my attention," he began, "that some business enterprise has been making incredible offers to those of you who have property bordering Benny's Lake." He paused long enough to let his blue eyes wander from Mr. Miller, whose tractor he had incorporated Dad to fix without charging a dime, to Mrs. Passino, the widow whose farm would have been no more if he hadn't helped her each morning, and finally to Old Man LeMieux, who would not let Kevin step foot on his property due to pride.

"I have to tell you, this scares me. And I shouldn't be the only one." Another pause, and another nudge from Brenda, who had sidled up next to me.

"If this developer gets all that property, then all the things 'Busco means to us will be taken away. It'll destroy us."

"Oh, now don't go scarin' the hell outta everybody, boy," mumbled Old Man LeMieux, who was slumped in a folding metal chair. "Ain't nothin' gonna happen to this town 'cept get improved some, eh."

Kevin drew closer to the crowd, raking a hand through his near shoulder-length hair. Sometimes he forgets to take care of himself. "Is that what you were told? Ever hear of something called 'rights of exclusion'? You people never got too picky about boundaries." He turned his attention to Mr. Miller. "It was kind of you to let me tap for syrup all these years, Mr. Miller—"

"Hell, you always gave me most of it, anyway." Mr. Miller pushed back the hunting cap on his head.

"And if you sell, I won't be allowed to do it anymore," he said. "And nobody will be able to fish in that water, because it'll no longer be considered riparian property."

"Kevin," Evelyn Smith said, "all these big words are impressive and all, but they mean very little—"

Kevin whirled around, his fists clenched at his sides, his face red. "We'd be losing our rights, Miss Smith. Plain and simple."

Carl Taylor, who was seated to Evelyn Smith's right, stood up and glared at Kevin. "We will not have our tempers raised here, young man."

Kevin's eyes locked on Evelyn Smith's. "We wouldn't be allowed any of the privileges we take for granted now. Maybe you can't appreciate what we have here, but that doesn't mean I have to stand by and watch it get destroyed."

Evelyn Smith's eyes, which had been lost in a sea of blue shadow, suddenly flared open, while her mouth, with lips painted that bright Avon red, clamped shut. She was a lump of a woman, and Kevin was right about her not being able to appreciate his cause, since she had her own. Close to forty and still unmarried, Evelyn Smith made herself available to any man who crossed her path. Apparently, she'd given up on the elusive Jack Finley a long time ago.

"Why don't you make your point so we can move on to other business," Carl Taylor said before sitting back down.

"My point is obvious," Kevin said. I could tell he was straining to keep his tone even. "We don't know what this enter...this business wants to do with all this property, but I can pretty much guess. It's just not going to respect it the way we do. The way I do." He hesitated then added, "They just don't know Benny."

How strange. Since that day all those years ago when Kevin and I were lolling on the boulder and he told me about the ghost of Benny, he'd never mentioned him to me again.

Glances were exchanged, and those sitting shifted in their chairs. Grandpa leaned over and whispered something in Dad's ear. The reporter scribbled on his notepad.

Brenda groaned. "He can't really believe that story. It's fictitious. And I should know. If Benny was to appear to anyone—"

A tiny gray head rose out of the midst. Evelyn nodded and said, "Mrs. Passino, you have something to add."

"Kevin," Mrs. Passino twittered, "I think you're just the nicest boy, but I can't do it no more. I mean, I'm thankful you helping me make it work this long, but it's just not enough."

Kevin raced down the aisle toward her and took her birdlike hands in his. "I'll never stop helping you, Mrs. Passino. You don't have to pay me a cent; not losing Benny's Lake would be enough. Together we could make it work." His expression hopeful, he looked out at the crowd. "All of us, if we worked as a team, could keep things as they are."

Mrs. Passino pulled her hands away and squeaked, "No, Kevin! It's too much since Fred's gone on." She did a one, two, three, four motion with her hand, causing Brenda to roll her eyes. "It's too much work," she continued, "and too much money to pass up." She lowered her voice. "I'm sorry, Kevin, but this way I have something to leave my children. They'll be taken care of; they won't have to work the way their father did."

"But wouldn't you want them to have what you have?"

"What?" she squealed. "Hard work, no money? Worrying about paying the bills?"

There were nods and some mumbling, until Kevin countered, "A bit of heaven, Mrs. Passino. What we have here is a bit of heaven."

I'd never thought about it that way, but it's true that 'Busco was a vast stretch of nature, with trees, streams, farmland, and fields that went on and on. I also began to feel guilty for having taken Benny's Lake for granted, a lake that offered swimming in the short summers, ice-skating in the long winters, and fishing all year round. There was just no money to be found in any of it.

Mr. LeMieux heaved himself from his chair, tottering and sputtering. He didn't wait for Evelyn or any other board member to acknowledge him. "It's nothin' but wasteland, boy. It takes a body down, buries it. Feeds it dust." He swayed, and his voice cracked. "You callin' it heaven. Well, it ain't. Can be nothing more 'en hell."

I thought back to a few years earlier, when Mr. LeMieux's four-year-old grandson was playing hide and seek with cousins and no one could find him for hours. I imagine the little fellow thought he had found the best spot. Who would find him crouched under a pile of hay out in the field? Meanwhile, his grandpa was doing what he'd done for no less than forty summers, except instead of using a pitchfork to load the hay on a wagon pulled by a team of horses, he'd succumbed to progress and invested in a baler, the teeth packing the hay into a tight square. Now, years later, the baler remained in the field where the accident happened and the grass grew wild, while Mr. LeMieux spends his days and nights at the ho-del keeping himself in a disconnected haze. I suppose most of the people in the room were thinking about the same thing.

Kevin's voice was soft when he replied, "I understand, Mr. LeMieux, but—"

"No!" A jarring ripple flowed through the room. "You don't, or you wouldn't ask me to stay." Knocking over his chair, he plunged through the crowd and pushed his way out the exit door. The sound of his work boots thumping down the stairs reverberated throughout the town hall. No one spoke for a moment, and then Grandpa raised his hand.

"Gerald, you got something to add?" Mr. Chase, who was sitting at the table, said.

"My grandson's got a point. Once it's sold, there's no turning back. Maybe we'd better find out more about what these city fellas want to do with all this property."

"Never had to struggle with farming, Gerald?" Mr. Miller said. "Never had to think about how you were going to make it from one season to the next?" When Grandpa didn't reply, he said, "Found it too damned hard to make it, like the rest of us. Besides, it don't much matter what anyone thinks; if we want to sell, hell, there ain't a soul who can stop us."

"He's right, Kevin," Mr. Chase said. "This issue really doesn't concern us. These people have a right to sell if they want to."

Kevin faced the board. "But I've been thinking this through. What if the town was to buy it instead?"

There were gasps and chuckles and the shaking of heads, the board as amused as the rest of the townspeople.

"Why not?" Kevin shouted over the murmuring and snickering. "Why can't we as a town own it?"

Mr. Taylor sneered and, in a syrup-filled voice, said, "Mr. Finley, I happen to know how much this developer has offered these people. We couldn't even come close."

"Yes," Kevin said, "but all we'd have to do is buy one of the farms. That way he won't get rights of exclusion. That's all we'd need to do."

"Won't work," Mr. Miller called out. "This business made it clear it wants it all or nothing."

Kevin turned toward the room again, his face filled with panic. "That proves my point! They have plans to do something drastic to this place."

"Nuttin' wrong with change," called out a voice from the crowd. Everyone looked to be in agreement by the way they were nodding. Except Dad and Grandpa.

Kevin began to pace. "Don't you care what's going to happen to this town if they take over the lake?"

Brenda muttered "no" loud enough to make some people turn and look.

"Dear God in heaven," he continued, "the wolves are finally coming back. And I heard Lester spotted a moose in his field just the other day. It's been years since we've had any wildlife here and now that they're coming back—"

"Who wants wolves around anyway?" shouted another faceless voice, prompting more nodding.

He lunged toward the crowd. "You just don't get it, do you?"

"Ah, get a haircut."

This time I could tell it was Brad Hunt who had spoken. His buddies surrounding him snickered and one of them mumbled something about "Mr. Bookworm" showing off. I glared at Brad and he responded by blowing me a kiss.

"Have you forgotten what this town stands for?" Kevin said.

"Being poor is all I've ever known," Mr. Miller shouted.

"Poor? The lake gives us fresh trout; the forest, berries and syrup. It's all there, and you're willing to let it go for a few bucks? Who knows if any of those trees will be left standing once Scoleri Enterprise moves in—trees the Iroquois planted hundreds of years ago."

Brad and his cohorts began making Indian war cries until the rap of the gavel hushed them.

"And we're willing to sell it to the devil."

Brenda whispered in my ear, "Aren't you embarrassed?"

I thought Kevin was a bit extreme with his comparison, but it didn't stop me from wanting to hit Brenda all the same. I also wanted to come to my brother's defense, but I didn't have the courage or words to do either.

Miss Smith stood. "Kevin, we all love this town, too but it's out of our hands. Now, we simply must move on to new business." She shuffled some papers and said, "Now then—"

All eyes rested on my brother. His hands became tight fists, and a rumbling from deep within him began to roll out. At first, I couldn't understand what he was saying, but then, as he started walking toward the front of the room, he punched one of those fists high in the air and tore into the silence by chanting, "Forever wild! Forever wild!" He circled the room, his pace quickening, chanting that odd chant over and over again.

"He's totally lost it," Brenda said, this time not bothering to whisper.

People began looking at each other in horror; the reporter writing furiously on his notepad. I tried to see what Dad and Grandpa were doing but couldn't because of the tears filling my eyes. I kept wishing someone would rise and join him, like in some sappy movie, so he wouldn't look so pitiful, so alone. The board members were standing, all trying to plead with him to sit down, but he acted as though he couldn't hear them.

Even Brad was stunned into silence.

"Kevin!" shouted Mr. Chase, his face blood red. "You have to stop this now!"

But Kevin had broken into a run, going round and round the room. "Forever wild! Forever wild!"

"What does that mean?" Brenda said.

This tirade was going to gain mileage, fueled by exaggeration, as it would surely get around town the next day. The truth was bad enough. I just wished he would stop, or that someone could stop him.

Then, rising out of his chair, my father stood. A triumphant sob escaped from me. Perhaps it would be like one of those movies. But Dad didn't say a word. With his head down, he shuffled by some people in his path and went to Kevin, placing a hand on his shoulder. His voice was low, but the room had become so quiet I could hear what he said: "Come on, son, that's enough."

My brother looked to be confused. He stared at Dad for some time, then glanced around the room at the sober faces staring at him. He pulled away, rushing down the aisle and stumbling over dozens of feet. But even as he tore out of the door and stomped down the stairs, he kept repeating that odd chant. I wanted to go after him. I really did. But in the same way my voice had betrayed me, my feet did as well.

Brad nodded to his buddies and started out the door, but my father, looking up to the challenge, with a form as stocky as Brad's, grabbed Brad by the collar and shook his head no. Brad scowled and then slammed his back against the wall, raising his hands as if in defeat.

I scraped the frost from the window so I could see Kevin opening and shutting his pickup's door. He pulled onto the road and drove away slowly. The room did not stir for a few moments, as though Kevin's electricity was still running dangerously through it.

When Kevin was a young boy and read to me each night, he'd read me stories about animals and nature, but he'd eventually rest the book on his lap and begin talking to me about our little neck of the woods.

One night he said, "You know, a long, long time ago, Indians named our town."

I gazed at him in wonder, the covers pulled up to my chin. "They did?"

"Yup. Know what it means?"

I shook my head.

"Place of Angels."

"Wow." I liked the idea of living where angels lived, where wars and violence could not gain access.

Yet, like the stories he read to me, where animals could talk and evil giants could be destroyed, I realized now it was nothing more than a fairy tale.

CHAPTER 7

True to Kevin's word, by the time the sap should have been flowing, we were no longer welcome onto the flourishing property surrounding Benny's Lake. I missed it more than I would have imagined, although Brenda said it was simply because I was being denied access. Maybe. Still, I missed the conversations I used to have with my brother out in the wild. He seemed more at peace, less restless, when we were deep in the forest. It was in those woods that I dared to tell him what I intended to be when I grew up. He was planting some saplings at the time.

"That makes sense," he said, leaning on the shovel.

"It does?"

"Vicky, you're always in the kitchen rustling up something good for us fussy old men. I just figured you'd want to be a cook."

"Not just a cook," I said. "A chef, in a nice restaurant."

It was also in those woods, a season or two later, that I found out Grace hadn't always been a Finley; she had begun life as a Dormand. It was late spring, and we were collecting the sap. Somehow, I managed to bring up the topic yet again.

"Brenda's got four grandparents," I said.

Kevin pulled the plug on the maple tree, picked up the bucket half-filled with sap, and went to the next tree. He was used to my hints and said, "We did too."

"We did?"

He then told me how our mother's parents had been killed on some highway during a terrible snowstorm. They hadn't lived in Churubusco, and he had no idea where they had lived. An only child, Grace had come under the care of her elderly Aunt Gladys in Churubusco, and Aunt Gladys had since died.

"She's got no ties here anymore," he said, trudging along the soft, wet ground, going to the next tree. "Well, except for us."

Now it was the end of March. The morning chill had been warmed by a powerful afternoon sun, which poured over Brenda and me as we pushed through the doors of Northern Adirondack High. As we walked, our arms laden with books, Brenda complained about how much homework we had been given.

"And it's the weekend!" she moaned, as if it were news to me.

As we headed toward our bus, I spotted Kevin's red Datsun. He rolled down the passenger window, calling me over.

"Hey," I said, "what's up?" Then it occurred to me that perhaps there was a problem back home.

"Thought I'd pick up my little sister," he said, without budging from the passenger side, which meant he was going to let me take the wheel. Now that Mrs. Passino had moved away, her farmhouse and barn leveled, Kevin had a bit more time on his hands. Not much more time, since most every day he worked from dawn to beyond dusk attempting to make the farm a financial success. It was easy to see he wanted to prove to those who sold out that they had made a mistake. So far, it didn't seem to be working.

I ran around to the driver's side and opened the door, but I stopped when I saw Brenda directly behind me. "Can we drop her off?"

Kevin tapped the console. "Not really. There's something I want to show you."

"Fine," Brenda said. "It'd be too crowded in that sardine can, anyway." With a toss of her head, she marched toward her bus.

Even though Kevin didn't act as though he cared he'd insulted her, I assured him she would get over it soon enough. I climbed in the Datsun without question and pulled away from the school. I'd only recently passed my permit test and was a little shaky behind the wheel, but Kevin seemed more intent on where we were going than how we were getting there.

"Veer left," he said, forcing me to take a familiar dirt path, which soon became nothing more than a crude trail that led to Benny's Lake. Hills of dirty snow bordered the trail, even though spring was nudging earth back to flora and fauna, but the season hadn't had a chance to come to its own just yet.

He made me drive until I could drive no further and had to slam on the brakes with a lurch. Directly in front of us was a sign that posted the message:

NO TRESPASSING. Beside the ominous warning, another sign stated: ***Coming Soon: Lake in the Woods Resort.***

I should have guessed the impromptu trip had something to do with "the destroyer." A couple of months earlier, the local sheriff had had to physically remove Kevin from Mrs. Passino's barn so that the wrecking crew could do their job. But later, when no one was around, he brought me back there and went through the rubble to show me what giving up looked like. The next day, the crew headed to Mr. Miller's place, then to Old Man LeMieux's the next. Each time, Kevin had to be removed and handcuffed, and he now faced a number of trespassing charges. It never stopped him though, because he would always return to see what the destroyer had done. Dad and Grandpa talked solemnly during supper about Kevin's behavior, about his sad intensity.

"He'll get over it," they finally decided; I think more to ease their concerns than for any other reason.

There we sat, facing the bold, menacing signs, not saying a word for a while. Finally, I braved a glance at my brother. His expression was somber, gazing inward. My throat became tight.

"At least we have our memories," I said, barely above a whisper. He did not respond. "Kevin?"

"This is killing Benny," he said.

Out of the corner of my eye I glimpsed my brother, and I was glad that Brenda hadn't come along. She would have had some snide comment to make just then.

I said, "Isn't it time to milk the cows?"

"I suppose."

"Why don't you eat supper with us tonight? I'm making spaghetti and meatballs, your favorite."

He didn't answer, so I simply put the truck in reverse and backed away while his gaze remained fixed on what had been.

If the sap wasn't flowing that spring, well then the gossip was. 'Busco was suddenly going to be the land of opportunity. The name Scoleri Enterprise poured off people's tongues in awed tones, and Kevin said the town was starting to think of this Mr. Scoleri—as yet unseen—as some kind of Santa Claus. He might have been right, because one Sunday morning while coming out of mass, I overheard Evelyn Smith chattering on to Ruby Dupree's mother, saying, "I hear these are gonna be tourists with money to spend and time to kill. I'm sure the women'll want to keep up with their manicures."

"I heard men with that kind of money get manicures too, you know."

Evelyn gasped. "You're not serious, eh."

"Yup. Can you imagine my Billy getting that done?"

Evelyn tottered away, giggling like a little girl on Christmas morning. Days later, when I passed her house, there was a sign on her front lawn: *Nail Technician*. In fine print below, it stated, *Both women and men welcome.*

I scribbled a note in study hall to Brenda about it, then slipped it between the pages of her French book and passed it to her. She scrawled back to me: *Just because she knows how to polish her nails doesn't make her a technician. She's probably hoping she can hook a rich man this way.*

I wasn't sure if Evelyn Smith cared if he was rich or not, as long as he was a man. Suspecting that Mr. Down was watching from the front of the room, I turned the page of my French book, feigning concentration before passing my written comment to Brenda. She let out a loud laugh and then hastily disguised it as a cough. She then wrote her response, folded the paper, and slipped it in the book. A surreptitious glance told me some minor commotion across the room had captured Mr. Down's attention. I took advantage and hurriedly unfolded the note.

Mr. Collings is looking for a cook for that restaurant. Interested?

Brenda's family was good friends with Mr. Collings, who had been the groundskeeper for Northern Adirondack Central School for years and had managed to get a job as overseer for Lake in the Woods Resort, where there was going to be a restaurant.

Struck with the possibility, I gazed at her. "Really? Think they'd hire me?"

"Vicky." Mr. Down was looking at me.

Reggie, who was leaning in his chair in the aisle across from me, said, "Yeah, behave Vicky, or he'll have you sit up in the front again." He then whispered, "That way he can stare at your boobs."

"Shut up," I said.

Mr. Down stood. "What did you say?"

"Nothing. Sorry."

For a few cautious minutes, Brenda and I kept our heads bent over our books, pretending to study, until Brenda mumbled, "It's going to be called Snack Shack. Mr. Collings heard about how you like to cook and asked me about it."

My elbow hit the book, knocking it to the floor. I went to pick it up, but Reggie got it for me, handing it to me with a warning: "Down wants you in the worst way."

Mr. Down was indeed watching me without reserve. I placed the book in front of me and made sure he saw me concentrating on irregular verbs. Once he sat back down, Brenda pointed at the book, as if asking another question. "This will be so excellent," she said. "Mr. Collings said I could work there, too. No more baby-sitting for a dollar an hour. We'll be able to save for Montreal!"

The moment Brenda had found out that Mrs. Fitz, my home economics teacher, planned to recommend me for an apprenticeship at a major restaurant in Montreal, she grabbed on to my apron strings, intending to come along for the ride—as if Montreal was the ideal place for her to get a license to cut hair. Still, my heart pounded as I pointed blindly at words on the page. She was right. And it would look good on my résumé. Snack Shack. Didn't sound too impressive, though. I flipped the page and whispered, "How big's the kitchen?"

She shrugged. "What difference does it make? It's our ticket out of here." She went back to her notebook and scribbled: *I just don't know why Kevin was so against all this.*

That's when it hit me. She must have seen my expression change.

"What?"

"Kevin."

"What about him?"

"I'd be working for the *destroyer*. I'm not going to be able to do it, Bren."

"What!"

Mr. Down got up and strolled toward us, while Reggie said, "Mayday, mayday, he's coming in for a landing," causing everyone in our vicinity except me to giggle. Brenda pulled her book closer and whispered, *"Baiser il adieu."*

"Miss Finley," Mr. Down said, standing over me, his eyes not actually on me. I rested my arms across my bosom. "Is there a problem here? Because if there is, I will have to ask you to move."

"Of course you will," Reggie muttered. Mr. Down ignored the comment.

"No," I said. "I'm just having trouble with this." I pointed at the book.

"Yeah," Brenda piped in, "Mrs. LaCroix is giving us a unit test tomorrow, and Vicky's not going to pass if she doesn't get it. I'm trying to help her get it."

Mr. Down reached over and leafed through the pages of my book, barely grazing me. "Perhaps I could help you...get it," he said.

Brenda said, "Well, it helps me to help her. I'm pretty good at French, but the practice helps." She then turned to me and said, *"Aidez-moi, s'il vous plait chez...uh...chez Snack Shack?"*

It must have sounded French enough to Mr. Down, because he strolled back toward the front, his hands clasped behind his back. And even though it was choppy, I knew what Brenda was saying to me, but before she let me respond, she added, "That resort's coming whether you work there or not. Someone else'll get the job, that's all. I mean, I thought you wanted to cook—and we'd be able to work together." She shook her head. "Sad that you'd pass it up because your brother has you wrapped around his finger like some obsequious fool."

I wasn't sure what 'obsequious' meant, but there was no mistaking what the word fool meant. "Does not," I whispered.

"Well, if he cared about *your* feelings, he'd understand this is an opportunity you can't pass up."

I thought about this, tapping my pen against the paper. She did have a point. Besides, even Dad and Grandpa thought Kevin was becoming a bit "crazy" about everything. Mr. Down was back at his desk, but if he listened with special care he'd be able to hear my "très bien."

Her freckled face broke into a wide, crooked-toothed grin. "Thank you, oh thank you!"

Everyone turned their heads, and Mr. Down stood up again. Brenda said in haste, "I mean, uh…oh, *merci beaucoup!*"

It was too late, though. He gestured for me to come to the front of the class.

"Me?" I said in protest. "But I didn't say anything."

He nodded, and Reggie said, "Yeah, but you're a lot more fun to have next to him than Brillo head."

Once I had settled into the seat directly in front of Mr. Down's desk, I ignored his blatant staring and opened up my worn copy of *Les Misérables*. It was required reading, but I was actually enjoying it. I believe I was drawn to Cosette, because she too lost her mother at such a young age. And she too had to overcome so much. Well, I wasn't living through a revolution, but I planned to overcome my circumstances.

The words blurred on the page as I started thinking about the kitchen at Snack Shack. I even heard the kettles rattling, felt the hot steam waft across my face. It obscured my thinking and made me forget about what my decision would do to my brother.

The ground had some occasional soft, wet spots causing my bike to sink if I went off the narrow trail, but as the sunshine had been intense the past few days, it was now compact. Brenda was traveling at a frantic pace and I found it difficult to keep up with her, but she was used to racing to get from point A to point B, coming from a house filled with clashing Hannigans. The bike she was riding was the coveted prize that she had stolen from her brother, James, to whom it had actually been promised for the day. Every so often I glanced over my shoulder, certain we'd be discovered then reprimanded—not for sneaking off with James's bike, but for trespassing. We couldn't claim ignorance, since the posted signs warned us that we'd be prosecuted. And yet, here we were, cutting through the woods on the makeshift trail recently pummeled into the earth by a construction crew. Between swerving around fallen branches using one hand and stilling my bouncing breasts with the other as I tried to avoid the ruts, I got farther behind Brenda than I cared to be. Eventually, she disappeared around a curve, and I decided to make the ride a leisurely one.

The woods no longer closed in on me the way I remembered them doing. Instead becoming more difficult to cut through, the path widened the farther I pedaled. Strewn along the way, glistening moist with sap, were dozens of tree stumps. A sinking feeling came to me as I imagined Kevin gazing on the carnage. I did what Brenda's mother always said to do when things looked down and I looked up. Okay, so she was talking about heaven and all things spiritual, but high above, buds just beginning to blossom on the remaining trees standing, was a sight just as hopeful.

A turn around the curve proved Brenda had opted to keep on going. Either that, or she had decided to hide behind some bushes and try to scare me as I passed by. She enjoyed frightening me.

"Kiss it goodbye!" I called out, continuing to pedal while streaks of warm rays streamed across me through the wide gaps overhead. If trees are left standing, soon a canopy of green leaves will crowd out any sunshine. I reached another bend and rattled around it, only to slam on my brakes at the sight before me. Brenda, her mouth open in awe, was clearly just as amazed.

We had stumbled into another world right here in Churubusco. A new world. It used to be that Benny's Lake was snuggled by woods and rocky terrain. I wondered if perhaps I'd taken it for granted. Now, there it was, massive, demanding to be admired, the shivering ripples lapping the shore, reaching for the jagged rocks and ageless trees.

But they were not there.

What had once been rugged shoreline was now smoothed down, with fine grains of beige sand traveling along an unfamiliar beachfront.

"What's that?" Brenda said, stretching her head to better hear.

There was a distinct rumbling in the distance. It was easy to guess what it was, but instead of taking flight, escaping from discovery, Brenda jumped on her bike and headed toward it. I'm not sure why, other than curiosity, but I followed. Soon I came upon a monstrous yellow machine leveling powdered sand, which was being dumped by an ugly, noisy truck spitting smoke from its tail end. Man and machinery were orchestrating the demise of what had once been a place for solitude. A few feet away, a tractor was dragging off felled trees. I rolled up next to Brenda and could do nothing but watch in horror.

"Wild, isn't it?" Brenda said, her freckled face lit up.

I tried to brush the tears away before she could see them. "It looks so...so ruined. So different." I envisioned the pain on Kevin's face. "It'll never be the same."

"Thank God."

I closed my eyes and there we were, Kevin and I, leaping from one boulder to the next, finally collapsing on the biggest and me always working the subject of Mom into our conversation.

Out loud, and without realizing it, I said, "Poor Kevin."

Brenda whipped around so hard her thick, red, bunched-up ponytail flopped to one side. "Don't you start changing your mind again. Vicky, so help me, Mr. Collings is depending on us."

"Well, Mrs. Scott did call and ask if I'd baby-sit for her this summer."

"Oh, that'll jumpstart your career."

"I told her I had a job, but still...he's going to hate me."

"What else are brothers for?" She hopped on the purloined bike and took off again.

I yelled to her, telling her that I was going to go back, but she didn't answer. How could she hear me, though, over the roar of the machines? I had to go after her, which was the excuse I used to see how much work had been done on Snack Shack. This was the carrot Brenda had dangled to convince me to trespass in the first place.

My tires crunched over pine duff, and it was getting more and more difficult to pedal. The rumbling and whining of machinery reverberated all around me. 'Spoilers of nature' was what Kevin had called them. I couldn't help but agree as the strong gasoline odor and bluish haze choked the forest. Off to the side were trees, appearing green and vibrant, piled into a horizontal heap. Finally, I spotted Brenda and struggled across the rutty path to get to her. One by one, the machines died down, and we were eyed by a scattered group of grimy, sweaty men.

"Don't you know you're on private property?" shouted a man crusted with dirt, dragging a shovel in his large hand.

"We're looking for where Snack Shack is going to be," Brenda said. "We're not really trespassing. Mr. Collings wanted us to check on its progress, because we're going to be working there."

"Really," said the man.

Brenda nodded, and did what she usually did when subterfuge failed to get the response she was looking for: She roped me in to her scheme. "Yeah, Vicky's going to be the chef."

The man looked at me and the lines in his face disappeared. He rested his weight on the shovel and smiled at me. "And you're Vicky."

A voice from above said, "Yep, Miss Vicky Finley, always the flavor of the month."

I looked up to see Brad Hunt sitting at the controls of the crane, his eyes alive and eager, settling too long on me.

"Hi, Brad," Brenda said. "Would you know where Snack Shack is? We're going to be working there this summer and—"

"You, too, pretty thing?"

When I didn't reply, Brenda said, "Well, it's just for the summer. We both have bigger plans. Someday I'll be the owner of my own cosmetology shops in all the big cities. But for now—"

Brad chuckled. His arm, thick and dusty, poking out of a rolled-up T-shirt, pointed down the path. Before another moment went by, I pedaled past Brenda, shouting for her to come, but I didn't get too far, as a tree limb was blocking my way. There was nowhere to go, since there was thick foliage on either side of the unwieldy limb. I'd have to move it, which wasn't going to be easy.

"Why don't you let me get that for you?" Brad said, his face suddenly inches from mine. But it wasn't a chivalrous offer, his voice filled with suggestion. He didn't attempt to move the tree. Instead, he stood over me, gazing down at me, making me feel exposed.

"I can get it," I said, realizing I'd first have to pass him to get to the limb, and he wasn't budging. I paid little attention to the men who had gathered, a solid collection looking much like the rocks they had been heaving, and slipped by Brad, smelling beer on his breath. The branch was heavy and awkward as I tried to move it. The collection of men murmured and guffawed, egging Brad on. Finally, I pushed the branch over far enough to get through. Trying not to pay attention to the breathing boulders, I picked up my bike and started to push it, until Brad grabbed the frame.

"Where you going?"

"Let go," I said.

He put his smirking, clammy face in mine. "How 'bout riding me, baby?"

Over the chuckles, I shouted, "I said, let go!"

To my surprise, he did. I took off over a bumpy trail, wondering if Brenda was behind me. I pedaled hard and not nearly as fast as I wished, wanting to put distance between him and me. I didn't stop until I came upon a foundation. The blocks of wet cement were a bright, clean gray. I used my bike for support while catching my breath. *Could this be it?* Seemed so small. No bigger than a hot-dog stand.

"Hey," Brenda said, huffing toward me.

"Why wouldn't you help me back there?" I shouted.

"I didn't want to interfere. He was flirting with you."

"Flirting! He's disgusting."

Brenda rolled her eyes. "God, Vicky, you're going to have to borrow some of Kenny's magazines and stop being so uptight."

This was the third time Brenda had mentioned her brother-in-law and his lurid reading material. Apparently, Jane let Brenda read it when she visited, the two of them giggling over *Playboy* and other magazines that Father Richards harped against from the altar. Brenda thought she was an authority on sex. Compared to me, I suppose she was.

She dropped her bike and walked over to the foundation. "This must be it."

"It can't be. It's too small."

"What were you expecting, one of those fancy restaurants you're always reading about?"

Maybe I had had something a bit more grand in mind, but this square of space was pitiful. Brenda looked into the gaping hole. "It seems small now, but wait 'til it's finished."

I dropped my bike next to hers and went over to scrutinize the space, to picture what it would look like when completed. "I don't know, Bren, there's hardly any room for the kitchen. And where will the dining area be?"

"Dining area?" She laughed. "I never said there was going to be a dining area. Mr. Collings did say something about picnic tables, though." She looked around, resting her sights at a stand of hemlocks. "They'll probably be there."

So it *was* nothing more than a hot-dog stand. I batted back the tears, noting the trampled shadbush, its cluster of white flowers crushed into the ground, a trail of tire tracks having beaten down everything in its path. *Spoilers of nature.*

It was at that moment I remembered the Great White Pine.

Without hesitation, I ran to my bike and took off as Brenda called after me. If she wanted me, she'd have to follow. The farther I got, the more I struggled over fallen limbs, the path closing in on me. I didn't know the woods the way Kevin did, but as long as the lake was in view, I was okay. I'd get a glimpse of the body of leaden-colored water through the occasional open patch, and I knew I wasn't lost.

The Great White Pine was sure to be the tallest tree in the North Country, but it was easier focusing on the trail if I focused on the ground. All I had to do was watch for where the big boulder cropped up along the lake's edge, since it was only a short distance from the tree. But what if the boulder and Great White Pine were no longer there? The thought sickened me. Then, I came to a sharp bend and there it was—the boulder, stubbornly rising out of the lake with sheer resistance. Across from that beautiful sight, branches open wide and welcoming, was the Great White Pine. I could barely see the top, the tree standing tall and regal, looking as calm as it did majestic. I let my bike fall and ran to the tree, grasping a prickly needle in my hand, the roaring threat of machinery in the distance.

Then a limb moved, caused to quiver by someone or something. I caught my breath and backed away. There was a shuffling sound beneath the fanned-out branches near the trunk. *Benny?* The thought that I could be in the presence of a ghost paralyzed me. I tried to call for Brenda, but nothing would come out.

"Scary, isn't it?"

I started to run, until I realized the voice was Kevin's.

"There you are," Brenda said, rolling up next to me. "Why'd you take off like that?" She noticed Kevin crawling out from under the branches and asked what he was doing there, as if he were the only one breaking the law.

"You don't think they'll cut it down?" I said, caressing the pine needles.

"You two are pathetic," Brenda said. "God, you're talking about a tree."

Kevin said, "You're right, Brenda. It's only a tree." He pointed to our surroundings. "This is only a forest. And that lake is only a lake. And we're here to destroy it all, just because we can."

She rolled her eyes and shifted her weight. "Aren't you afraid they'll arrest you again?"

"It's nothing more than a rape."

She clicked her tongue. "Everybody thinks it's going to improve this town. Campers will come from all over and spend their money here. Mr. Collings said that they might tear down the old schoolhouse and build a grocery store there. That's just good business. Who knows, maybe someday I could open a smaller version of one of my salons right here."

"Seems the whole damn town sold out."

Brenda's cheeks flushed until her mass of freckles got lost in burning red, which I knew meant trouble. "There's nothing wrong with making money, Kevin."

"Except when it's dirty money."

I did not want this conversation to be happening. I hadn't found the time to tell Kevin about my plans to work at Lake in the Woods, and this was not how I wanted him to find out. I said, "Hey, don't you have chores to do?"

Brenda rolled her bike directly in front of Kevin, looking to challenge him. I caught her by the arm, willing her to keep quiet, giving her the warning: "Kiss it goodbye, Bren."

Kevin put a finger to his lips, signaling us to be quiet. "Hear that?" he whispered.

I paused. He often played this game with me when we were in the woods, making me guess what kind of bird might be chirping; often, it was not a bird of any sort, but a chipmunk. Now, all I could hear was the not-so-far-off rumblings.

"Sounds of modern man," he said, his eyes bugging out.

"Yeah?" Brenda said. "Music to my ears."

"Used to be I could sit under this tree and hear the hammering of a woodpecker. I've had deer meander right by me to get a drink from the lake."

"Ooh, I got goose bumps," Brenda said.

"Kiss it goodbye," I mumbled to her.

"You think that's going to ever happen again?" He looked from Brenda to me. "Don't count on it."

I dropped my gaze to the ground. How could I look him in the eyes?

"I can't believe the lake's not even Benny's anymore," he said.

I fiddled with the pedal of my bike with my foot, twirling it round and round, wishing for an excuse to get away. I said, "It'll always be Benny's Lake, Kev."

"Well, someone should've told Scoleri Enterprise. They've gone and put up a sign across the lake where I suppose the main entrance will be." He sneered. "'Lake in the Woods.' Real original."

Barely above a whisper, I said, "It's not so bad."

"Not so bad?" They're going to have some sort of hot-dog stand back there. Knocking down trees hundreds of years old so people can cram their faces with hot dogs!"

My throat tightened as I heard the words come out of Brenda's mouth. "Least it's gonna make us money so we can get out of this place."

I turned toward her, yelling for her to shut up. When I dared to look at Kevin, he was studying me.

"*Us*? You too, Vicky?"

"Yeah," Brenda said, "and we're going to make more than minimum wage."

Sentences I'd been practicing for days jumbled in my head, prepared explanations of why I was doing the unthinkable had vanished. He didn't say anything, but there was disappointment on his face and in his walk when he trudged off. I wanted him to say something to me, yell even. But he just kept walking.

You're a lot like Mom, after all.

The words didn't come from him; still, I heard them.

"Oh, let him go," Brenda said with a shrug.

"I told you to kiss it goodbye!" I said. "Why didn't you just kiss it goodbye?"

"Stop with the histrionics, Vicky. It's no big deal. He'll get over it."

"Why didn't you let *me* tell him?"

"When was that going to happen?"

I didn't say anything. Couldn't.

"You have to admit, he's getting more and more weird. Love struck over a bunch of trees."

"Shut up."

"Don't you think it's sick he's never had a girlfriend?"

"I said, shut up!"

"Fine. Let's go." She started to pedal away. When I didn't follow, she turned around and called to me.

I didn't answer.

"I'm not going to wait for you."

"Suit yourself."

Moments later, I was standing alone. Brenda was probably waiting for me right around the bend, planning to try and scare me, then laugh and pretend the fight never happened. Well, she could wait all day. She had no right to tell Kevin a thing. I kicked up some pine duff, hating my life right then more than I ever had. I couldn't get his sad image out of my mind. He'd always been Kevin, alone. Now, I suddenly felt responsible for it.

The voices of men approaching interrupted my thoughts. I dropped to the ground and crawled beneath the expansive branches. The forest floor was musty. I sat quietly and waited. I couldn't make out what the men were saying, but I saw two sets of work boots clomping along the path. Soon, Brad Hunt was in full view, swinging a small cooler at his side. Another worker I didn't recognize was walking in step with him. I doubted they would notice me hidden beneath the branches, but they might see the bright red chrome of my bike a few feet away from where I was hiding. They broke from the trail and headed over to the boulder—Kevin's and my boulder. Brad opened the cooler and pulled out a six-pack of Genesee. He ripped a can free from the plastic ring and tossed it over to his buddy. They both flipped the broken metal tabs into the lake and began guzzling. Brad's throat vibrated as he swilled. When he finally stopped to take a breath, he let out a belch, punctuating it by tossing the can into the lake.

"Hey!" I scrambled out from beneath the tree, not thinking about anything but Kevin's passion and the disappointment I had caused him. However, once Brad and his buddy saw me, wearing mixed expressions of surprise and amusement, I realized I might have made a bold yet foolish mistake.

Brad mumbled something to the other guy, and after he also polished off his beer, he handed the empty to Brad.

"Could this be what you're yapping about?" He swung his arm back and tossed the can far into the lake. It dipped and lurched on a gentle wave.

"There's a law against littering," I said, my mouth feeling dry.

"Littering, eh? Why we ain't littering. Are we, Jim? We're what you'd call decoratin'."

Jim chuckled and handed Brad another beer. Brad, in turn, offered it to me, his mouth twitching. When I wouldn't respond, he hopped down from the boulder and swaggered toward me. I glanced at my bike. Chances are, if I ran for it, he'd be sure to catch me. Besides, Kevin had once told me never to turn my back on a wild animal to run. He said I'd be good as dead. The way Brad was approaching me, I felt as though I were being stalked. I stared the creature in the eye and took my toughest stance, all the while concentrating on not shaking.

"So, what's the problem, Miss Vicky Finley?"

"I...I...just don't think you should be polluting the lake."

"And you'd be right." He raised his can in salute to me. "But if you don't tell on me, I won't tell on you."

"I don't pollute."

"But you did trespass, eh?" And that's just as illegal, wouldn't you say?" He took another swill then said, "What, your brother got you spying for him?"

"Brenda told you why we're here. She's going to be back any minute."

"Don't think so. She passed us some time ago. Said she was heading back home. Couldn't help but notice you weren't with her. Saw your brother, too. What, some kinda family reunion out here in the woods today?" He turned to Jim and called, "Hey, remember that asshole tryin' to stop us from coming in here a few weeks back?"

Jim nodded, popping open another beer.

"This is his pretty little sister." Brad eyed me with one long, sweeping gaze. "Ain't you somethin', though."

"A rare breed," Jim said, bringing the can to his mouth.

"Such a shame. Won't even look at me." He grazed my cheek with his rough, stubby finger.

There was no more debate. I went for my bike, but just as I started to pick it up, a work boot clamped it back down. I looked up to see Brad grinning at me.

"Let me go."

"First gimme a kiss."

"No."

"Ya know, I should bring you in for trespassin'."

"Then bring me in." It would be safer than being deep in the woods with a couple of drunks, both constantly grabbing their manhood in crude fashion. Calling his bluff made his big round face turn purple.

He grabbed my arm, squeezing it tight. "I should, ya know. Unless you choose to be real nice to me."

"Let go. You're hurting me!"

"You think you're too good for me, don't you? Rather have one of those book-smart assholes, like your brother." He yanked me, pressing me into him. He was rock solid, with a bulge here and there. "You're probably doing him, eh?"

"Hunt, let her go," Jim said. "We don't want no trouble. How 'bout another beer?"

He stared at me with squinty eyes then turned toward Jim. "Sounds good to me," he said. Just as he went to catch the can sailing toward him, I pulled the bike from his foothold. I thought I might make it until he blocked me from shoving off, the can landing at his feet.

"You like to dance? You and me gotta go dancin' sometime."

I'd been too close to getting away to risk being trapped again. As hard as I could, I rammed my bike into Brad's groin. He doubled up, grabbing himself, yowling. I pushed off with all my strength and veered around the bigger branches, ignoring the brambles that scratched my legs. Behind me were enraged curses and seething promises of revenge, but I kept going, whirring by the monster machines, ignoring the wolf whistles, keeping my pace fast and furious. My heart pounded, and didn't stop racing until I reached the main road. That's when I dared to slow down and look behind me. Gratefully, no one was there.

In spite of what had just happened—or worse, what could have happened—Kevin was all I could think about. That night, I fried up a batch of perch, prepared my homemade tartar sauce, and placed it on a plate with potatoes au gratin. I walked it over to the little house, but when I got to his door and turned the knob, the door did not budge. It was locked. Kevin never locked his door.

It was a message I couldn't ignore.

CHAPTER 8

If there was a lesson I learned that spring it was that money makes things happen. And big money makes things happen faster. Creating a resort where none existed in a matter of months is the fastest of happenings. It had a dizzying effect on 'Busco. Around the end of June, long and luxurious camping trailers began pulling into our small town, recreation vehicles more glamorous and classy looking than the stationary trailer homes many of the locals owned.

Odd thing, too: since all those RV's started coming in, one with Manitoba plates and another all the way from California, Brenda started talking less about getting out. What she did keep harping on was how eager she was to meet the Scoleris of Scoleri Enterprise. Apparently, she was impressed with how quickly they got things done without having to worry about money. She'd asked Mrs. Passino, before Mrs. Passino packed up to move a couple of towns away to the new mobile home she'd recently purchased, if she'd met any of the Scoleris during the sale of her property. She had not. However, Mrs. Passino spoke of the mystery men in glowing, almost messianic terms. "All my grandchildren are going to college," she said. "Without that money, it never could've happened."

Lake in the Woods was the hot topic in the area. The reporter from the *Plattsburgh Press* did a cover story on it, inserting Kevin's photo near the bottom, his hair unkempt, his eyes wild. The caption read, "Finley's Futile Fight."

Even though he wasn't talking to me, I continued to bring him supper. Since his door was always locked now, I would bring him a plate covered with aluminum foil and leave it on his front steps. Sometimes I'd hear him rustling around inside and I would knock, but then the rustling would stop. I was sure I could hear him breathe, though. It was a cold war I wanted no part of, and sometimes I'd bang on his door until my knuckles were red. Still, he would not let me in.

One day, I found a package on his front steps with a note.

༄

Vicky,

I just need for you to understand me. Maybe this will help.

Kevin

I ripped open the package to find a worn copy of *Adventures in the Wilderness*, by a Reverend William Murray. I wasn't familiar with the book, but leafed the pages yellow with age, some feeling as though they'd crumble at the touch.

I tried reading it; honestly I did. It was so boring, though, and my mind kept wandering with thoughts of marinades and sauces, certainly not trees and wildlife. However, he had made the effort to reconnect, which meant there was hope.

Grandpa pointed a gnarled finger across the table toward the bowl of sweet peas and when I started to pass them, he shook his head and waved his hand harder. The older he got, the less he wanted to say. I reached for the platter of roast beef and he nodded. He took the platter and scraped off two large slices, dropping them on his plate.

With a mouthful of potatoes, Dad said, "You gonna have time to cook like this with that job of yours?"

"I'll prepare what I can ahead of time. It might run a little late, but—"

"How late?"

I cleared my throat. "I don't know yet." I saw that I needed to change the subject and rattled my brain for some topic. Then it dawned on me: "What kind of car you working on now?"

I'd seen the rusty blue vehicle sitting in the garage earlier when I'd come home from a bike ride with Brenda. We'd clocked how long it would take to get to Snack Shack: Twenty-seven minutes. Not too bad.

He ignored the question and said, "I'll talk to Mr. Collings."

"It's my job, Dad." I felt panic rising within me. "So, did you sell that other car?" The other car was some gray-colored tank he'd been working on for months. I knew Dad had actually sold it, but I couldn't think of anything else to say to change the subject. The topic of old jalopies was going nowhere, though.

"I'll let him know you have things to get done here."

"Dad, I need the money for Montreal."

"It's a waste. You'll get there, meet someone, get married. Where's the cheese?"

I should've known better than to leave it off the table. It was his way of reminding me that he contributed more than laconic comments and an occasional icy stare. Leaving it off the table was my way of showing I didn't care. I went to the refrigerator and pulled out the familiar plate of mozzarella, Muenster, American, and cheddar. I decided Dad could take the plastic off for himself and slammed the plate down next to him.

"I don't plan on getting married," I said. Then went to the sink, squirted dish liquid in, and blasted on the water.

"So," Grandpa said, "tomorrow's the big day, eh?"

I muttered yes and then opened the door, responding to Conroy's bark to be let out. When I did, Kevin was walking into the shed.

"Hi," I said. "I have your plate ready, but you could come inside and eat with us." He didn't respond, but called Conroy, and the two of them headed out to the barn.

I went back to doing dishes. There was a small mirror above the sink with painted green ivy bordering the glass. For as long as I could remember that mirror had been there, and I had always assumed my mother had put it there. I'd see her getting ready to go out on Saturday night with my father and making that mirror her final stop to check the lipstick and hair before running out the door. I refused to look at myself in that mirror, because whenever I happened to catch a glimpse of my reflection, it wasn't me I saw but the woman in the three-by-five Polaroid.

I washed the dishes in silence, just as I did every night while my father finished his cup of coffee. I didn't have to look to know he was leaning on the table, his plate pushed away, his cup in front of him, and a distant look in his eyes. He got up and shuffled by me, heading in to the garage to turn the piece of junk sitting there into something salable.

I went to the table to collect more dishes. Grandpa was swabbing his plate with some bread to soak up any remaining gravy before getting up. He used the table to support his feeble body. I went back to the sink and dropped the dishes in the water. Then it occurred to me what I could do to make things right with my brother. I wasn't sure why I hadn't thought of it earlier.

"He loves ya, Vicky." Grandpa was standing behind me, patting my back. "It's just hard for him."

I glanced in the mirror at Grandpa's reflection, his filmy blue eyes lost in a face rippled with lines.

"I know, Grandpa. Still, I feel bad."

"Ain't no call for you to be feelin' bad."

"I shouldn't be working there. It's like a slap in Kevin's face."

"Kevin? I'm talking 'bout your bitter old man."

I stopped washing the pot and turned to look at him.

"He's not too crazy with your talk 'bout running off to Montreal."

"I'm not running off, Grandpa."

"What's wrong with Plattsburgh?"

"Grandpa, that's not where the apprenticeship is. Anyway, I think it's *you* who's not crazy about me going to Montreal."

He pinched me lightly on the cheek then headed toward the front porch, where he likes to sit each night to watch the sun give way to the rising moon.

The sound of the jalopy's coughing and wheezing came from the garage, then there was a choking noise and a sudden revving down of the motor. Cheese and cars—that's how I thought of my dad. Cheese was for security, cars for chasing away the time.

Once the dishes were done, I ran up to my room and lifted my mattress. I pulled the picture from the pages of my diary. I wrapped it in some paper along with a note telling Kevin I thought it was his turn to have the photo for a while. I placed it, along with his supper, on his front steps then went back home to work in my garden.

I poked around the dirt and pulled weeds for a while as dusk settled over me. The row I was presently in would be cucumbers, which made me think of a recipe from my French cookbook that I planned to try. *Concombres farcis* wouldn't work at Snack Shack, but I was already planning on suggesting deep-fried vegetables. I'd serve them with a variety of dips. There'd be eggplant, carrots, squash—

"What does Brad Hunt drive?"

I jumped, startled, and then caught my breath when I saw Kevin standing at the end of the row. "What?" I said, wiping sweat from my brow.

"What does Brad Hunt drive?"

Brad Hunt? I shrugged.

"He just went by real slow about five minutes ago. Didn't you see him?"

I shook my head, looking out toward the empty road. Some days not a car goes by for hours.

"Seems to be going by quite a bit lately."

I stood, wanting to run over and hug him. He was talking to me!

"Maroon," Kevin said. "Chevy pickup."

I wasn't thinking about maroon pickups.

"Would you know why he keeps going by here?"

"No, but does this mean you're talk—"

He pulled something from his back pocket and tossed it at me. "I don't want to see this ever again." As he strode off, he said, "I'd watch out for him."

I bent down and picked up the Polaroid, which now had a crease running down my mom's face.

CHAPTER 9

Dusk began to settle around Brenda and me while tiny ripples lolled up to shore and wet our bare feet. We'd closed Snack Shack for the evening awhile ago, but instead of heading home as usual, we had wandered down to the shore and collapsed. Earlier, the beach had been littered with campers, most coming over to Snack Shack for a soda or maybe a small order of fries, something to hold them over until the night's festivities took place on the other side of the lake. I was still angry with Brenda for not telling me about Moonshadows—the other dining choice at Lake in the Woods. Actually, from what I could tell, it was the *only* dining choice. Clearly, I was working on the wrong side of the lake.

On our first day at Snack Shack, I said to Brenda, "That's where I should be working. Not this hot dog stand."

Passing by and dragging a garbage can, Mr. Collings said, "No way. They hired a chef from France to make fine cuisine. What do you know about fine cuisine?"

Even though Mr. Collings couldn't tell me exactly what the fine cuisine was, the campers could, leaving me to realize that perhaps Mr. Collings was right: I knew nothing about fine cuisine.

"The bouillabaisse was out of this world," Mrs. Edwards, the gynecologist from Toronto, said. Even Randy Daniels, a boy younger than Brenda and myself, said, "The crème brûlée was awesome." His brother David added, "I'm getting it again tonight."

I didn't know what bouillabaisse or crème brûlée was, but I was willing to learn. More than anything, I was dying to know what the kitchen at Moonshadows looked like. Chances were, I'd never get to see it, since the culinary extravaganza was for guests of Lake in the Woods only. Locals were not permitted to taste the caviar or sip the expensive champagne.

I wasn't the only one who was frustrated by the blatant elitism. Brenda kicked up some sand and smashed her fist to the ground. "It's not fair," she said. She'd been talking less of Montreal when the world was actually driving in to 'Busco, but now it seemed that same world was elbowing her, and the rest of the locals, toward the sidelines, and each day she was feeling more and more slighted. Earlier, while the sun shone and our side of the lake was filled with activity, I hadn't been upset that there was going to be a party across the lake, a combination Fourth of July and grand opening celebration, but then the sun began to set in the purple sky and Moonshadows shone in the distance like a sprawling, glittering, tormenting diamond. From a distance, the private club looked like a glass palace, lit with thousands of twinkling lights.

I rested my head on my raised knees. "I wonder how many stoves it has."

Brenda sighed. "You're crazy. Wouldn't you rather be over there all dressed up, gabbing on about…about…well, I don't know. Maybe current events."

"Like what?"

"I don't know. Like…what do you think those men were doing in that apartment? My dad says Nixon's being set up."

"Maybe they were looking for the kitchen." I gazed across the lake. While the lonely sounds of croaking frogs and chirruping crickets surrounded us, an occasional shriek of laughter mingling with music drifted over from the other side. I glanced at Brenda and thought I detected a tear slipping down her cheek, which was not a common sight for the brazen redhead.

I nudged her. "Another glass of champagne, darling?" When she didn't laugh, I tried again. "A canapé?"

"Stop! This just doesn't piss you off? I mean, what if *she* was over there?"

There was no need to guess who Brenda was referring to.

"What if she was over there with some rich man, knowing you're only minutes away, and she—?"

"Why do you have to say mean things like that?"

"Because you don't. Come on, Vicky, you must think about her."

"Why should I? She left, not me." It sounded tough and cold; but in truth, not a day went by that I didn't think of her. No one had to know that, though, especially Brenda.

When we were younger and had play dates, Brenda insisted on playing a game she called Runaway Mom. Brenda would pretend she was me, and she always instructed me to be my mother. On one occasion, my bedroom was a grocery store, my bed and dressers the shelves filled with cereal, pickles, and other items I'd borrowed from the kitchen to make the scene authentic. Brenda, playing an older version of me, would walk by, pretending to be pushing a cart, and suddenly act shocked to discover I, her mother, was shopping in the same grocery store. She'd start yelling at me, telling me how bad I was to have walked out, which was when I'd stop the scene and give direction.

"No, don't yell. Cry and hug me. Then I'll say how hard I've been trying to find you."

Brenda rolled her eyes. "That wouldn't be true. She knows where her home is."

"I don't want to play anymore," I'd say, and would gather up the cereal and jar of pickles, carting them back to the kitchen.

Now, after a few wordless minutes passed, filled with distant music and laughter, Brenda said, "Still, what would you do?"

"If I saw her?"

"Yeah."

I had every possible scenario played out and I knew that once the day comes, because there was no doubt that the day would come, my reaction would be nothing at all what I dreamed it would be.

"Vicky?" Brenda prodded.

"I don't know."

"I know what I'd say: Go to hell!"

"Brenda! You're talking about my mother. I'm sure she had a good reason for leaving." I just hadn't discovered what it was yet.

Across the lake, inside the glass palace, specks of people moved about. I imagined her laughing, tossing her head back, a glass of wine in her hand…no, champagne.

"Oh, I guess you're right," Brenda said. "She was probably going to come back, but just got too busy. You know how life can do that."

I stood.

"Don't go," Brenda said. "I'm sorry. Really." She reached up and grabbed my hand, pulling me back down. "Besides, the fireworks are going to start soon."

Rumor had it that the fireworks were going to be spectacular, a sight this town had never before seen. Supposedly, some camera crew was in town to film it for the eleven o'clock news, and some company called Pyrotechnique had been preparing for the show all day out on the lake. Earlier, some of the guys had even come over for hot dogs and drinks. One of them told me his name was Greg and asked if we could get together after the show. I told him I'd see without actually meaning it.

Another rumor was that some of the Scoleris of Scoleri Enterprise were in town for the celebration, making it an official grand opening party. Brenda had looked for them all day long, but when they didn't appear, Brenda said that we were going to have to go scope them out.

"Whoa! WhoaWoe! Woe!" Mr. Collings interjected. "You can't just go over there. There's security and everything." He was a small, wiry man with unmanageable tufts of hair cropping up from his balding head.

"Security?" Brenda and I said in unison.

"These Scoleris have more money 'en God. They know people in big places."

"You met them?" Brenda said.

He nodded and sucked up some air, hitching up his pants as if he were one of the important people in the know.

"Then maybe you could see if it'd be okay if Vicky and I went over there for a little while. Tell them we work here and wouldn't cause any—"

"Brenda, you just don't understand. These guests pay big bucks to belong to this club. If they saw you two mingling in the crowd, they'd be pretty upset." Mr. Collings took off, leaving Brenda pouting at the counter. That's when the subject of taking flight from this town came up again. I could see her mentally packing her bags so that she could make her own mark in the world.

We sat quietly while the sky drank up the purple and filled to a rich black with hundreds of stars appearing first here, then there. Tucked between the trees behind us along the beachfront were empty RV's, the campers having boated over to Moonshadows, leaving behind soft ripples in their wake.

All day long, there had been a flurry of activity in the middle of the lake on the small tanker, until it became too dark to see much of anything. Now, finally, a shriek filled the air and the sky overhead exploded with color. Benny's Lake reflected the radiance. I gasped. I couldn't help it; I was struck by the array of images splashed across the heavens. From the other side of the lake, there were cheers and applause. Brenda leapt up and joined in, clapping so hard her hands must have hurt.

She turned to look at me. "I bet they can see this all the way into Canada."

"Probably," I said. It was a certainty that Kevin would be able to see it from wherever he was. We hadn't spoken since he had approached me in the garden, but each morning, I'd see the supper plate I'd brought him the night before resting in the dish rack. Sometimes, I'd see him out in the fields working with

Don, a farmhand he'd hired. I'd wave, but Don would return it. With each day that passed, I wondered if our cold war would ever end.

A grand finale of fireworks erupted in a continuous explosion of reds, whites, and blues, until finally the sky dimmed to its original black canvas dotted by stars. The applause dwindled and the crowd, looking much like a troop of ants, trailed back into the glass palace. The thumping of percussion streamed over to us, and the ants started bopping.

"I can't wait till next year," Brenda said.

"Yeah," I agreed. That's when we would be packing up for Montreal, where she planned to focus on cosmetology and I on the art of cooking. I'd make bouillabaisse and crème brulée, for sure. We were going to share an apartment together. A year seemed like an eternity to Brenda. For me, it seemed like a year.

"Hey," I said. "You'll be an aunt by then." Her sister Jane, who'd moved to Syracuse after she'd married, was due to have a baby any day.

She didn't seem to hear me. "I wonder what they look like," she said, still standing, gazing across the lake.

"Who?"

"The Scoleris."

"Probably fat, ugly, and bald."

"Who cares? I'd be blinded by the dollar signs."

I shook my head and strolled toward my bike. "Nahnahnahnah, nahnah-nahnah, hey, hey, hey, goodbye…kiss it goodbye."

"Dare to dream, Vicky," she said, catching up to me on her very own bike, which her parents had given her for her birthday. "Dare to dream. Nothing wrong with that."

Still, she started singing our anthem with me and laughing, the two of us coasting along the dirt road, heading home.

CHAPTER 10

While Mr. Collings counted the day's profits, I dawdled, pretending to be doing some last-minute straightening, even though Snack Shack was finished for the night, the window where we served the burgers and fries closed by an aluminum shutter, and the side door locked. Mr. Collings was making fewer and fewer appearances during the day, leaving Brenda and me unsupervised while he went off to ensure the campers were content, as well as following the campground rules. At least that's what he told us and anyone within hearing distance. There were times, though, when I saw him sitting on his bony backside, leaning against a tree, his cap over his eyes, while he snored as loud as a chainsaw. However, at the end of the day he was wide eyed and eager, sitting at his makeshift desk, consisting of a crate and an overturned bucket. He had a look of satisfaction as he thumbed the stack of fives and tens.

I put the mustard and ketchup on either side of the napkin holder then back again, watching Mr. Collings finally wrap a rubber band around the last bundle of bills and place it in his pouch. He glanced up at me. "Another good day."

"We're trying."

"Brenda left?"

I nodded.

"All excited 'bout being an aunt, eh?"

Another nod. Brenda had tried to act as if Jane's baby was no big deal, but I saw the way she jumped on her bike and tore out of the campsite after her brother, Mike, who was winded and flushed, tore in on his ten-speed with the news.

"What'd she have?" Mr. Collings said.

"A boy." Brenda's mother was taking the five hour ride to Syracuse, and Brenda wanted to go with her. "I told her to go ahead, that I'd clean up."

He surveyed the eatery. "Good job."

"Oh, no big deal."

He stood clasping the pouch close to his chest. "So, you need a ride or somethin'?"

I shook my head. "I…I wanted to talk to you about something."

He cleared his throat. "Listen, Vicky, I told you, they already have a full staff over there, and—"

"Oh, no. That's not it." I sucked up the nerve and blurted, "Brenda said she thought you might let me try some of my recipes here, and I was wondering if I could. At least I could make something interesting for lunch," I said.

"Like what?" he said.

"French-fried vegetables."

"Vegetables?"

"Well, yeah, instead of just potatoes, we could have zucchini, carrots, cauliflower, sweet potatoes—"

"And you make them like French fries?"

"Well, first you coat them in a batter. They're delicious, and it doesn't take too much time to make them." His doubtful expression forced me to go at him from all possible angles. "Brenda's family is crazy about them. You can ask Mr. Hannigan." *Mr. Hannigan…that would be your close friend.* "They all think the campers would like the variety."

He patted the thick pouch. "We're doing good, Vicky. Wouldn't want to jinx it or cause more overhead to cut into the profits."

"We wouldn't stop making other stuff. We could just introduce it slowly and see how it goes. And I'd be willing to show Sandy and Kelly how to make them on my days off." Sandy and Kelly worked at Snack Shack when Brenda and I didn't.

He seemed to think about it, then said, "What would you need?"

"Just flour and eggs. I'd get the vegetables from my garden. I wouldn't charge you anything for the trial period."

"Whoa, whoa. We got room for all that?"

"Sure. I've figured it all out. I could cut the vegetables on that counter, and the stove is big enough to hold a pot to deep fry them."

He hesitated longer than I would have liked. Then: "Well, I guess we could give it a whirl. But if I don't see a profit, it gets canned."

His pencil-thin mustache twitched at how I leapt and squealed. This was why I'd gone against Kevin, why I'd put up with my brother's cold shoulder for the past few months. Finally, I saw that it wouldn't be for nothing.

Soon, Mr. Collings was rolling out of the campground in his Jeep, the pouch tucked under his shirt. I was left on my own to find my way out, the only light a pale half-moon suspended in a charcoal-gray sky. I had to pick my way out along the dusky trail, leaving behind a resort filled with an active community of campers, and enter the solitude of a back road leading me home. I'd asked Grandpa that morning if he could make sure the chicken pot pie had been heated through by the time Dad came home. I'd prepared it the night before, since Brenda and I had decided that the next day after work—today—would be a good time to approach Mr. Collings about the French-fried vegetables. I would have preferred having Brenda at my side, but Jane having her baby couldn't stop me since I wouldn't be able to stay late again without hearing it from Dad.

As I pedaled, I began to miss the chats Brenda and I had as we rode home. We got a lot of mileage out of gossiping about the campers. They might have had money, but many of them lacked much else. Just the night before, Brenda had gone on how the Ducharmes from Ontario resembled the dogs that they kept on leashes near their camper. Jowly Mrs. Ducharme resembled Ralph the boxer, and Mr. Ducharme, with a beer belly hanging over his skimpy swimsuit, lagged behind his wife like their basset hound, Bob. Brenda did have a funny way of describing people.

I came upon the gate that kept out anyone other than those who belonged on the campground and waited for Stuart to raise it for me. "Late night, huh?" he called.

"Yeah, but a good one," I replied. My tires hit pavement and I began to glide. It was a relief to leave the woods, whose tree limbs looked like they could come to life and grab me. However, I was still wading through darkness along the opened road. Who would have guessed an exclusive society existed beyond that thick of woods? Perhaps that's what made it so special, so exclusive. Imagine, something like that in 'Busco.

I whirred past the four corners, strands of hair blowing free from my ponytail. Eggplant and yams would be my first two choices. I'd give away samples first to whet the campers' appetites. No doubt, they'd be a refreshing hit, keeping Mr. Collings busy at night counting the profits. Perhaps it would even open the door for me to Moonshadows.

I entertained the fantasy of the chef racing over to Snack Shack, eager to meet this culinary prodigy, until a roar came up from behind, rocketing by within inches of me. I screamed and sailed off the road into the ditch, flying free from my bike.

I tried to break my fall with my hands and felt the rough brush scrape against my palms and knees. One glance up and I saw that the vehicle had skidded to a halt, its brake lights on. I made out that it was a truck, a Chevy pickup. It was too dark to tell, but if I had to guess, I'd say it was maroon. Then I noticed the back-up lights brighten.

I scrambled to find my bike in the bushes, all the while aware of the chunk of metal tight to the shoulder charging in my direction. It got close enough that it kicked up pebbles and sand, stinging my face and eyes. Then, legs as thick as tree trunks headed my way. I groped for my bike, my thumping heart filling my chest. When the tree trunks were only a few feet away, I gave up on the idea of the bike and started running. I didn't get very far, though.

"Oh, no you don't, cunt." Brad grabbed my ponytail, stopping me. "Nothin' but a goddamn cock teaser." He let go long enough to push me onto my knees and into the branches.

A nightmare was swallowing me, one from which I could not crawl out. It had become so dark that I wasn't sure what was sky and what was ground. Clambering to a hunched stance, I tried to escape deeper into the woods, but came up against a barbed-wire fence. Once again, Brad slammed my face down to the ground. Still, I scrambled, fighting against the incline of the ditch.

"Think you're better 'n me, you and your ed-u-ca-ted brother." His weight fell on top of me, crushing my face to the ground. His thick hand found my breast and cupped it in a painful squeeze. I howled, vomit churning inside me.

He raised himself enough to flip me over, using my ponytail as a handle, the acrid odor of beer hovering above me. I tried not to throw up while attempting to punch him with hands I could barely lift from the ground. He laughed at my hopeless fight while lifting my blouse and groping me, leaning over and licking me. Perhaps getting sick was not such a bad idea. Attempting to give rise to vomit like some powerful poisonous geyser, I choked up some spit and sent it soaring. In the next instant, his hand came hard across my face. I reached up and gouged at his eyes, making him yowl before he got a hold of my arms and pinned them back to the ground. He brought his mouth to mine and pressed on it.

I felt around for anything that I could use as a weapon, and my hand came across twigs, grass, and dirt before settling upon a branch. It didn't feel too thick, but did feel solid. He tugged at his belt buckle, muttering how I was going to get what I deserved. I wrapped my hand around the branch. There was the rip of his zipper, then his hands yanking on my denim cutoffs. There wasn't any time, and just as I was about to strike him over the head with my weapon, he miraculously flew out of my reach, his doughy belly suspended over me in levitation. Then he vanished out of view.

In my daze, I heard the sound of bone against flesh. I rolled away, snapping my shorts, and scrambled out of the ditch and into a blinding light.

"I warned you, Hunt!"

I moved out of the glare and saw Kevin's fist connecting with Brad's nose, over and over again, the headlights of the Datsun illuminating the scene. It wasn't long before Brad's arms were limp at his side, his head lolling to his chest and his pants opened, resting below his hips.

"What the hell you tryin' to do, tough guy?" Kevin screamed, his words winded. His lean body stood locked in a fighting stance, but Brad simply tottered, blood gushing from his nose and mouth. He swayed to the right and Kevin went behind him, steadying him in a chokehold. That's when Kevin looked at me.

"You okay?"

Was I? I could barely nod, but I did.

"Did he...?"

I shook my head.

"He's got a CB in his truck. See if you can get someone to get the cops here."

I didn't budge until he repeated the instructions, and then I wobbled, groping my way toward the truck. Then I stopped, turning to see the two beams of light streak across Kevin, who was maintaining his hold on a stunned Brad.

"What are you doing here?" I said, my voice trembling.

"What?"

"Why are you here? Where'd you come from?"

"Vicky, just get help."

My mind was having trouble making sense of what had happened, what was happening. "No," I said.

Kevin gazed at me, bewildered. "No?"

"I'm not calling anybody."

Brad shifted, and Kevin tightened his hold. "What are you saying?"

"Let him go."

He stared at me. "Vicky, if I hadn't come along, he would've—"

Brad sputtered, "You heard her, Finley. Let me go."

"Not on your life, asshole. We're pressing charges."

"Not me!" I shouted.

"Vicky, what the hell is wrong with you?"

"Me? You haven't talked to me in months, and now all of a sudden you show up to save me? I had things under control."

He looked at me as if I'd become a stranger, and he might have been right. "You had things under control?" His tone was incredulous.

The way I saw it, this was no longer about Brad and me. Sure, I felt the blood trickling down my shin, and my face stung, but the weeks of silence and the crease running down my mother's face hurt more. "Yes," I said, "now let him go."

He didn't though. He said, "You're not thinking clearly, Vicky. He tried to—"

I screamed, "What do you care! Now let him go."

"Then *I'll* call the cops."

"Yeah," Brad sputtered, "they'll believe you. Ain't they tired of your face?"

Kevin seemed to absorb what Brad was saying. He'd gained a reputation as a rabble rouser. The law didn't take kindly to rabble rousers.

Not until I had screamed the demand again, and not until he had tightened his grip around Brad and made him promise to stay away from me, did Kevin let go. Brad dropped to his knees and crawled a few feet away before getting his footing and stumbling to his truck. I moved out of his path, watching him hike up his pants and struggle to pull himself into his cab, using one hand to cup his bloody nose. Moments later, the engine revved and he spun away, the truck kicking up dirt and pebbles.

"I don't get you," Kevin said.

"Me? I don't get you! As far as you're concerned, I haven't existed for months. Now all of a sudden you decide to care?" Tears began to spill. Because of my pride, I had let that idiot go, and I was already regretting it.

"All of a sudden? Vicky, how can you say that?" He trudged into the ditch and lifted my bike, swinging it across his shoulders. He tossed it into the back of the truck. "If there was anyone I wanted on my side..."

He stopped and looked into the woods. I followed his gaze and gasped, sure that the person standing there was Brad, until I realized that didn't make sense. Then the shadow vanished, just like that—if it had been there at all.

Why had I let him get away? Now I'd be looking over my shoulder every waking moment.

I went next to Kevin and touched his arm. "I am on your side. I've always been on your side. It's just that—"

"I know," he said, taking a deep breath. "I know, this is something you've got to do."

"You're right, it's just a hot-dog stand. But it's a beginning, a stepping stone."

"Those stones are leading you out of 'Busco."

"You know, not everyone who leaves doesn't come back."

"Nah, you won't be coming back." He looked me up and down and touched my face, causing me to wince. "You okay?" he said.

My knees and elbows were scraped up pretty good, my face hurt, and my whole body felt like one giant bruise, but Kevin was talking to me again. "I'm fine," I said.

He said, "I should have never let him go. I don't trust that bastard."

"I think you scared him."

"For now, but we're going to have to keep our eyes opened."

"Kevin, why did you come when you did? I mean, how'd you know Brad was watching me?"

"Word got around that you ticked him off in front of some buddies. He's not the type to let things go. Then, tonight, when I didn't get my supper…well, I knew something was wrong."

"I told Grandpa I'd be late.

"He didn't mention it to me. Glad he didn't."

"Me, too." Seeing my brother act like a wild man, using fists as weapons and not to just punch the air, caused me to recall the meeting several months earlier. We stood for a moment before I said, "Kevin?"

"Yeah?"

"Remember that night at town hall when you kept repeating that phrase over and over?"

"Forever wild?"

"Yeah. What did you mean?"

He dropped his sights to the ground. "Guess you didn't read the book I gave you, did you?"

I couldn't look at him. "I tried."

He nodded and cleared his throat. "Let's get you home so you can get cleaned up."

I climbed in the Datsun and Kevin put it in drive. I wanted to thank him for watching out for me, but I didn't know how to put it into words. In silence, we whirred past the woods, leaving the shadows behind. Or so I thought.

CHAPTER 11

I didn't think much about Brad Hunt or what he'd tried to do. I guess I figured that Kevin's relentless warnings with his fists would be enough to protect me. More importantly, Kevin and I had made peace and my burden of guilt was lifted. It seemed every day was filled with gilded rays streaming across the lake reflecting puffballs of clouds that sailed along a blue sky. It was a season of pine duff and French-fried vegetables.

Word of mouth and a great advertising campaign kept Lake in the Woods occupied throughout the summer. One article in a travel magazine compared our popularity with Aspen in winter. I cut the article out and stuck it on the refrigerator at home, hoping my father would read it. Not for the Aspen comment, but for this:

> Clearly, Moonshadows is the place for evening fare for guests of Lake in the Woods, who are no strangers to eating with a view of the Seine or dining in four-star restaurants, for that matter. Chef Antoine, who was lured away from the urban, elegant kitchen at Les Mignardises, must have been given an "offer he couldn't refuse." However, even in daylight hours one can satisfy the most discriminating palate at a tiny eatery known as Snack Shack, which sits on the other side of the lake. The burgers are thick and juicy, the French fries abundant. Unlike the usual hot dog stand, Snack Shack offers unique tasty edibles created by blond beauty Vicky Finley.

My brother was talking to me again, and at just seventeen years of age my cooking was being praised. Things could not have been any better. Well, unless if my mother had been there to witness it all. I fantasized about her reading the article and being inspired to seek me out. It was a wish I kept to myself.

Before I knew it, it was the middle of August, and the weather was dry due to the lack of rain all summer. Business was non-stop, to Mr. Collings delight. Lots and lots of campers pulled in, many of them with young, attractive men, to Brenda's delight. Usually, Brenda would flirt with them from behind the counter, but now she broke that barrier, sashaying over to a couple of these male magnets while I went about the routine of pouring a big bottle of oil into a large pot on the stove and turning on the burner. Usually Brenda coated the vegetables with a batter I would concoct before work, but she wasn't nearly as inspired by the kitchen as I was and was becoming more and more distracted by what was going on away from Snack Shack. I wanted to be angry at her for her blatant attention seeking, but I understood why she did it. Brenda Hannigan was one in a mess of Hannigans, who all craved attention one way or another. Being the only girl left at home made her loneliness even more acute. So, I decided to coat the green beans with the batter myself. While I did, I pondered what working under a chef in Montreal would be like. As I often did when performing a mindless task, I pretended I was working in the kitchen of a thriving restaurant, keeping up with the frantic pace, until my fantasy was interrupted.

"How ya doing, sweetheart?"

"Fine," I replied, not bothering to give Mr. O'Hare, the backslidden Mormon from Utah, the satisfaction of looking at him. I knew he was standing at the counter, watching me with his squinty, eager eyes. "What can I get you?" I said.

"That's okay. I'm here for the view."

"How's Mrs. O'Hare?" Far as I knew, there was only one Mrs. O'Hare in the Mormon's life, and she usually hid in their camper doing needlepoint while her stomach grew with her fourth child.

"Don't worry about her," he said. "What I want to know is why a pretty thing like you is sweating over a hot stove instead of being off in Paris modeling for some rich designer."

A glimpse told me that Brenda didn't plan on returning any time soon, since she was sitting on the table twisting a strand of her red hair with one hand while using the other to cover her mouth. She was flirting shamelessly, desperately even. I checked the oil, and it wasn't quite ready.

"You like to cook so much, I could provide you with a kitchen and a ton of people to feed each night. Ever been to Utah?"

I hadn't finished coating the beans yet, but I escaped to the stock room to take refuge. Seems guys were all the same. When would Brenda discover that? She couldn't understand my distaste for the same attention she hungered. I banged pots and cursed Mr. O'Hare, hoping if I let enough time pass, he'd be gone when I went back out. But before that happened, I heard shouts. Not the usual hungry voices at lunchtime, but voices laden with panic. I ran out, and right there on the stove leapt bright orange and red flames, just beginning to lick at the wall.

"Get out of there!" someone yelled.

The flames would have to be quenched, but the sink was beyond the stove. I'd have to try to get past the fire to get to the water, but the heat was already pressing on me, holding me back. That's when I spotted a towel. I grabbed it and smacked it on the fire, but the heat forced me to keep my distance.

"Vicky, get out of there!"

Inches from the wild, dancing flames, I saw the lid to the kettle. I stretched my arm as far as it could go, the blast of heat almost unbearable, the oil spitting at me. I couldn't think about what I was doing; I just grabbed the lid, and, as if playing ring toss, I flung it. It landed on the pot, partially covering it. I then grabbed a long-handled wooden spoon and used it to push the lid completely over the pot. Someone behind me was spraying the wall with a fire extinguisher, which I'd forgotten existed. Finally, the fire was out. One of the guys who'd been sitting on the picnic table with Brenda dropped the extinguisher on the floor and asked if I was all right.

I couldn't speak, staring at the charred wall, watching a hand reach over and turn off the burner.

"Man, I bet this never happened to Julia Child," Brenda said, suddenly standing beside me.

"It was an accident," said the guy, his ruddy complexion bright, his blond hair tousled. I could see Mr. O'Hare standing at the sidelines, a comforting arm around Mrs. O'Hare.

"Holy shit!" Mr. Collings said, running over. "What the hell happened here?"

"Vicky had an accident," Brenda said. "The oil spilled over, but Clark took care of it."

Mr. Collings looked from me to the blond-haired guy, who now had a name, then to Brenda.

"Only thing we should worry about now is her," Clark said. "She's got to get to a hospital."

I followed his gaze to my arm and saw that a large patch of skin had bubbled. I don't remember when it happened, but the oil must have splattered on me.

"I can take you," Clark said.

"Good," Mr. Collings said. "Brenda, you help me clean up."

"Can't I go with them?" she said.

"I need you here."

"Well, maybe I should go find Kevin," she said. "It'd be better if he took his sister."

"I wouldn't suggest waiting," Clark said. "It looks pretty bad, and we don't want her going into shock."

"Well, uh...I just think I should go, too." Brenda offered one suggestion after the next that included her, causing me to feel embarrassed for her for the frantic pirouettes and leaps she was doing to get Clark's attention. Without a doubt, she wished she were me just then, stinging with rising blisters and all.

I followed Clark to his car in the parking lot on the far side of the woods, and during the twenty minute ride to the hospital, I tried to keep Brenda on his mind by talking about how good she was in French and how she wanted to be a hair dresser. Clark never gave the topic much consideration.

"It's been a dry summer," he said. "You're lucky those flames didn't get a chance to jump."

In my mind, I saw the whole forest in flames, the Great White Pine having survived the recent destruction only to be burned down by my carelessness. I also thought of all the remaining wildlife that would have lost homes. But it was Kevin's stricken face that I envisioned most of all.

It turned out my burns were only first degree, and during the drive back, Clark tried to make me show my gratitude for the time he'd spent taking me to the hospital by pulling off the road and getting me to kiss him. After a slap to the face and a stern vocal demand, he put the car back in drive, and by the time he dropped me off at Snack Shack, we weren't speaking. I might have been a little harsh, confusing Clark's advances with Brad's forceful assault a few weeks earlier. When I slapped Clark across the face, perhaps it was Brad I was slapping. Once we returned to the campground, he and his buddy split.

"It was just a kiss," Brenda said, defending Clark's amorous attempt. "And Brian and I were hitting it off. We could've double dated."

"Well, I wouldn't have been up to a wrestling match," I said, waving my bandaged arm.

Soon, summer came to an end, and the campers rolled on out. Snack Shack closed up shop until the next summer. Mr. Collings promised me the charred wall would be painted over by then. My blistered arm had almost healed, as well. As the leaves began to turn and storm windows replaced screened ones, I began to wonder if Lake in the Woods had been just a dream. Brenda was wondering if the Scoleris were the phantoms, and not Benny, since they had never actually showed themselves to our side of the lake.

I began my senior year full of anticipation, as did Brenda. We talked more and more of Montreal, even taking Amtrak there one Saturday and exploring the busy, steep streets for possible locales in which to live. We'd wandered into Le Palais, the restaurant I would be training at, but after being seated and having our water poured, we saw the prices on the menu and immediately excused ourselves. The school Brenda would be attending was quite a number of blocks away from the restaurant, and we'd decided it would be best to rent an apartment at the midway point.

All in all, our optimism abounded, even after the unsettling occasional phone calls. Once in a while, I'd answer the ringing phone, but no one would respond to my hello. I could hear the breathing and imagined that the breath smelled like beer. I'd then drop the phone down and remind myself that soon I'd be a safe distance away. Until then, I made sure never to be alone, especially when riding my bike to and from work. I began to avoid the ringing phone and spent my time attempting culinary creations, which often disappointed me. I was becoming more and more eager to learn the true art of excellent cuisine.

Winter was upon us again, and one November night, when I was getting ready for bed, I noticed from my window a light shining from the barn. Months ago, Hercules had come back for another successful encore, and another calf was due any moment. My guess was that the moment had come. I slipped a coat on over my pajamas and put on a pair of sneakers before running out to the barn. There was something about the process of birth that excited me. I also suppose Kevin's high hopes made me want to participate somehow, or at least be an audience to the miracle. But once I ran into the barn and saw Kevin and Dad kneeling next to the cow, lying on her side, her breathing labored, I knew the occasion was far from triumphant. Off to the side was a formed mass covered with blood—Kevin's hope gone stillborn. The rest of the cattle had been let out to pasture after being milked hours earlier.

Dad stood. "It's got to be done, son." He walked out of the barn and into the milk station.

"Kevin?" I said.

He sniffed, lifting his head. "Takes a certain kind of man to do this. Maybe I was asking too much of everybody."

"What happened?" I drew closer to the calf. Other than all the blood and its absolute stillness, it looked perfect.

"Seems it didn't want to be born just yet." He reached over and stroked the cow as she lay on her side. "She just got tired." The cow wheezed. She seemed to be straining to see her baby, but she had no strength to do so.

"She's a good mother," he said. "She did her darndest."

Dad walked in with a rifle in his hand.

"What's that for?" I said.

"Vicky, go back to the house," Dad said.

"What are you doing?" I said.

"I'm not doing anything. Now go."

"She'll get better," I said, my voice quivering. "She's just tired."

Dad shook his head. "Kevin," he said, holding the gun out to him.

Kevin wiped his eyes and took the gun. I was horrified by the sight.

"Vicky, I said go," Dad said.

"No." For some reason, I felt that if I stayed, the cow had a greater chance to live. I watched as she looked to be gasping for air. I said, "She just needs to catch her breath."

"She's in misery, son," Dad said, turning his attention to Kevin.

"Can't you call the vet?" I cried.

"The vet's not gonna help, 'cept put her down himself and charge us for it."

Kevin stood there sniffling, wiping the tears from his face. He wasn't a man, but a little boy just then—in my eyes, anyway. He raised the gun and pointed it at the cow's head, his arms shaking. Time passed by, his finger toying with the trigger.

"Sometimes you have to know when to let go, son," Dad said.

"You don't have to do it, Kevin," I said.

With that, the blast of the gun went off, not once, not twice, but numerous times. With each angry cock, another bullet riddled the cow's head and heart. Dad ran over, grabbing the gun from Kevin and grasping him while Kevin collapsed and sobbed.

I found myself on the barn floor, shaking while Mr. LeMieux's words haunted me: "You callin' it heaven. Well, it ain't. Can be nothing more 'en hell."

Just how deep that abyss was, I had no idea.

CHAPTER 12

The combined aroma of vanilla and cinnamon filled the house, along with the Christmas songs from a record album I'd found mixed in with a box of ornaments. It was a Sunday afternoon, and Brenda had escaped her mad house to help me bake cookies. Out of the corner of my eye, I watched her press the rolling pin back and forth over the dough, flattening it so thin you'd think she was making wafers. Just as she was about to roll yet again, I blurted, "That's enough."

She stopped, giving me an insolent look.

"If it's too thin, they'll burn."

She dropped the rolling pin on the table and walked to the sink to wash the sticky dough from her hands. It was clear I was exasperating her. First, without asking, I had handed her a rubber band to pull back her hair.

"*Seventeen* magazine says those things cause split ends," she said, refusing to take it.

"Well, why don't you take off that sweater," I suggested. "You'll sweat to death."

"I like to sweat to death," she'd said. Now she was drying her hands in meticulous fashion for my benefit.

"What's your mom making for Christmas dinner?" I said, trying to ease the tension.

"Turkey. What else?"

I cut out Christmas trees, bells, and Santas from the dough, while "Pahrumpumpumpum" played in the background. "I have this great recipe for a glaze sauce for baked ham. Think I'll make that."

"Fascinating."

"Will Jane be coming home?" I placed the shaped dough on a cookie sheet while Brenda's first, and apparently only, batch went into the oven.

"Yeah. And all her baby paraphernalia. God, I never want to have a kid. It's like she brings her entire house when she comes to visit now."

"Ho, ho, ho," Kevin bellowed, tramping into the kitchen with Grandpa behind him, the two of them dragging a large pine tree. "You should see the saplings, Vicky. They're already up to my waist." A few weeks had passed since he'd lost the calf and her mother. Hercules had since returned, and so had Kevin's optimism.

"It's so big. Is it going to fit in the living room?"

"It'll be snug," Kevin said, "but Christmas only comes once a year."

Christmas. Ever since I was little, it was a holiday I anticipated until the very day, yet I would always find myself wondering what my mother was doing and with whom she was spending it. Each year I'd also look for the Christmas card that was certain to arrive from her, and each year I'd be disappointed, with nothing left to do but wait for the next.

"The lights are in the smaller box on the end table," I said as they dragged the tree through the house.

"When we have our apartment," Brenda said, "let's get one of those fake white trees. They look so pretty."

The phone rang, saving me from throwing dough in Brenda's face. For the last few months, I avoided answering the phone, afraid it was Brad on the line. My excuse this time not to pick up was the flour all over my hands. Brenda didn't wait for another ring, and picked up.

"For you," she said, stretching the phone out to me. I hesitated until she added, "It's Mrs. Scott."

I dusted off my hands and took the receiver.

"I know it's kinda late, and you probably already have plans for New Year's Eve," Mrs. Scott said, "but Fred wants to go out in the worst way, and I was wondering if you'd be interested in babysitting for us."

I thought about it for a moment. Last New Year's, Brenda and I sat at her house taking care of her brothers while we snuck a beer or two to her room and pretended to get drunk. Well, I pretended after two small sips of the bitter brew. I couldn't be sure about Brenda, though, and I ended up doing most of the babysitting.

As if trying to elicit both pity and guilt, Mrs. Scott said, "The kids asked for you. They missed you this summer with your working."

"Well," I hesitated.

"I'll pay you two dollars an hour."

"Really?" Now that I was no longer making any money, that sounded just fine by me. I said, "Okay."

"Thanks, Vicky. The kids'll be thrilled. I'll pick you up around sevenish, okay?"

"What'd she want?" Brenda said the second I hung up. When I told her my plans for New Year's Eve, she shrieked, "Are you nuts? Rich is going to have a huge party! Call her back and tell her you can't."

"Brenda, it's good money."

"It's also our senior year."

"Bren, kiss it goodbye. How else are we going to afford our apartment? You know, the one with the tacky fake tree?"

Kevin called to me and I went into the living room to see the tree was fanned out so wide that it filled most of the room.

"I told him it'd be too big," Grandpa said.

"Dad's not going to like it," I said.

Grandpa sniffed the air. "Something's burning."

"Ohmygosh, the cookies!" I ran back into the kitchen and opened the oven door. Smoke gushed at me, causing my eyes to tear.

"Guess you were right," Brenda said, surveying the tray of blackened discs. "They were too thin."

I tossed them in the garbage, wanting to toss Brenda in with them.

"Man, what is it about you and food?" she said. "Always burning something."

"Can we stay up just a little longer?"

It was Jamie who was asking, but I could tell Jonathan had put her up to it.

"Your mom'll be mad at me. She said no later than ten, and it's already past that," I said.

"But I wanna watch the ball drop."

The Scott kids were sitting at the kitchen table drinking milk and eating the cookies I'd brought for them. Jamie was only three. What did she know about a ball dropping on New Year's Eve?

I laughed. "Come on—let's get you two up to bed."

"Can't we finish our castle first?" Jamie said, pointing to the pile of blocks on the worn linoleum floor. I suppose with a great amount of imagination, the stack might look like a castle.

"I won't touch it," I said, "and you can finish it in the morning."

Jonathan twisted his mouth, showing defeat. He was eleven. "Come on, Jamie, let's go."

I trailed behind the kids as the three of us went up the lopsided, creaky steps. Sleet spit at the windows, and the wind grew from a whistle to a roar, shaking the old farmhouse. The kids' eyes widened and they took each step hesitantly. I tucked Jamie in first.

"I didn't pray," she said, as I brought the blanket up to her chin.

"Oh," I said. "Sorry, go ahead."

She sat up and made a careful sign of the cross. "Dear God, thank you for Mommy, Daddy, Jonathan, and me. Please help them find Uncle Lou and keep him safe. Amen." She dropped back down but then sat up to make a closing sign of the cross.

"Who's Uncle Lou?" I said, tucking the covers around her.

"Mommy's brother. He's stupid."

"Jamie! That's not nice."

"No, he is," Jonathan said, standing in the doorway. "He stays at a special place with people like him. He can't hear or anything."

Jamie covered her ears as if testing the very idea, but her window rattled and she shot a frightened look at me. "He ran away the other day, and nobody knows where he is. Mommy's real worried 'bout him." Her bottom lip began to quiver.

That would explain why Mrs. Scott had told me to call her at the ho-del if anyone from Massena Center called the house. She hadn't explained why, though.

I said, "I'm sure he'll be fine. He probably just needed to get away for a while." It sounded lame, and I could tell Jamie thought so, too. I patted her on the head then crossed the hall to find Jonathan already in bed, a stream of light from the hallway casting his room in shadows.

"You don't hafta tuck me in. I'm almost twelve."

"Well then, goodnight," I said, starting toward the steps. A big gust of wind shook the entire upstairs.

"Vicky!" he called.

"It's okay," I said, going back to the door. "It's just the wind."

"I know," he said, sitting up. "I'm not ascared. I just wanted to know something." He stopped.

"What?"

"Do you have a boyfriend?"

"A boyfriend?" I stifled a smile. "No," I said.

"Really?"

"Yes."

"Mom told Dad you're something every boy wants. She said if you weren't so nice, you'd be dangerous."

I swallowed hard, knowing I wasn't supposed to be hearing this. "She said that?"

"Yup, we all think you're real nice. But I know things."

I knew he was baiting me, but I went for it. "You do?"

He nodded with certainty. "I know your mom went away a long time ago and never came back. My mom says she ran away with a man."

My mouth went dry.

"Mom says she wouldn't be surprised if you did the same thing someday. She won't let Daddy pick you up or drive you home."

"Goodnight, Jonathan," I said, heading downstairs.

One way or another, I'd heard all the rumors about why Grace Finley had abandoned her family. My father didn't help to squelch any of the gossip with the truth, since he refused to talk about her. I turned off the light at the bottom of the steps just as another gust of wind shook the house.

"Vicky!"

"What?"

"Jamie likes the light on," Jonathan said.

"Do not," Jamie called. "You're the scaredy cat."

"Am not."

"It's okay," I said, turning the light back on.

I went to the kitchen and cleaned the plates and cups off the table. As dingy as it was, the kitchen was the brightest room in the house. I figured I'd pass the time by mixing up a cake, but after rooting through the cabinets, I found only a half-cup of flour in the canister. I washed and dried the kids' milk glasses then put them away. There was nothing left to do but sit in front of the television. With the weather as nasty as it was, perhaps the Scotts would come home early. The money no longer seemed as important.

I wandered into the living room and discovered that the lamp in the corner, the one missing a shade, had a burnt-out bulb. The dried-out Christmas tree had only a few twinkling lights, hardly enough to brighten the room. The kitchen adjoined the living room, so I kept the overhead light on in there. Mrs. Scott was a farmer's wife who helped in the fields and got up at the crack of dawn with her husband to milk the cows. It was clear she didn't have time to create a homey atmosphere. Even the windows lacked curtains or blinds. Just beyond the pane of glass was a sea of black, obscured by an ice-caked window. There was nothing to view anyway, since the house sat back about a mile from the road, the driveway nothing but a crude, narrow tree-lined path.

Earlier, while Jamie and Jonathan were watching some game show, one of them had put the broken TV knob somewhere. But where? It took awhile to find it, but after lifting cushions and feeling beneath the couch and finding only crumbs and goo, I found the knob under an old Sears catalog on the wobbly stand next to the couch. After finally getting the knob in place and clicking the TV on, the room suddenly went from darkness to a gray dreariness. There was more snow on the TV screen than outside. I played with the antenna until I could make out the form of Times Square, filled with a New Year's crowd. Dick Clark was going on about the number of celebrants who had gathered to watch the ball drop. He then reminded us there was another half-hour to go before we could welcome in the New Year.

The weather appeared calm in New York City, even though Dick was huddled in a heavy winter coat and his cheeks were rosy. Outside the Scott's house, the wind was roaring, the heavens spitting ice. Concern prodded me to get up and survey the outdoors from the kitchen window. Across the yard stood the barn. A powerful light near the hayloft beamed brightly on icicles weighing down wires that were connected to I don't know what. They sagged so low, it seemed they could snap at any moment.

For no other reason than boredom, I went to the refrigerator for a glass of milk. I took it to the living room, along with a plate of cookies, and settled on the threadbare couch. Just as I dunked my first cookie, the phone rang. I scrambled off the couch and into the kitchen to grab it before the ring woke the children.

"Hey," Brenda said, her tone depressed.

"Happy New Year."

"Yeah, right."

"You're in a good mood."

"Why'd you say you'd baby-sit?"

"I don't know anymore," I said, "but the party sounds pretty dull."

"I'm home," she said. "Rich's parents said the roads were getting slick and sent everyone home before we had to spend the night there."

"So I didn't miss anything, and making money besides."

"Yeah, but we could've at least hung out together. Now I'm sitting here looking at Dick Clark's ugly face."

"We could—" Crackling sounds interrupted me. "Brenda, you there?"

"Yeah, barely," she yelled.

"We might get cut off." More static. The image of the sagging lines came to mind.

"I'm here," Brenda said, her voice at a normal pitch. "So, what's cattleman doing?"

"Probably asleep," I said.

"He's become an old man already. Makes you wonder—" We were cut off again by crackles. Then, she came across loud and clear. "Hey, you want to hear this month's story?"

"No," I said, not at all interested in the erotic tales she loved reading to me.

Silence. We'd been cut off, or so I thought, until Brenda said, "Come on, it's such a hot story."

"Will you stop?" I said.

"Hey, has Brad called you lately?" she said.

"I wouldn't know," I said, since I had refused to answer the phone.

"What if he—" Static interfered again. It was just as well, since I didn't want to talk about Brad.

I said, "I can hardly hear you. I'll talk to you tomorrow, okay?"

"Fine," she said, "but. "But if you hadn't said yes to the Scotts, we could be hanging out."

Not long after I'd hung up, the huge glittering ball inched its way down the pole in Times Square, with Dick Clark leading the countdown.

"Seven, six, five…"

In a whisper, I joined in, "Four, three, two…"

A winter advisory for the entire northeast region scrolled across the bottom of the screen. A gust of wind rattled the windows as a confirmation.

"One…Happy New Year!" The crowd tooted their horns and cheered. It made me feel lonely. I huddled in the corner of the couch, watching people hooting and hollering for the camera. Then I heard a discordant whimper. And it didn't come from the television. I got up, turned the volume down, and listened. There it was again. Jamie?

I went upstairs to see her jaw slack, her breathing even. Jonathan was curled in a ball, snoring lightly. His blanket was on the floor, so I tiptoed in his room and tossed it over him before going back downstairs and into the kitchen. Outside had become a crystal wonderland. I hoped the sand trucks were out already; otherwise, it would take eons for the Scotts to get home. Just getting up the driveway would take them forever. There was little to do but wait.

I pulled out the afghan shoved in the corner of the couch and wrapped myself in it. Dick Clark was gone, and some old black-and-white movie was now on. I turned up the volume to keep me company and lay down, surveying the tree, its limbs bowed as if exhausted by the holiday season. Nonsensical but comforting murmurs droned on while I dozed, until everything suddenly became silent as stone—both the television voices and my dream ones.

I opened my eyes. Or thought I had.

Darkness surrounded me. I fought the blindness, until I made out the square of the TV. It was off. As were the Christmas lights and bright overhead light from the kitchen. But there was the eerie sounds of the house groaning, having been cut off from its life source. If I'd been smart, I would have looked for candles or a flashlight earlier. Now I was lost in a sea of black. Nothing to do but sleep until the Scotts showed up.

Just as I was about to drift off, the spitting on the living room window became scratching. I held my breath, watching as ice was being scraped away by a hand. I forced myself not to scream, when a face pressed up against the glass. I remained motionless, unable to make out the distorted face as the head swayed this way and that, eyes searching the darkness of the room, maybe even seeing me. Then, the face disappeared, but footsteps crunched along the perimeter of the house. At that moment, I couldn't remember if I'd locked the door behind the Scotts when they'd left for the evening.

It seemed to take forever to untangle myself from the afghan. Once I did, I groped my way through the dark and into the kitchen. I forgot about the castle Jamie and Jonathan had built earlier and knocked into it, blocks scattering at my feet, tripping me. I let out a scream, but then clasped a hand over my mouth to muffle it. As I reached the door, the knob jiggled. My fingers scrambled to find the skeleton key resting in the hole, but the lock had not been engaged. The second the door started to open, I threw my weight into it, struggling to get it closed. I braced my feet and pushed, but whoever was on the other side was determined to get in. However, the intruder was shrewd enough not to speak. Then, a hand, icy and meaty, latched on to my wrist. I clawed at it with ineffectual nails, and when that didn't work, I rammed the door, once, twice, three times against it, until the hand finally let go. I then immediately slammed the door shut, found the key, and fumbled for an eternity until it turned over. I backed away, hugging myself, trying to stop shaking, my heart feeling as though it would fly out of my chest.

"Who is it?" I called.

No reply.

The hand, that cold, groping hand, reminded me of a hand from several months earlier, and that head swaying in the window began to fill in, becoming a face. Even though there was silence from the other side of the door, I heard the voice, threatening me.

Before I had a chance to figure out what to do, a beam of light zoomed in on me from the living room. I whirled around, squealing, ready to charge, discovering too late that the small, shrieking figure gripping a flashlight was Jonathan, his body trembling, his sleepy eyes widening.

I rushed over to him, scooping him in a hug, hushing him.

"You afraid of the dark, too?" he said, his voice shaky.

I couldn't let him know who was on the other side of that door. "Could I...uh...could I borrow your flashlight?"

He gazed at me with wondering brown eyes. "I got it in my stocking. Jamie got a pink one just like it in hers. She still believes in Santa Claus."

"Jonathan, I need the flashlight," I whispered, trying to listen to what might be going on beyond the door.

"I'll go find Jamie's and—"

"Jonathan," I snapped, "there's no time. Please give me your flashlight."

He hesitated, and when I was about to make his decision for him, he handed it over, but not without mumbling, "The batteries are gettin' weak already."

I trained the light on the phone on the wall and began to dial, grateful there was still service. I wondered if he was right outside the door, waiting. Or had he moved back to a window to look inside, to see where I was?

Static crackled over the ringing. *Please, please, please pick up.* Finally, a voice, thin and distant, muffled by static, answered. It was the voice I wanted to hear.

"Kevin!" I had to stop myself from choking on tears. "I'm still at the Scotts'. Brad's trying to break in. I don't know what to do."

Kevin sounded as though he were across the ocean instead of just a few miles away. All I could make out was a tinny sound that might have been words. I had no idea if he could make out what I was saying, so I started to repeat myself. Before I finished, the static stopped.

"Kevin? Kevin! You there?"

The phone had died. I called his name again, but then dropped the receiver back in to the cradle. He must have heard me. He'd be on his way. It was all I could count on.

"Who's Brad?" Jonathan whispered, wide eyed. Something slapped against the kitchen window and we both screamed, lunging for each other. Another slap, and I dared to look this time: nothing more than a snapped wire.

"Who's Brad?" Jonathan repeated.

"Just someone who's not very nice."

"Does he want to kill us?"

The question stunned me. I mumbled no, but the idea didn't seem so impossible if he was willing to stalk me in weather like this. Brenda had told me she'd heard a rumor that the sheriff was instructed to keep an eye on Brad, after Kevin had made a formal complaint against him. But even if that were true, how serious would the sheriff take my trouble-making brother? Again, I chastised myself for letting Brad go, for not telling anyone other than Brenda about the threatening phone calls.

"Call the police," Jonathan said.

"Oh, yeah," I said, my entire body shaking. It hadn't occurred to me to call them. Kevin had been the one to protect me the first time, and I was hoping he could do so again. My hands shaking, I picked up the phone and dialed the operator. But the line was still dead.

"Hope he doesn't figure out how to git in the cellar from outside," Jonathan said.

I was now paralyzed with the thought that he could already be in the house. Frantic, I searched the room and then grabbed one of the metal chairs from the table, the plastic cushions torn, and scraped it across the floor, ramming it up against the cellar door. It would never stop him, but I was hoping to slow him down so we could get out. But where would we go? And I wasn't willing to leave Jamie alone in the house with him. *Please, Kevin, please hurry*.

"Jonathan, where does your dad keep his gun?" I couldn't believe my voice had said those words.

He gaped at me. "We're not allowed to touch 'em. He's got five of 'em."

"But I bet you know where the key is."

"There's no key."

"Where does your dad keep them then?"

"In his closet."

"Jonathan, I'd never shoot anybody, but I'd feel safer if we had one—you know, to scare him away."

"Jamie and me aren't allowed to touch 'em."

"You won't be. I'll tell him it was my idea. Besides, it's my job to protect you and your sister."

Just then, there was pounding at the kitchen door, and Jonathan lunged at me. Or I may have lunged at him. At least Brad hadn't found his way into the cellar. He had to have gotten drunk, somehow found out I was babysitting for the Scotts, and decided to pay me a visit.

"They're upstairs," Jonathan said, his voice shaky. "I'll show you."

With the flashlight guiding our way, we walked up the creaky steps, through the darkness, and into the Scott's bedroom. The smell of Old Spice greeted us. Jonathan opened the closet door, and there were the guns, in a rack against the back wall. I had no idea which one would be best, but I figured any one would be enough to keep Brad at a distance if he did manage to break in before Kevin came.

"The bullets are up there," Jonathan said, pointing to the shelf overhead. "I'm not s'posed to know that, though."

"I...I don't think I really want to use bullets," I said. "I'll just use the gun to scare him."

Another round of pounding caused Jonathan to jump and grab my arm. "What if he has a gun, with bullets?"

"I...I...can't do this. I just can't." I started to cry and prayed for Kevin to arrive soon, prayed that he had heard my pleas.

Using a lower shelf as a stand, Jonathan climbed on it and felt around the top shelf until he found what he was looking for. He took the gun from me and pulled the chamber; he dropped in a bullet and then closed it. He handed it back to me with the instruction not to cock it unless I planned to shoot.

"And don't tell my mom I know how to do that," he said, the two of us groping our way back downstairs. "She'll get mad at Dad."

I scoped the downstairs, half-expecting Brad to come out of hiding. The pounding had stopped, which made me uneasy.

"Let's wait on the couch," I said. We sat down, the gun resting across my lap. The flashlight was becoming weaker, as Jonathan had warned, so I turned it off.

"Hey!" Jonathan said. "Turn that back on."

"It's okay," I said. "Our eyes will adjust."

We sat in vigilant silence, every groan of wind and slap of wire causing us to huddle closer together. I listened for shuffling feet, a door opening, finding the gun on my lap a comfort. Then, finally, from that sea of darkness, lights, welcoming lights, flashed across the living room walls, flooding the entire room. We stumbled to the window and watched as headlights on the high-beam guided a car up the length of slippery driveway. It crept, sliding first to the left then all the way to the right. It wasn't Kevin's pickup—that much I could tell. The window framed us as we stood like hopeful, grateful children, willing the car to inch closer and closer to the house then drive by, following the path to the back door.

"It's Dad!" Jonathan said, taking the flashlight from me and running to the kitchen.

"Jonathan," I shouted, "don't open—"

But it was too late; the sound of the click echoed all around me as Jonathan unlocked the door. I stumbled behind him, shouting for him to close the door while he called to his parents to hurry. The paltry beam of light barely penetrated the darkness. Mrs. Scott climbed out of the car, crossing the ice-slicked driveway on unsteady legs.

"Mom! Mom!" Jonathan yelled. "Be careful."

But still she tripped at the threshold. "What on earth?" she said, a groan coming from where she stood. Jonathan shined the light on a huddled figure lying outside the door. The figure groped at Mrs. Scott's legs. I screamed for Brad to let her go; then I remembered I had the gun in my hands. I raised it and pointed it at him, my aim shaky but determined.

"Lou!" Mrs. Scott screamed. "Fred, it's Lou!" Mr. Scott came up behind Mrs. Scott and said, "Well, I'll be darned."

The figure lurched, as if breaking from a frozen glaze, swinging its arms. Mrs. Scott grabbed them; then, once he stilled, she turned Lou's face toward her. She tugged her gloves off and made frantic signals with her stubby fingers. With hands that moved in slow motion, Lou returned the gestures.

Then they both stopped and looked at me.

"He...he tried to break in," I said.

"Uncle Lou's not a bad man, Vicky," Jonathan cried out, his tone accusing. "He's just dumb." He fell on the icy gray lump and wrapped his arms around him. Lou looked to have dissolved into passive gentleness, grinning a toothless grin.

"You must be frozen through and through," Mrs. Scott said, pulling Lou up, leading him into the house. "He didn't understand why no one would let him in."

"It's wicked out there. Amazing he survived it," Mr. Scott said. He stopped and gazed at me. "Vicky, what you got there?"

I glanced down at the gun in my grip and couldn't speak.

"She made me get it," Jonathan said. "I told her the rules, Dad, but she thought some man was going to kill us."

Mr. Scott took the gun and opened the chamber. "Christ," he muttered, dropping the bullet in his hand. He placed the gun in the corner, slipped the bullet in his shirt pocket, and instructed Jonathan to shine the flashlight in his direction. He stood on a stool and pulled a lantern down from the top of the cabinet.

"Poor soul must've been out of his wits," Mrs. Scott said, pulling Lou's rubber boots off while Mr. Scott lit the lantern. The smell of kerosene and a yellow glow poured into the room.

"Better call the center now so they know where he is. I can't believe he came all this way in this kind of weather." The dishes rattled in the cabinet as Mrs. Scott thumped across the room. She picked up the receiver and announced, "It's dead."

I stood in the middle of the kitchen, wondering how I could make them see the way it had been. To me, it hadn't been a poor, helpless soul beyond those doors, but a drunken threat eager to break in and cause harm, perhaps even death. Lou studied me, his eyes narrow, his head down slightly. He used his hands to say something to Mrs. Scott.

"He's wondering why we have no electricity," she said, her fingers offering a response.

"Whole North Country is in a black out," Mr. Scott said, jangling his keys. "They say it's the worst ice storm in years. I don't think it'd be a good idea for you to drive Vicky home in this, Mary," he said.

"That's okay," I said. "Kevin should be here any minute. I called him before, before the phone went out." From the way they all looked at me, I knew I was the unwelcome guest, a floozy not only trying to seduce Mrs. Scott's defenseless husband but the one who had tried to kill her pitiful mute brother.

"Couldn't you tell him I'm sorry?" I said. "I didn't mean to—"

"She thought it was a bad guy," Jonathan said.

Mr. Scott took the chair from the cellar door, dragging it through the fallen castle and putting it back at the table. "We'll have to find a safer place for the guns," he said.

"It's not Jonathan's fault," I said, crouching down and gathering the blocks, tossing them in the box.

"No one ever said it was," Mrs. Scott said, peeling Lou's coat off him. She hung it in the corner with a pile of other coats and then turned back to him and flicked her fingers again, this time bringing a wide grin to his stunned face.

She shrugged her coat off and wobbled around the kitchen, taking milk out of the refrigerator and pouring it in a pan. After a strike of a match, the gas burner puffed on. "Making hot cocoa," she said, "if anyone wants some."

Jonathan ran to the cabinet and pulled out a mug. He brought it over to the table and put it in front of Lou. It was a Santa, his arms akimbo serving as the handles. Lou grinned again.

Not much later, they were all drinking their cocoa while I stood at the living room window with my coat on, waiting for my brother. Once they'd finished and Mrs. Scott made a bed for Lou in the spare bedroom, she said, "Probably couldn't make it on these roads and decided to turn back. He'd call if the phones weren't down."

I couldn't argue with her, but there was no way Kevin would have turned back after my cry for help. That's when I realized he had never actually heard me. The connection had been so bad that he probably hadn't made out my voice. His was garbled, and I only recognized it because he was the person I was calling. Chances are he was sound asleep in the warmth of his bed.

"Why don't you sleep on the couch?" Mrs. Scott said. "I'll take you home in the morning."

I nodded and tried to apologize again, but she was already shuffling upstairs.

CHAPTER 13

Through the deep, black hole seeped in Brad Hunt. He leaked in as an unpleasant vapor, smelling like stale beer. I was in that hole, trapped and naked, unable to get warm, and there was nowhere to run, my supine body unable to budge. Then, as a drunken threat, Brad materialized, suspended over me. His cold hand reached out to me, touching me, tugging on me. I tried to scream for help but had no voice.

"Vicky! Vicky!"

A beam of light poured into the dark hole. I flailed in protest, until the beckoning began to sound less like Brad and more like my father.

"Vicky."

I squinted, trying to adjust my vision. Dad was standing with Mr. Scott, the two of them looking down on me as I lay on the couch. The room was chilly and I groped for the afghan, finding it on the floor. The dim lighting of the room came from the kerosene lantern in Mr. Scott's hand. Brad was nowhere to be seen.

"Vicky, come on now, wake up."

"What?" *What time is it?*

"You spoke to Kevin last night?" Dad said.

I rubbed my eyes, attempting to make sense of what the two blurred figures standing over me were saying.

"Vicky! Mr. Scott said you tried to call Kevin last night. What did you say to him?"

I cleared my throat. "I thought someone was breaking in." I recalled how Mrs. Scott had helped Lou up the stairs. He had been helpless, defenseless—his clothes damp, his steps uncertain—certainly not a threat. In a small voice, I continued, "It was only Mrs. Scott's brother."

Dad turned to Mr. Scott. "He's out there, somewhere."

I sat up. "What's wrong?"

"Kevin didn't show up to milk the cows. Don came to the house to see if we knew where he was. Since you never came home, we hoped he was here with you."

"Except he never showed up," I said. "What time is it?"

"Almost five," Mr. Scott said.

"But I called him…hours ago!" I clambered from the couch. "He's off the road somewhere, Dad. He must've gone in the ditch."

"No. He took the Ski-doo."

"He never got here."

"He's out there somewhere, Fred," Dad repeated, his voice tense.

Out where? Through the rime-covered window, dusk was drinking up the dark and dawn seemed to have calmed the sleet and wind. "We have to find him," I said, searching for my coat.

"It's wicked cold out there, and you're not dressed to be in this weather," Mr. Scott said. "Jack, we'll use my sled."

I watched in silence as Mr. Scott dressed and then nodded to Dad, signaling that he was ready. They hustled out of the house, and moments later I heard the snowmobile roar by, taking to the fields. Mrs. Scott was probably already out milking the cows. I scrounged around until I found a piece of paper and jotted down my apologies yet again for what I had done; then I propped the paper against the grimy plastic salt and pepper shakers on the table. I took my coat off the back of a kitchen chair, put it on, and tugged the zipper up to my chin. Then I slipped on my gloves and pulled my wool hat over my head. Outside was a world of glistening ice. I had no choice but to take it slow over the crusty, rutted driveway, passing power lines that drooped to the ground and snapped tree limbs. As I walked, I shouted Kevin's name, hoping he'd hear me and call back, "Right here, sis!" But all I heard was the echo of my own tremulous voice.

Soon, the sun began to rise, although it offered no warmth. It was amazing how bright the day looked—the sky a crisp, hopeful blue, without a single cloud to mottle it up. I saw this as a promising sign and continued shouting my brother's name, pausing for a response, then shouting again, my breath puffing out as I trudged on.

Once I came to the main road, I stayed at the edge, searching the ditches, peering through the wide gaps of trees, many of them damaged by the ice storm. The shouts became frenzied screams as I walked on, my feet numb, my sneakers poorly suited for this trek. My face felt as though it would shatter and my fingers burned, and I had a good mile to go. Still I screamed, ineffectual squeals of desperation.

Eventually, I reached Mills Road and saw the welcome sight of my house. Grandpa's hunched form appeared on the front porch steps. I couldn't make out what he was saying, so I imagined it to be something about Kevin sitting in the warmth of the kitchen, sipping hot cocoa. When I reached Grandpa, he pulled me into a hug.

"Why didn't you come home last night?"

"The roads were bad, Grandpa. Mr. Scott couldn't drive." But I didn't care about me. I said, "Is Kevin back? Did he come back?"

We must have heard the sound at the same time, as we both turned toward the wide stretch of open field. At first I saw nothing, but I recognized the buzzing in the distance. Soon, a snowmobile glided into view, jouncing across the glazed surface of ice-crusted snow. I kept hoping it was Kevin, ready with an explanation, wearing an apologetic grin. But as it roared closer, I saw Mr. Scott standing at the controls. Once he spotted Grandpa and me, he stopped, waving his arms wildly, shouting for us to get into the house.

Instead, I took a step closer.

"I said get in the house, goddammit!"

But I wandered even closer, staring at my dad, who was sitting on the back of the sled cradling a bundle. There was a persistent moaning. I eventually realized it was coming from my father. Then the most horrid wail of protest I'd ever heard came from my grandfather. Staggering toward the scene, he cried my brother's name.

CHAPTER 14

The last part of my senior year of high school was a wide gap of numbing emptiness, with me floundering from one day to the next. At night, I'd go to bed before the sun set and sob, draining my body of emotion to put myself to sleep. Sometimes the dreams were welcoming, and Kevin was very much alive. Other times, the horror repeated itself. It wasn't until a stifling day in June that I began the gradual climb out of that cold chasm. I was shuffling down the auditorium aisle behind a line of fellow classmates, all garbed in the same purple gown and mortarboard. "Pomp and Circumstance" accompanied us as we paraded in the fierce, blinding sun, and I found myself caught in a knot of glowing parents and chattering graduates. It was Brenda who appeared and freed me. Tommy was in her arms.

"Jane thinks this is a thrill for me, showing off my nephew." She rolled her eyes. "Like a baby's something new for the Hannigans." She reached over and flipped my tassel to the other side.

"Congratulations, girls," Mrs. Fitz said, placing a hand on my back. "Vicky, may I speak to you?" She led me away from the crowd and grasped my hands. "I know how difficult this year has been for you." Her eyes brimmed with tears. "And I'm so proud of how you continued on."

Continued? If continued meant staring blindly at the pages of my books, if continued meant walking zombie-like from class to class, if continued meant continuously hiding in my room, then, yes, I did continue on.

"In all my years teaching home economics, I've never seen anyone so talented. Chef Dupuis is really thrilled to have you." She squeezed my hands, turned, and dashed away. It took me a moment to remember that Chef Dupuis was the Master Chef at Le Palais, a four-star restaurant in Old Montréal. I vaguely recall taking a ride with Mrs. Fitz to see the robust man with cauliflower ears and bulbous nose some time ago for an interview with him. Days later, I had received a letter in the mail congratulating me on having been assigned to his program. Mrs. Fitz had been more excited than me.

Brenda came up alongside of me. "You shouldn't have just stood there, Vicky. She passed you without you turning in a single thing. You should thank *all* your teachers. They let you slide. Man, you're so lucky."

Lucky?

"So, you ready?" she said, switching Tommy to her other hip. "Di's probably already putting out the beer and chips."

I shook my head. "I'm going home."

"Oh, right, your dad might be having some big celebration waiting for you." A wave of regret immediately washed over her face. "I'm sorry. That was mean, even for me. It's just I hate seeing you miss out on everything. The prom, now this. It's supposed to be one rocking party, and she hired the Frozen Sunshine to play. The *Frozen Sunshine*, Vicky."

Tommy spotted Jane and stretched out his arms toward her. She took him, resting him on her hip. "You be careful tonight, Bren. No drinking," Jane said.

"I'm eighteen now. It's legal," Brenda said. Then, to me, "So, come on. Let's go."

"I can't. Really. But thanks for asking."

"Fine." She flung her arms in the air. "But I'm not driving you home."

Earlier, she'd picked me up in her Chevette, a graduation gift from her family. It was a hand-me-down, so rusty the original color was indistinguishable, but Brenda was simply thrilled to have a means of transportation.

"We'll take her home," Jane said.

"Great," Brenda said, nudging her sister. "Maybe if you hadn't opened your big mouth, she wouldn't have had a choice but to go with me."

The Hannigans were all shouting at once while the van rumbled along Route 11. Even Tommy, who was sitting on Jane's lap, let out an occasional squeal.

"She'll be the best hairdresser around," Mr. H. called out. I could see his reflection in the rearview mirror. His usual rosy cheeks were now burning a bright, glowing red.

"*Stylist*, Dad," Jane shouted. "It's called *stylist*. At least, in Syracuse it is."

"Point is, once your sister makes up her mind 'bout something, there's no changing it."

"Wonder who she takes after," Mrs. H. said, reaching over and tousling her husband's hair. She then craned her neck to look over the bushy redheads, all at various heights, and said, "Vicky, you still plan on going to that cooking school, don't you?"

Everything came to a sudden hush, and all eyes fell on me. A slight nod was all I could manage for the mass of freckled faces, but if I had to be honest, until Mrs. Fitz had mentioned it, I hadn't thought much about the culinary world in quite some time. It seemed as if it had been someone else's desire.

"You just can't let what happened stop you, honey," Mrs. H. said. "Life goes on."

The back of Mr. H.'s head bobbed. "Yup, keep on keepin' on, Vicky. That's our motto!"

I pressed closer to the window and gazed out at the passing fields while the van roared down the highway. Excited chatter began to build again, then fade, while green fields turned brown then grow white with frost, the leafy, erect trees becoming bare and bowed with the weight of ice. I began to shiver from the cold.

Once again, I was reliving that bitter first day in January.

There is that disturbing moaning that sounds at first like the engine of a snowmobile, but then I discover it's coming from my father, who is cradling an awkward bundle. Mr. Scott bellows for Grandpa and me to go into the house, but we don't listen. Instead, we watch my father stumble from the sled, his knees buckling as he travels in circles, unsure where to go with the burden he's carrying. His face is blanched, his wails guttural. I see that the coat he had been wearing earlier is now swaddling his armload.

My father drops to his knees and Kevin's head lolls lifelessly out of the overcoat. My heart feels as if it is choking me with its incessant thumping, and my mind begs: *Please not Kevin. Don't let it be Kevin.* But each time I relive this horror, it is Kevin's head, hanging precariously, and along his neckline there is crusted blood. I shout for my brother to help. *Kevin! Kevin!* But he, a motionless heap on the ground, is of no help. And there is the matter of his face—with its bluish hue and opened eyes that stare at nothing.

Kiss it goodbye. Kiss it goodbye.

No one heeds the warning, and a flurry of confused activity goes on around me, while I, unable to budge, try to make sense of what is happening. Conroy is now on the scene, and he skulks over to Kevin, inspecting him, whining, pacing around him, until he braves to draw closer and begins to lick Kevin's face and neck.

After seconds go by, or a lifetime—I can't be sure which—a haze of people blur in front of me, a red light streaking intermittently across the action. I hear words come out of my mouth.

"Get him to the hospital! My God, someone help him."

But no one listens.

Mr. Scott is holding up my father as he's answering a stranger's questions. Parts of the conversation drift in my direction.

"He couldn't have known John fenced his property." He shakes his head. "Sliced him right across the jugular. And to make it worse..."

Conroy is licking Kevin's shirtsleeve, lapping where there should be a hand but is only a gnawed off stub. It takes me some time to realize this.

"A pack of 'em," Mr. Scott is saying. "Here he's been defending them, and..." He hesitates then says, "Chased 'em away with the sled. Let's just hope to God he was gone before they got to him." That's when he notices Conroy and runs over, kicking him, causing the dog to yelp and scurry away. "God-damn dogs!" he yells. Then he covers his mouth and races to the side of the house. He leans on it and shudders. My father has crumpled on top of Kevin, sobbing, pleading. Grandpa is leaning against the fender of the ambulance, staring off, shaking his head.

I want this to stop. I want to still be asleep on the Scott's couch.

No, I want to be in my crib when my mother comes to kiss me.

And she decides to stay.

I stagger into the house and go directly to my room. I kick off my sneakers, crawl under the covers, and pass out before another thought enters my mind. When I open my eyes, my bedroom is cast in early-evening shadows. I study the small figure at the foot of my bed until it takes a familiar shape.

"Brenda?"

She sniffs and wipes her nose with a crumpled tissue. "You okay?" she says, her voice quivering.

I sit up, wrapping my arms around my knees. "What happened?"

She gazes at me, her eyes swollen and red. "You don't know? They said you were there."

I cocoon myself in my blanket but cannot get warm. "He's...he's dead, right?"

"I'm so sorry, Vicky. I never meant all the things I said about him."

It is then that I first cry. "You know what happened?" After a moment of no reply, I look up and press her. "Do you?"

She nods.

"Tell me."

"But you know."

Do I? I am not sure. "Tell me anyway."

"Oh, Vicky, please don't make me—"

"Tell me!" I demand, and she jerks in surprise.

Her bottom lip quivers, and her thick head of hair drapes over her face. Her voice is small and strained. "He wanted to get right to you. It was dark; he didn't see the posted signs."

I squeeze my eyes closed, but can still see the barbed-wire fence. Brenda stops, picks at her cuticles. Finally, she continues.

"He lost so much blood, Vicky. There was just no way."

Who suddenly puts up a fence? All these years no fence, and now...

I don't know how much silent time goes by, but I eventually ask where everyone is.

"Gone to take care of the arrangements."

"Arrangements?"

"At the funeral home."

I sob, then sputter. "But he was going to buy a combine, bring Hercules back." I cover my face with my hands and cry. When I can speak, I say, "Who's going to tell my mother? We have to tell her. She needs to know."

Brenda doesn't say anything, and I curl up in a ball, unable to stop shivering, exhausting myself crying while a song from a long time ago goes round and round in my head: *Four little monkeys jumpin' on the bed, one fell off and bumped his head...*

"Vicky?"

I look up to see Mrs. Hannigan, along with the rest of the Hannigans, gazing at me. "You okay, honey?" she says.

Although rumbling, the van sat motionless in my driveway. I wiped the tears from my face and climbed over a tangle of legs so I could get to the open door.

"Give everyone our best," Mr. H. said.

I mumbled a thank you and headed toward the house.

"Oh, Vicky!" Jane called, running over to me. "Your tassel," she said, handing it to me. "Must've fell off your cap." She hesitated, then pulled me into a hug. "Why don't you come to Syracuse sometime with Brenda? We'll stay up late and make popcorn and—"

I nodded and said, "Yeah, that'll be fun."

She ran back to the van and I returned the Hannigans' waves as the vehicle backed out of the driveway. When I turned, I tried not to look at the empty pasture, its cows having been sold some time ago. Finley Farm had become a statistic. Don's services were no longer needed, and he had departed as well, but it was the occasional sight of Hercules that I missed more than the farm-hand.

My tassel crumpled in one hand, my diploma in the other, I went into the kitchen to find Grandpa sitting at the table. He was wearing a suit and tie.

"Tried to get him to go," Grandpa said. "But he just couldn't."

I nodded and sat down next to him, looking at Kevin's little house through the kitchen window. Grandpa and Dad had summoned every ounce of strength to sell the cows and machinery, give the gutters one last cleaning, and basically bury Kevin's dream along with him. I had intended to help by taking care of the little house and clean up what had been his, but could not find it in me to do so. How could I admit that my brother was not coming back? Once or twice, I had even made him his hot plate out of habit. Without saying a word, Grandpa would pick it up and toss its contents in the garbage.

"It was my turn to go," Grandpa now said. "Just doesn't make sense."

I placed my hand over his and we sat together without saying anything for some time. Dad walked in to the kitchen, his suit pants on. An attempt, anyway. The white T-shirt, however, proved he wasn't capable of going through any such thing as a graduation ceremony. I felt his eyes on me and had to say something.

"I did it." I waved my diploma as proof.

He headed out to the garage without a word, and soon I could hear the hood of the Mustang creak open. He'd been working on this latest jalopy since early winter. I went out to watch him for a while. I'm not sure if he knew I was there, but when I saw he was looking for a specific tool, I took a chance and handed him a wrench. He looked at me and then seized it without comment.

Conroy gamboled by. Dad said, "How you doin', boy."

Before losing Kevin, Dad and I rarely spoke. Not a whole lot had changed. But there were two words I wanted to say to him. No matter how I tried, though, they always got stuck between the reasoning that they were too weak and the fact that they wouldn't make up for anything, anyway.

"Dad?"

He cranked the wrench, turning and turning. He hadn't changed from his suit pants, and now they had a spot of grease on them. I edged closer and saw that the wrench was clutched to some cap that refused to budge, but Dad did not give up.

"Dad?" I repeated, somewhat louder.

The cranking stopped.

"I...I'm sorry. I didn't mean it. It should've been me."

The wrench suddenly became a hammer, and he bashed at the engine. He said, "Why the hell don't you just leave?"

The door between us had never been open very wide, but now he had slammed it shut.

"Go play your goddamn music and leave us the hell alone."

My music? "Dad? What—"

"Jack!" Grandpa shouted.

When had he come in to the garage?

"That's enough."

"Nothing but a goddamn whore," my father said.

In an instant, Grandpa placed himself between my father and me, as if attempting to protect me from the words. Conroy dashed out of the garage, and I followed. I ran and ran until I was out of breath, collapsing on the front steps to the little house where I'd once put Kevin's hot plate during our cold war. My hand shaking, I opened his unlocked door and went inside.

I nearly doubled up, overwhelmed by Kevin's redolence. I closed my eyes and saw him trekking through the woods or tossing bales in the hay field. I saw his determination, his drive, and also his watchfulness for me. After some time, I opened my eyes and wandered through the house. On a shelf in the living room, he had a row of Future Farmers of America badges lined up, and next to them was a photo of me. I looked to be about twelve and was carrying the first birthday cake I'd baked for him, my face glowing brighter than the nineteen candles.

Among the clutter of books and papers on his kitchen table was a marble notebook. At first, I was sure it was the same marble notebook where he had kept our mother's photo before giving it to me. I sat down at the table, eager to read his thoughts. But as I leafed through the pages, I saw that it was nothing more than a log with modest financial figures and notations of when to bring Hercules back; I smiled to think that he'd adopted the name with which Brenda and I had christened the bull. In smaller handwriting, he wrote, "Benny was near the Great White Pine today." A few pages later, there was another entry, this one claiming that Benny had paddled by in his canoe. Also tucked in the pages was a copy of the article about Snack Shack and me. There were also mentions of Grandpa and Dad and another scribbled note: "Grandma would've been seventy-five today. Guess that's why Grandpa isn't getting out of bed. Sad day all around. Lost one of my best and her calf today."

One name was missing altogether, and I realized then that Kevin had been able to do what Dad had not: clear his mind of Grace Finley. Apparently, seeing her likeness in me day after day had done nothing but haunt my father.

Well, in a few months, I'd be off in Montreal, and he would be free. I just couldn't be sure there'd be any reason for me to return to 'Busco, and I ached with the thought.

CHAPTER 15

❧

That summer, the air was so thick and sticky that even walking through it was difficult. Campers came in droves, but once they arrived, they stayed molded to their chaise lounges. If they entertained the idea of cooling off with a swim, they had to do battle with the swarms of gnats suspended over a lake that looked nothing but stagnant. It was a summer that contradicted the one that had preceded it, and it felt right to me: The world was mourning the loss of Kevin Finley, finding it impossible to flourish.

I took comfort immersing myself in the woods, though, and would take long breaks and sit beneath the Great White Pine. When my shift was over, I'd often tell Brenda to go on ahead without me and would sprawl across the boulder, close my eyes, and relive the hundreds of conversations Kevin and I used to have. I barely paid any attention to the campers who were around me, but if they struck up a conversation, I would tell them about how I used to tap for syrup with Kevin Finley or about Benny and how his spirit was nearby.

"Yeah, right," one doubtful young camper said, while taking surreptitious glances at the Great White Pine. "Did *you* ever see him?"

I nodded. It wasn't exactly true, but if Kevin said he existed, then as far as I was concerned, Benny existed.

Lake in the Woods had become my sanctuary, a place that provided me with a multitude of memories, and I believe it was my saving grace.

Brenda scraped a stool over to the counter and pulled a wad of paper napkins from the holder. "Thank God this is our last year," she said, patting the sweat from her forehead and nose.

I took a damp cloth and wiped away anything that would attract bugs, swerving around Brenda's cup of 7-Up. "Sixty-two days," I said, not sure if I was looking forward to Montreal more for the culinary training or to relieve Jack Finley of my presence.

The campground was lifeless, the campers sleeping in after a night of celebrating both the Fourth of July and the one-year anniversary of Lake in the Woods. I wished someone would wander over and order something. There was too much time with nothing to do but talk.

"I'm going to make sure our apartment has air conditioning," she called to me as I went to the sink to rinse the cloth.

Odd, but I had a difficult time carrying plans I'd made in the past over to the future, when there'd been that awful, time-stopping gap in between. The forms and applications had all been filled out and sent in with Brenda's forceful help, but I couldn't seem to get past the mental image of packing a suitcase and saying goodbye.

"How about we go next week to check out the apartment situation?" Brenda said. "Before you know it—"

She abruptly stopped, and I followed her gaze. Mr. Collings was down by the lake's edge with two young-looking men.

"Ohmygod!" she said. "It's *them*. Mr. Collings said they might get over to this side of the lake today." She ripped her hair out of an elastic band and began finger brushing. "Oh, it's just a bushy red mess with this heat." She looked at me. "I wish I had your hair." When I didn't respond, she said, "Do you know who they are?" Without waiting for an answer, she whispered, "It's the Scoleris of Scoleri Enterprise. They were at Moonshadows last night for the party."

She twisted the elastic band around her hair to make a taut ponytail, tossed her half-cup of soda in the garbage, and pressed a sponge into my hand. "Better look busy." She rushed to the counter and began straightening napkins and condiments that weren't in need of straightening. The men stopped a short distance away and pointed at the trees, shaking their heads.

"I knew they'd be good looking, but man, they are knock-out, drop-dead gorgeous. And look how classy they dress."

I scarcely took in the white linen pants and navy blue polo on the bigger of the two men, trying to hear what he was saying about the fortunate trees still standing.

"Which one do you want?" Brenda whispered, switching the napkin holder to the other side of the counter, where it had been moments ago.

I shot her an incredulous look then immediately returned my attention to the conversation the men were having. "So, if we were to clear this out," the bigger man said, waving his arms across the expanse of woods, "we could bring in dozens more campers. Maybe down the road, build some cabins for the winter. Keep this place operating year round."

"Clear what out?" I said, loud enough so they heard me.

Brenda gasped, and they all looked in my direction. The one in the navy polo lifted his mirrored sunglasses and gave me the once-over before letting them fall back to the bridge of his nose. He strolled over and extended his hand. When I hesitated, he reached over and grabbed mine. "I don't believe we've met. "I'm Frank Scoleri. And over there is my little brother, Vinny."

"Vincent," little brother corrected. "My name is Vincent." Vincent was wearing khaki shorts and a pale yellow cotton shirt, the sleeves partially rolled up.

Frank Scoleri still had my hand in his. I'd never felt a man's hand that was so smooth. His arms, however, were so hairy he looked liked he was covered in fur. And there was a chunky gold chain resting in a bed of fur poking from the neckline of his shirt.

Pulling my hand away, I said, "You were talking about clearing something out, Mr. Scoleri. What did you mean?"

He took his sunglasses off and gazed at me, his expression amused. "Call me Frank."

Brenda leaned over the counter, stretching out her hand. "It's a pleasure to meet you, Frank. I'm Brenda Hannigan. I just love what you've done for this town. I mean, I've never gotten to see Moonshadows, but I hear it's just—"

Frank barely paid her any attention, his sights still on me. Mr. Collings interjected, "It's usually much busier here, Frank. But everyone seems to be partied out from last night."

"Could also be the oppressive heat," Frank said. He lowered his voice. "We don't talk about that in our brochures, though." When he laughed, Brenda and Mr. Collings joined in.

Vincent came over and extended a hand. "I don't believe I got your name."

"I never said it," I said, barely touching his hand.

"Ooh, shot down!" Frank said.

"Could you cut it out for even a minute, Frank?" Vincent said.

"Vicky," Brenda said. "Her name's Vicky Finley."

"Vicky," Frank said, as if storing it for future reference.

"You were telling Mr. Collings about clearing something out," I said. "What did you mean?"

He raised his eyebrows on his evenly tanned face, a face shadowed by stubble that looked intentional. "You're quite persistent."

Mr. Collings cleared his throat and said, "She's the one who made all those deep-fried vegetables last year I told you about. We're trying to talk her into doing it again this year."

"Mr. Scoleri," I said, "it's just that—"

He raised his hand. "Again, the name's Frank. Let's not make me sound any older—"

"Would you let her speak," Vincent said. "She obviously has something on her mind."

"It's just that I care very much about this place," I said. "I'd hate to see anymore damage done to it."

"Damage!" Frank said. "Seems to me we kicked some life into this deadbeat place."

"You can't even imagine," Brenda said. "This place was nothing but moribund."

"Was not," I said, knowing the word meant something negative. "There used to be a ton of trout in that lake; now you're lucky if you can find even one."

Frank chuckled. "I find it commendable that a young woman such as yourself is so…so…environmentally conscious." He slipped his sunglasses back on and sighed.

"Vicky," Vincent said, "we had to turn a large number of applicants away this year, and we're overbooked as it is. Wouldn't you want them to see what you have here?"

"It wouldn't be the same." I thought of the Great White Pine. Who would protect it? "Please understand," I said, wanting to sound strong and forceful but sounding pathetic instead.

"You see, Vicky," Frank said, "the Scoleris are men of vision. We see something all it can be, and we don't rest until it is."

"I think it was all it could be already for Vicky," Vincent said, his tone gentle. "We just came in and ruined it." He may have been Frank's brother, but he appeared to be from different stock. I agreed with a nod and briefest of smiles.

Brenda leaned in his direction and whispered, "She's still upset. Her brother died a few months ago, and he was the one against all—"

"Brenda!" I glared at her, even though she wasn't looking in my direction.

They both offered their apologies, while Vincent suggested to Frank that they move along.

"Well," Brenda said, leaning on the counter, "I miss him, too. He was like a brother to me. Some days I just feel like I can't—"

I ran to the back and slammed the door. I was sure Brenda would be along any second, and I was ready to tell her what I thought of her play for attention at my brother's expense. But she did not come. Instead, she continued in her pitiful chatter, heard easily from the back room.

"In September," she said.

"Montreal is a pisser of a town," Frank said.

"Yeah, can't wait to party! I'm going to open my own hair salon. Maybe I'll have several branches, become a real entrepreneur like you two."

"Yeah," Frank said, "you should open some in New York."

"Wow, that's where you're from?"

"Is Vicky going to be a hair stylist, too?" Frank said.

"Oh...no. I thought of all sorts of names for it, though. 'Crazy Cuts,' or—"

"So, what's Vicky going to do while you're doing wonders with hair?"

Brenda hesitated. "She wants to own a restaurant. She likes to cook. She's a very homey type." She lowered her voice and I heard her add in singsong, "Boring!"

"Think we can get Vicky out here to cook something for us?"

"Frank," Vincent said, "let her be."

"Wouldn't you prefer something from across the lake?" Mr. Collings said.

"Actually, no. I'd prefer something from here. I want to see what all these raves are about."

"You're such an asshole," Vincent said. "I'm going down by the lake."

Mr. Collings' tone was managerial when he told Brenda to get me. A heartbeat later, she pushed open the back door. "He wants you to—"

"I heard."

"Come on, you can't be rude. Besides, maybe he's thinking of hiring you at Moonshadows."

"Yeah, because burgers and fries are such tricky fare." Still, I felt I had no choice. I went back out to see Frank eyeing the menu.

"What's a 'Michigan'?" Frank said.

"It's a hot dog on a roll with meat sauce," Brenda said. "If you want, you can add onions and mustard."

"Sounds like what we New Yorkers call a chili dog. I'll have two of those."

I headed toward the back, certain his eyes were watching me, suddenly feeling exposed in my short denim cutoffs. I threw the two hot dogs on the grill.

"He wants the works," Brenda said, over the hiss. When I ignored her, she said, "You know—mustard, onions."

I jabbed a fork in the hot dog and it spit at me.

"What's your problem?" she said. "The richest guys we've ever met are actually paying attention to us, and you treat them like dirt. What's with you?"

It would have been nice if she, my best friend, could have figured it out on her own. Sometimes I think the only reason we were best friends was happenstance.

Not caring if the hot dogs were done, I dropped them on two rolls, slopped on some meat sauce, loaded them with raw onions, and, finally, squirted two lines of mustard down their length. After plopping the whole mess on a flimsy paper plate, I brought it over to the counter and slid it in his direction. It stopped just before falling off the edge. "Bon appetite," I said; then went straight to the storage room and shut myself in the cramped space. I sat down on the overturned bucket. *How can I stop them from doing more damage to this place?*

Brenda flew in. "Vicky, you're never going to believe this!" she said as she pranced before me. "We're invited to Moonshadows! Tonight!" She grabbed my arm and squeezed me. "It'll be a double date. He said it, not me. Vincent is kinda cute, don't you think? We're invited as their guests. Frank says he feels bad we never saw it and wants to—and I quote—'show us a good time!'"

"Have fun."

"What do you mean, 'have fun'? We're both invited."

"Well, I'm not going."

She backed away, gaping at me. "Why not?"

"He gives me the creeps."

Her eyes flared open. "That gorgeous man?" she said, pointing beyond the door to where Frank was surely cramming hot dogs into his obnoxious hole. "That man out there gives you the creeps?"

"Yes!"

"Vicky, you want to go to Moonshadows as much as I do. Remember that chef you're dying to meet? I bet it could happen tonight."

Frank called to us and Brenda went to the door. "Be right there." She turned back to me. "Come on, Vicky. It'll be so cool."

"I said I'm not going. Go without me, because I'm not going."

She sighed in exasperation and went out the door, but it wasn't long before she was standing in front of me again, staring me down. "He says it won't look right if it's just me. Please, Vicky. Can't you just give this pity party a rest?"

Pity party?

"Hey, Bren," Frank called, "maybe another time. And, Vicky, those were the best Michigans I ever had."

"They were the *only* Michigans you ever had, asshole," I muttered.

Brenda ran out, but was back seconds later. "What's wrong with you?" she cried, stomping her feet. "We might never get another chance like this. Never. He was only being nice, and you treated him like he's some enemy."

"You heard him. He wants to cut down more trees."

"So, why should we blame him?" She slammed herself against the wall. "First, you're mad at Mr. Hamilton for putting up a fence. He didn't do it on purpose, Vicky. There were signs posted."

"He couldn't read them; it was too dark, and he was going too fast."

"Then that scene you had with Brad. God, I was never so embarrassed in my life."

I'd forgotten about that. Brenda had just been given her car as an early graduation gift and wanted to take me for a ride. She was so excited to be filling it up with gas for the first time. We pulled into Phil's. Right away, I spotted the maroon pickup at the pumps. Without hesitation, I jumped out of the car and ran up to Brad, who was pumping his gas.

I pounded the barrel of his chest. "It was you outside that door, wasn't it? It was you all the time!"

He pushed me away, the nozzle popping out of the tank, gas spilling on our feet. He said, "I don't want no trouble. Bren, if the cops come, you'd better tell 'em I didn't start this."

"It was you who made those phone calls. I heard you breathing on the other end." I went back at him with both fists, until he grabbed them, stopping me. Brenda had to pull me from him.

"Phone calls? I don't know what the hell you're talkin' about." He rammed the nozzle back into the pump, paid Phil, and leaped into the truck. "You're one crazy bitch, ya know." The engine roared. "Cops should be watching *you*, not me."

"You can't keep running," I screamed, as the truck squealed away, kicking up dirt.

Brenda hadn't said much that day, but now: "You got to stop blaming everybody."

"You're right," I said. "I should've never called him. No one says it, but everyone thinks it."

"It was an accident, Vicky. An accident."

"I let him down, over and over again."

She stomped her foot and screamed, "You have to stop this! I can't keep giving, Vicky. I just can't."

Just then, someone from out front called, "Can we get some service out here?"

She left to take care of the customer, but once she returned, she said, "I want to be there for you. But sometimes I need someone there for me, too."

"I'm here for you."

"No, you're not. You're lost in some other world. I really wanted to go tonight, and what happened just proves to me what I know is true."

"What do you mean?"

"I'm nobody without you. Frank wanted you to go tonight, and I know if it had been just you, he wouldn't have cared what it looked like to anyone."

"Oh, Bren—"

"No. Listen to me. It's like I'm your shadow, but sometimes people eventually look past you and finally see me. But it's better than when I'm not with you, because then I'm nothing more than a red-headed pixy who's good for a laugh." She was crying, and I wasn't sure what to say. She sputtered and said, "Now you're scaring me. Last summer, you would've done almost anything to go to Moonshadows, to taste their food and stuff. I keep thinking you're going to do the same thing to me when it's time to go to Montreal."

"I'm going to Montreal, Bren. I promise."

"Really?"

"Hey, didn't I fill out all the paperwork and send it in?"

Just then, Vincent poked his head in the doorway. Brenda and I both jumped. "Sorry," he said. "Didn't mean to scare you. But if tonight's not good, I just wanted to invite you both to Moonshadows for Friday night."

I caught Brenda's cautious look at me.

"It'll be my way of apologizing for my brother's rude behavior."

"You don't have to—" I said.

"Oh, I know. No pressure. It's a theme evening. 'A Night at the Tropics,' I believe they've called it."

Brenda was finding it difficult to behave subdued, tapping her foot, her face hopeful.

"Sounds like fun," I said, trying to be insouciant.

Without hesitation, Brenda blurted, "You'll need directions."

"Directions?" he said.

"Yeah," Brenda said, "to pick us up."

"Oh, um...you have a car, don't you?"

She nodded.

"Good. I'll leave your names with the guard at the gate. Should be a good time. Things should start hopping around nine."

The moment he was gone, Brenda turned to me and attacked me with a grateful hug. "He is *so* hot!"

CHAPTER 16

Friday night came too fast for me, though obviously not fast enough for Brenda. From my bedroom, I heard the whine of her feeble horn, prodding me to hurry. I gave myself a cursory look in the mirror and sighed. I felt a tightness in my chest, and breathing was difficult. I wished I hadn't told Brenda I would go. It didn't feel right to be where there was laughter and music, but I knew Brenda would never let me back out now. It was all she'd talked about since Vincent had invited us.

I grabbed my purse and went downstairs. Dad sat shriveled in his chair in front of the television. The entire country was absorbed in the drama coming from Nixon's White House just then, but my father didn't seem to care how it would play out, impeachment or no impeachment. He stared at the screen without seeming to care what was going on. We hadn't exchanged any words since he'd spoken to me so viciously, confusing me with my mother, and I avoided him when I could. Without saying anything, I walked out onto the porch. Grandpa was sitting in his usual spot, gazing out the window. I went to him and kissed him on the forehead.

"Ain't you a pretty thing. Where you off to?"

"Out with Brenda."

He nodded then said, "Say goodnight to your father?"

I shook my head.

"He didn't mean it, Vicky. He loves ya."

I didn't want to dispute my grandfather, but I felt my dad's actions had proved otherwise.

"I'm trying to get him to talk to Father Richards," Grandpa said. "He's just not right; his thoughts seem to be all jumbled."

I didn't know what to say. I was saved by another weak honk from Brenda's horn. "I shouldn't be too late. About twelve, okay?" I ran outside.

"Will you come on?" Brenda shouted, tapping her steering wheel. I climbed in and she shoved a cassette in her tape player. "Let the party begin," she said as Led Zeppelin blasted from the speakers.

"So," I said, examining the clingy black dress hiked up to Brenda's thighs, "is that what you got at The Blitz?"

"Yeah, isn't it great? My dad almost made me change," she said, backing out of the driveway, "but I reminded him that I was eighteen and he couldn't tell me what to do anymore. Boy, did that set him off." She took a quick glance at the yellow shift I was wearing. "You should've come with me. The Blitz has all the latest styles."

I hummed in reply.

"This is going to be so awesome," she said. "Frank really likes you, you know."

"He's a gorilla." I straightened my scarf, which matched my dress, then checked my faux gold earrings before settling back into my seat.

"I hope Vincent remembered to give the guard our names."

"If not, we'll just go home."

"Yeah, right," she said, putting the headlights on. Evening was fast approaching. "Zeppelin rules," Brenda said, turning the volume up.

And Zeppelin did rule—for the entire ride—until we pulled up to the gate to the private driveway and Brenda hit the eject button. I turned down the static. A guard lumbered over from the booth and scrutinized the car with a stupid grin.

"Sure you're in the right place?" He bent down, poking his large, round head through Brenda's window.

"Sure are," Brenda said. "Vincent Scoleri has us put on the list. Brenda Hannigan and guest."

He looked to be thinking. "Nope. No Brenda Hannigan."

"You're not even looking at your list."

"No need. There's only one name here. Is one of you Miss Finley?"

"That would be her," Brenda said, pointing to me.

He leaned further into the car to get a better look at me. He whistled. "Makes sense." He then checked out the interior of the car. "This thing really runs?"

"It gets me where I want to go, and right now I want to get through that gate."

"Better be careful." He swaggered toward the gate, raising his voice. "Most folks get to Moonshadows by boat. Not many take this route. You're gonna find quite a few sharp turns."

We rolled in, the car rumbling. He shook his head, clearly amused at the sight of such a battered mode of transportation.

"Someday I'm going to buy a car he'd never be able to afford, and I'll drive in using my membership card."

"Bren, if he's still working here by that time, I don't think you'd need to prove anything to him."

Turns out he'd been right and there were a lot of turns. It was as though we'd entered a world where darkness swallowed light. Huddled over the wheel, Brenda eased the car between the trees, riding both the brake and clutch as we crept along a crude path cut through an eerie, dense forest. Neither of us spoke while the car rattled up and down twisty hills with gnarly, grotesque shadows looming overhead.

"I'm going to tell them this road sucks," Brenda said, going back and forth from the brake to the gas pedal. "It's so creepy."

We drove under tree limbs that arced over us, their branches meeting in a skeletal grasp. Then, finally, the path opened to a panoramic view of Moonshadows. Up close, it was a real glass palace, shimmering with thousands of tiny sparkling lights. The car coasted to a stop and Brenda and I stared in silence. Having emerged from the other world, the brilliance was a welcome sight.

Her voice low, Brenda said, "Unbelievable. We still can't be in 'Busco." She took the keys from her ignition, leaving the car on a patch of grass, and slid out of her seat. While she bopped to the beat of tinny Caribbean music flowing from the glass world, I trailed behind her. French doors magically opened for us. She looked back at me, all aglow. Yes, the evening had a Cinderella feel to it—Moonshadows, the Grand Ballroom.

"Welcome to Jamaica!" boomed a large, dark man wearing a shirt decorated with pineapples. Dressed in Bermuda shorts so white, he looked like no one I'd ever seen before. His curious accent confirmed he was like no one I'd ever met before. "I'm Abdul. You must be the Finley-Hannigan duo. We've been expecting you." He laughed riotously, causing me to wonder if he found us amusing.

"You have?" Brenda said, obviously thrilled to have her surname on the evening's roster.

"Indeed, my fiery lady! Tonight we're celebrating warm sunshine and white, sandy beaches." He waved his muscular arm, gesturing toward the huge illuminated room strewn with palm trees and the most colorful flowers. I recognized many of the guests from having served them only hours ago, except now the women were dressed in bold print dresses and dancing with men wearing floral shirts and white pants.

"Are Vinny and Frank Scoleri here, yet?" Brenda said.

"Not to my knowledge. Were you expecting them?"

"Yes," Brenda said, her tone certain.

"Well, once they arrive, I'll tell them you're here." Abdul clapped his thick hands in a quick double time. "Gloria will seat you. If you need anything, be sure to let me know."

A slim, black woman in a sarong appeared and introduced herself as Gloria. She signaled for us to follow her across a shiny black floor, which reflected light from a tremendous chandelier. The music had stopped and the floor had cleared, and I knew we were being watched as we were led to a table in the corner by a window. Brenda's eyes gleamed as bright as the brass pedestals of the glass table at which we were seated.

A waiter dressed in white appeared. He took the cloth napkin from the table and snapped it open, placing it on my lap. He did the same for Brenda, who was trying to behave as though she were used to being catered to. I wasn't thrilled with the idea of being pampered on the Scoleris' dime, but I was beginning to thaw from the nasty chill of winter. It did occur to me, though, that once the Scoleris arrived, I would have the opportunity to share my concerns about anymore possible damage happening to the resort area.

After water—"moving water" was how the waiter referred to it—had been poured for us, Brenda reached over the table and squeezed my hand. "Did you see the looks we got? Everyone's dying to know how we got in."

The Caribbean sounds we'd heard moments earlier started again, played by a band across the room. The musicians, looking like hot fudge pouring life into an otherwise cool vanilla crowd, were invoking the mood of the tropics using a vibraphone and steel drum. One by one, people left their tables to rumba or cha-cha—I couldn't be sure which, but it was fun to watch the way couples mimicked each other while moving in time with the music. Brenda's legs were jittering, which meant she was eager to become more than an observer.

From my vantage point, I was watching tray-laden waiters going back and forth from what had to be the kitchen. To me, beyond those double doors was where the real action was happening.

"Good evening, ladies. What may I get you from the bar?"

Pulled from my reverie by a waiter standing at the table, I ordered a Coke. Brenda ordered one as well, but asked for rum in it. The waiter did not ask for proof of age, but once he left I gave her a scolding look.

"Oh stop," she said. "We're eighteen now."

"Yeah, but…"

"Lighten up. I feel like partying." She surveyed the room. "Just wish Vinny would get here. We need some younger blood."

Along with our drinks came a procession of dishes. After the shrimp cocktail, we were served mini-raviolis with a white cream sauce on gold-rimmed plates. Brenda kept busy watching the activity while I swept a square of pasta through the sauce and savored every crabmeat-filled bite.

"They're here," Brenda said, pushing away her plate, having barely touched her food.

I looked up to see Vincent and Frank at the front door in serious conversation with Abdul, who looked to be kowtowing by the way he nodded each time he was spoken to. Then he pointed in our direction.

Brenda let out a muffled squeal, straightening her dress, pushed up her strapless bra to give her something that might resemble cleavage, and finally took a deep breath.

"Good evening, ladies," Frank said, pulling out a chair and drawing it close to me. Vincent paused, then took the empty chair. Brenda shifted hers slightly closer to his. Immediately, a waiter appeared, and Frank ordered drinks for the table.

"Brenda, you're driving," I said, "and. "And it's going to be just as difficult getting out of here as it was getting in." Even as I said it, I knew I was wrong: Getting her out of this Shangri-La would be near impossible.

Frank draped his arm across the back of my chair. "Don't worry; I'll see you get home safely." He leaned in. "Whether it be tonight or tomorrow."

I lifted his hairy arm off my shoulder and stated, "It's going to be tonight, and it's going to be with Brenda."

He studied me with a brief hardness then forced a laugh. "Still worried I'm going to do something to your beloved trees?"

"Frank, cool it," Vincent said.

"Yes," I said, "I am."

Mrs. King, the ex-wife of some congressman from Albany, tapped Vincent on the shoulder to say hello. This opened the dam: one woman after the next, all looking old enough to be their mother, came by our table, ignoring Brenda and me, panting for the men's attention. Rail-thin Mrs. Nelson, who never ordered anything from Snack Shack but sugarless iced tea, sashayed over and bent down to say something in Frank's ear; she then threw her head back, laughing, while playing with her draping pearls.

After she left, Frank leaned over and whispered, "Don't be jealous. It's part of my job to flirt. It keeps them coming back."

"I'm not jealous," I said.

The music slowed and the men and women on the dance floor began to sway in each other's arms. Frank stood and put his hand out to me.

"No, thank you," I said.

"No thank you?"

"Vicky, come on. Dance with him," Brenda said. She looked hopefully at Vincent.

"No, Brenda. I don't feel like dancing."

"What are you, some ice queen?" Frank said.

"Frank," Vincent said, "leave her alone."

"Listen, Vinny, you should shut the fuck up. She's blowin' it big time." He reached over and pulled Brenda from her chair. "Come on, sweetheart. You look like you know how to party."

Brenda hesitated for a second, looking from Vincent to Frank, and then took Frank's outstretched hand and let him lead her to the dance floor. It wasn't long before she was up against him, her body swaying, her head resting against his chest. They almost looked humorous—tiny freckle-faced Brenda engulfed by a large, hairy creature wearing khaki shorts and a black polo shirt. Whenever she faced my direction, her eyes widened with shocked amazement.

Vincent sipped on his gin and tonic until Mrs. Nelson charged at him in a high-heeled clip clop.

"You're not getting off that easy, Vincent Scoleri," she said, pulling him from his chair. He wasn't actually bucking, but it was clear he was being dragged against his will. He shot me a comical look of horror as she led him to the dance floor, making me smile. I tried not to watch but couldn't help myself. He looked comfortable in his black denim jeans and white shirt, but he was clearly uncomfortable with the way Mrs. Nelson was wholeheartedly offering herself. She made a better match for Frank, who seemed to be having trouble keeping his hands off particular regions of Brenda's body.

"It's limbo time!" a rousing voice from the band called out, and the torpid, spellbinding beat picked up. Mrs. Nelson squealed and was the first to approach the horizontal stick. Vincent took the opportunity and escaped, sitting down in what had been Frank's chair.

"Don't you like to dance?" he said.

I shrugged and said, "I'm trying to work myself up into trying some of this." I pointed to the platter of seafood on our table. I had already tried a clam on the half shell and a chunk of lobster, and I was now debating the escargot.

"These?" Vincent said, eating one and smacking his lips. Nothing like a good snail to whet your appetite."

I picked one up with some hesitation, but hoots and howls drew our attention to the dance floor. Mrs. Nelson was leaning on the lug while Brenda, bent in half, was nearing the stick, her thick bushy hair sweeping the floor, her body taking cautious hops.

"How low can you go?" the musician challenged.

Apparently, Brenda was going to prove how low and hiked her dress as she approached the stick. She made it without so much as grazing it. Frank met her on the other side and scooped her up, swinging her around in mid-air. The abandoned Mrs. Nelson looked to be ready to go back on the prowl.

After swallowing the escargot, I turned to Vincent and said, "The food is phenomenal. That must be some kitchen."

"I suppose. The food is all right."

"Just all right?"

He shrugged.

I felt disheartened. I'd never created anything remotely as good as the dishes placed before us, and he thought it was "all right." I obviously had a lot to learn.

Flushed and walking on air, Brenda was back at the table, the lug in tow. He said, "Hey, little bro, you moving in on my chick?" He chuckled then flipped what had been Vincent's chair around so that it was backwards. He sat down, draping his hairy arms over the back in a relaxed fashion. He took Brenda's fork and swirled ravioli in cream sauce from her neglected plate and shoved it in his mouth. Barely swallowing, he said, "Barbara here is one hell of a dancer."

"Brenda," Brenda said.

"Yeah, yeah, Brenda. Just testing you." He motioned for the waiter to bring us another round of drinks. I rebuked Brenda with a glare, but she ignored me and changed the subject.

"Ew," she said. "What is that?" she pointed to the platter of seafood.

Sucking a clam from its shell, Frank said. "It's fruit from the ocean, sweetheart."

"Fruit from the ocean," she said, her tone worshipful. "Wow. That's poetry."

"Yeah, me and fucking Whitman. We're in the same league." He looked pointedly at me. "So, Vicky, you always such a wallflower? I could teach you to dance, ya know. I can do a mean lindy." He picked up the glass the waiter had just set on the table and swilled down a few gulps. Then he said, "Wait. Ice queens don't dance, do they?"

Vincent said, "Frank, will you shut the hell up?"

"Hey, I could've called her a frigid bitch, but thought I'd keep it nice."

Vincent stood and offered me his hand. I took it.

"Hey, where you going?" Frank said.

"To show her the kitchen. Let me know when you decide to apologize." He led me across the room and pushed open the double door.

Immediately, I forgot the gorilla's rude behavior, overwhelmed by the sight of steaming pots and cooks choreographing their moves as they prepared one dish after another, shouting orders to the officious waiters. Vincent introduced me to Chef Bresette.

"This is Vicky Finley," Vincent said. "She's intrigued by all this."

"I'm going to Montreal to be an apprentice at Le Palais in the fall," I said, hoping to gain the chef's respect. Instead, his face clouded over.

"But you are a woman! This is a man's world."

I smiled, thinking—hoping—that he was teasing me, but when he did not smile, I said, "Julia Child is a woman."

"You don't look like no Julia Child," he said with a shrug. He then hurried back to a sizzling frying pan. I watched in wonder, feeling that perhaps he was right and I had no business trying to be a part of such a world. As though reading my mind, Vincent leaned over and said, "I think that was a backhanded compliment."

I couldn't be sure. After I watched the activity for several minutes, trying to stay out of the bustling waiters and staff's way, Vincent suggested that we see if Frank was ready to apologize. I doubted there would be any sort of apology and by the time we reached the table, Frank was gone. As was Brenda.

"Where do you suppose they went?" I said.

We found Abdul and asked if he'd seen them.

"I believe Mr. Scoleri is going to introduce Camille to the fiery young lady."

"Camille?" I said.

"I hope your friend knows what she's doing," Vincent said.

"What do you mean?"

"Come on," he said, leading me outside and along the beach to the dock. We got there just as a cabin cruiser, with *Camille* looped out in fancy gold script along the boat's side, was chugging away.

"Frank!" he shouted. I joined in by calling Brenda's name, but the boat picked up speed, churning black water in its wake. A mist skated across the boat's beam of light. Eventually, the only sound was that of the docked boats rocking in the waves that *Camille* had stirred.

"There's nothing to do but wait," Vincent said. "Why don't we go inside until they get back?"

I shook my head. "You go. I want to be right here when she gets back."

He blew a low whistle. "Somebody's angry."

"I'm fine," I said, attempting to sound so.

"I doubt your friend will be when she gets back." He sat on the edge of the dock and patted the spot next to him, but I kept pacing, searching through a building fog for the cruiser to return.

"What happens? Your car turns into a pumpkin at midnight?" When I didn't laugh, he said, "Am I making you uncomfortable?"

"This whole night is making me uncomfortable. I mean, what kind of friend would just take off like that with some jerk." I realized the jerk I was referring to happened to be Vincent's brother, and I apologized.

"No, you're right," he said. "Jerk is an understatement." He looked up at me. "You going to keep standing?"

Holding the hem of my dress, I sat down next to him. I stared out on the lake; it was as if the boat had dissolved in the darkness. Calypso music drifted from the glass palace some distance away.

"Thank you for showing me the kitchen."

"Sorry Chef Bresette wasn't very kind. We hired him, since Chef Antoine decided to stay in France this year. Not *all* men are jerks, you know."

"I know." I thought of Kevin just then, feeling a sudden pang of loneliness. "If I close my eyes, it's like none of this is here." I did close my eyes, remembering that where I was sitting, on the border of what had been Mrs. Passino's property, there had been nothing but trees and rocks. "It was so quiet, except for maybe the chirping of a bird or a rustling breeze." And there was Kevin, sitting at the lake's edge, tossing back his fishing pole and then casting it forward, followed by the plunk of the sinker hitting the water.

"You're worried, aren't you?" Vincent said.

"You should've seen this place before all this was here," I said.

The calypso eased into a smooth, slow number, and Vincent stood. "Would it be safe to ask you to dance?"

I gazed up at him, at the way his brown eyes searched me. "Here? Right now?"

"Why not?" He took my hand, helping me up. We moved, gingerly at first, the dock creaking beneath us. I breathed in his cologne, felt his muscles against me. We danced until the song ended, but he didn't let go. Instead, he took my face in his hands and brought my lips to his. After a few lingering moments, he stopped and looked me in the eyes. I wanted to pull him back to me, to have him kiss me again, although I didn't understand at all the feelings he was stirring in me.

"You know, you really ticked off Frank. He's not used to being rejected."

"Well, I'm sure Brenda's feeding his ego."

"Not that she's not pretty or anything, but...well, she's not you," he said. "Frank always scopes out the most beautiful woman, claims her, and makes his attack."

"You're making him sound dangerous," I said, the dew clinging to me. When I looked, I saw that the fog had thickened so much that the lights of the crystal palace could barely be seen. "Maybe he can't find his way back," I said.

"They'll be okay. Frank's a pretty good navigator. Has to be. After all, he's a Scoleri."

It was an uneasy reminder of who he was. "You seem..." I hesitated, but he prodded me to continue. "Well, it's just you and your brother seem so young to own all this. To be businessmen."

"Oh, trust me, Senior Scoleri has the final say in all our decisions."

"Senior?"

"My father. He's the one who's really in control."

Off in the distance, a small beam of light nudged its way through the fog. Vincent and I stood at the edge of the dock and waited. Several minutes passed while the cruiser coasted and maneuvered into the space, churning up the water. Finally, the engine died.

Brenda emerged from the cabin below, her hair wild and uncontrolled. She took Vincent's offered hand and leapt on the dock. Her purse was open, pantyhose spilling from it. Frank then appeared, vaulting over the side in one fast swoop, the dock swaying under his jolt of weight.

"Hey, our own welcoming committee." He pulled Brenda, who appeared shell-shocked, up against him.

"I want to go home, Bren," I said.

She looked through me, as though I weren't there.

"Home!" Frank said.

I walked up to Brenda, "You okay?"

"Is she okay!" Frank said. "Of course she's okay. She's terrific."

Brenda nodded, seemingly coming out of some spell.

"We really do have to go, Brenda. I'm not—"

"You are one boring broad," Frank said. "The night's just beginning." He looked at Vincent. "The boat's all yours, if you want to give Vicky a tour." He chuckled. "Maybe you'll get lucky."

Vincent took a step toward Frank. "Shut the hell up."

"Chill, little brother." He gave me the once over. "Then again, with ice queen here—"

Before I realized what had happened, Vincent's fist made a sweeping arc, connecting with Frank's chin. Frank lurched backwards, but remained standing. Brenda grabbed him, screaming.

Wrapping an arm around Brenda, he said, "It's okay, baby. He's just ticked off I'm on the mark."

"You owe this lady an apology," Vincent said.

"I don't owe anyone shit," Frank said, squinting. "Bren, let's get outta here." He led her back to the boat.

"Bren, we have to go!"

Frank turned. "Listen, *Vicky*, Bren's spending the night with me."

"Brenda," I shouted, "your parents are expecting you home tonight."

Frank lifted her into the boat then jumped in behind her, rocking it. She said, "I'll call them and tell them I'm staying at your house." Frank praised her with a hug before they disappeared into the cabin.

"How am I going to get home?" I shouted at her, but she didn't answer.

"Come on," Vincent said, "I'll take you."

Stunned, I watched the boat chug away once again.

Unlike Cinderella, who went to the ball in a golden carriage and returned home in a pumpkin, I had come to Moonshadows in Brenda's jalopy and was being chauffeured home in a white Mercedes sports coupe, its leather interior sumptuous.

Vincent navigated us out of the private entrance, sharp turns and all. We finally hit the main drag, but had to maneuver through thick fog, going no more than twenty miles an hour. As dangerous as it could be, I kept thinking about Brenda and the situation in which she was putting herself. Eventually, with my direction, we pulled into my driveway. Vincent cut the engine and turned toward me.

"You're quiet."

"I just feel as though this whole evening was a bad dream."

"A bad dream, huh? Wow."

"Oh, not you. You're very nice." I felt myself blushing.

"You know, not every Scoleri is an asshole."

"I never said they were." I paused, then added, "I should go in."

He walked me to the door and gave me a kiss goodnight, softly on the lips. "May I see you again?"

"If you want to."

He smiled. "What about you? What do you want?"

I thought about it for a moment and was surprised by my answer: "To get to Montreal, to begin my life." Even as I said them, something about those words distracted me.

He caressed my hand and said, "You're going to be a great chef, Vicky. I just know it." He gave me a gentle squeeze before walking away.

I waited until his car turned the corner before I went into the house. Grandpa and Dad had already been in bed for hours. I groped my way through the living room, only to stop and imagine she was waiting for me on the couch. She'd rub her eyes, turn off the TV, and pat the couch, inviting me to sit with her and tell her about my night.

"He was so nice," I'd say. "His name is Vincent."

"Vincent," she'd repeat. "Will you see him again?"

I thought of the way he left and couldn't be sure.

"Think Kevin'll get mad?"

"Why would he get mad?"

"Vincent's a Scoleri."

"Oh, well. Doesn't much matter now, does it? Kevin's dead."

And there it was. No more would I have my brother's approval or disapproval. I was on my own to triumph or fail. Either way would have no bearing on the man who had been my own private cheering squad all my life.

The thought was unfathomable.

CHAPTER 17

After an unsuccessful attempt to chase my anxious thoughts away, I finally fell into a state of subconsciousness. I couldn't really call it sleep, my mind too busy doing twisted things and traveling bizarre places. One of those places was a tunnel, whose never-ending length I floated down, carried by a strong wind. There was fog as thick as gravy, clinging to me. No matter how hard I tried, I could not rub it off. Then there was a strange white mist hovering at the end of this tunnel. Whatever it was, I knew it was waiting for me. The closer I got to this mist, the more distinctive it became. At first, I thought it was a tree, an oak perhaps, its trunk tall and slender, its limbs long and thin, skeletal. However, once I drew closer, I saw it wasn't a tree at all, but a person. No, not just any person.

It was Kevin.

"Do you have any idea how long I've been looking for you?" I screamed at him. "We've all been looking for you!" I wanted to run, to find Dad and tell him Kevin was okay after all. I also wanted to go to my brother, to touch him, to hear him breathing, to smell him. But when I tried to get closer to him, he'd recede farther and farther away, shaking his head, where there was no mouth but parchment-like flesh. His eyes looked to be pleading.

I reached out for him, but when he raised his arms, instead of hands, there were two gruesome stubs.

"What happened?" I screamed, looking into his eyes for answers, but they abruptly became two agate orbs whirling uncontrollably like erratic marbles in a pinball machine.

"Kevin, please talk to me."

When nine o'clock came and there was no sign of Brenda, I realized I would have to get to work on my own. I couldn't very well call her house, since she was supposed to be staying with me. My bike would have to be my mode of transportation. I went to the garage and dusted it off. The tires were a little soft, but what other choice did I have? Well, there was Kevin's pickup parked in front of the little house, but I couldn't bring myself to drive it.

By ten o'clock, after I had brewed the coffee and Mr. Collings had dropped off the donuts and croissants, which were now in jars, there was still no sign of Brenda. I began to worry. Frank Scoleri proved himself an asshole, but could he have been something more sinister? Just when panic was about to prod me to fink on Brenda to Mr. Collings, her rusty Chevette pulled up. She climbed out wearing a pair of jeans and T-shirt. She stumbled past me, mumbling something incomprehensible, and poured herself a cup of coffee.

"Since when do you drink coffee?"

"Since now."

"Rough night?"

With an air of authority, she waved me off. "You wouldn't understand."

"What did you tell your mother?"

Three packets of sugar and four creams went into her cup before she took a sip. "You know."

"Brenda, you put me on the spot. What if she called and wanted to talk to you?"

"But she didn't. She would've said something when I went home to change this morning."

"I was worried about you."

"I'm a big girl, Vicky. I can take care of myself." She took another sip of her coffee. "So, what happened with you and Vinny?"

"His name is Vincent, and nothing happened."

"What a waste. He's cute, too. But Frank's so…so masculine."

A different word came to my mind, but I didn't offer it. Thankfully, Mr. and Mrs. Stiles, a retired couple traveling around the States, ambled up to the counter and ordered coffee, tea, and a plain donut to share. Brenda didn't budge, so I took care of them.

"You girls have a good time last night?" Mrs. Stiles said.

Brenda stretched and practically purred her reply: "Glorious!"

The Stiles exchanged disapproving glances then took their breakfast to a picnic table a short distance away.

"Bren," I said, "you blew me off last night, and I wasn't thrilled with having to get a ride home from some stranger."

"It's time you grew up," she said. "You know, Frank promised he'd visit me in Montreal. We'll have to work out some kind of system when we're entertaining our boyfriends."

Three children ran up to the counter, all shouting for lemonade.

"He told me I drive him crazy," Brenda said, disregarding the trio of faces barely able to see over the counter.

I poured the lemonade, took the money, and watched as they ran toward the lake.

"Can you believe it?" she said. "There you and I were, and he came after *me*." She got up and poured some more coffee in her cup and repeated the routine with the sugar and cream. "Please don't be angry, but he admitted he didn't care much for blondes. He said redheads were his cup of tea."

I had a difficult time imagining "cup of tea" coming out of that gorilla's mouth.

"Brenda *Scoleri*. Now that has class."

She talked as though she were walking on clouds, but looked more like she'd been slogging through muck. We began to have a steady flow of customers, and Brenda eventually pitched in. There was little time for any more talk, and I welcomed the break. When there was finally a lull in our work, Brenda, who was wiping up spilled ice cream, said, "You think he'll come back? He said he would, but maybe he was just trying to make me feel better."

"Feel better?"

She sighed and went into the back, and when she reappeared, her eyes were black from runny mascara and her nose was red. But then her face lit up, and she said, "He's here!"

Down the dirt path, the white Mercedes kicked up dust as it headed in our direction. Not many cars cut through the crude roadway, other than those belonging to the employees, and none of the employees at Lake in the Woods could have afforded such expensive means of transportation. Brenda shoved her T-shirt in her jeans and tucked a few loose strands of hair back into the elastic band.

I handed her a wet paper towel. "Clean your face." I motioned to her eyes.

The car pulled off to the side and the door opened, but it was Vincent who climbed out. He was carrying a bouquet. When he reached me, he placed a dozen pink roses in my arms. He said, "I hope you like daisies."

"Daisies?" I said, cradling the roses.

"By any other name, they smell as sweet."

Again, he stirred something in me, something I couldn't define. I touched the soft petals, so perfect and vibrant. "I love daisies," I said.

He scowled. "Real daisies or...?"

I laughed. "These are beautiful."

"Where's Frank?" Brenda said, sidling up to me.

"He had to go back to Long Island," Vincent said.

"He's gone?"

Vincent nodded. "He...it was an emergency."

"I hope he's okay. He is okay, right?"

"He's fine," Vincent said with a sigh.

"But he'll be back, right?"

His jaw tightened. "Brenda, I came to talk to Vicky. Would you mind?" To me, he said, "Can you get away for a minute?"

I told Brenda I'd be right back, and Vincent and I walked a short distance away into a wooded area. A large group of children were playing hide and seek, so we weren't actually alone. Some towheaded kid was facing a tree, his eyes occasionally darting around while he counted.

"Hey there," Vincent said, "no cheating."

The boy squeezed his eyes shut and shouted in singsong, "Eighty-one, eighty-two..."

The sun was bright, pouring through the leaves, casting warm rays over us. Vincent said, "I was wondering if you'd go out to dinner with me tonight?"

"Tonight? Gosh—"

"Le Café de Paris."

I caught my breath. "That's in Montreal," I said. I'd read about it, about it being nestled in the Ritz-Carlton, and its excellent cuisine, but didn't think I'd be dining at the four-star restaurant anytime soon—if ever.

"You're it!" shouted a young girl in long braids to a boy who looked to be about her age.

"Well then, how about it? I'll pick you up around six-thirty?"

Six-thirty. That would give me enough time, since there was a pan of lasagna thawing for Dad and Grandpa. All I'd have to do is put it in the oven for forty-five minutes, and, while it cooked, toss a salad, put some bread in a basket and the plate of cheese on the table, and figure out what I was going to wear.

"Sure," I said, wondering if I was actually going to go through with it.

"Good." He smiled.

"I'm thirsty," called one of the children, prompting all the children to tear out of the woods. I didn't have to guess where they were headed.

"I'd better get back and help Brenda."

"Hey," he said, slipping my hand into his as he walked me to Snack Shack, "why aren't you making those French-fried vegetables I've heard so much about?"

True to Mr. Collings word, he'd had the burnt wall fixed, but I was still gun shy.

I said, "Got to be more of a pain than anything." I dropped his hand, went to the other side of the counter, and helped Brenda pour one soda after the next for the kids.

"Vincent," she called over, "do you have a number where I could reach Frank?"

"Listen," he said, "give it up. He doesn't like being tracked down. If he wants to call you, he'll call."

Abandoning the sodas, Brenda stumbled to the storage room. I finished serving the children, and after I took care of the last one and collected the money, Vincent leaned over the counter and kissed me on the cheek. ""Six-thirty, then."

I watched while he strolled over to his car and drove off. I wondered how I could back out, grief still keeping a tight hold on me.

Brenda looked pitiful when she reappeared, her eyes red and puffy. "Frank'll be back," she said with conviction.

The very idea worried me. I think she knew in her heart that if Frank did come back, it wouldn't be for her. I knew it, too. What I didn't know was why.

❦ ❦ ❦

"Vicky," Grandpa said, coming into the kitchen just as I finished washing the last plate from supper. "Someone's here for you. I invited him in, but he said he'd wait in the car for you."

I dried my trembling hands on the dish towel. Earlier, I'd sat down at the table during supper and picked at the bit of lasagna I'd put on my plate, wondering how I could get out of the impending date. Like every night at supper, silence abounded, so I was left with my worrisome thoughts.

"He seems to think he's taking you out to eat," Grandpa said.

"I'll tell him I can't go," I said, the words coming out weak and shaky.

"Why can't you go?"

I felt a tear slip down my face. "I just can't, Grandpa."

"Oh, my sweet angel." Grandpa scuffed over to me and pulled me against him. I could feel his ribs jutting out. I began to sob. Conroy got up from the rug and came over to me, whining.

"How can I go and have a good time, Grandpa?"

He took my face in his hands, and said, "Because someone in this house has to keep on livin', Vicky. I'm so goddamned tired of how stale everything is anymore."

"But I miss Kevin so much," I sputtered.

"We all do, sweetheart. I miss Kevin, and I miss the old Vicky. Now, why don't you go upstairs and get on somethin' proper for this date, and I'll go tell this young man you'll be out in a few minutes."

I sniffed, still unsure.

He said, "Do it for me."

I gave Grandpa a tight hug and then ran up the stairs.

"They fly this in all the way from New York," Vincent said, spooning a dollop of shiny caviar onto a wedge of black bread. Having never tasted caviar before, I nibbled off a small amount, letting it rest on my tongue to savor it. Vincent, on the other hand, brought an entire caviar-covered wedge to his mouth.

Even though everything seemed perfect, I was still uncertain I was where I should be.

"What are you thinking?"

"How out of my element I am." I'd once considered the simple beige dress I was wearing to be elegant, but now it felt dated and unrefined. Vincent was wearing a designer suit. He reached over and took my hand.

"Enjoy it. If you're going to be the chef you want to be, it won't be often that you'll be the one who's being wined and dined."

It was a clear, warm night, and we decided to eat al fresco. We were seated on the outskirts of a duck pond surrounded by flowers. A waiter freshened our champagne while another placed mixed salads in front of us. I gazed at my glass, at the way the bubbles continued to rise to the top. I was feeling lightheaded, but couldn't be sure if it was from the candlelight, sitting by a pond rimmed with gladiolas, geraniums, and orchids, all perfuming the air, or, yes, maybe even the champagne.

"Vincent," I said, pushing radicchio around on my plate, "how did Scoleri Enterprise discover Benny's Lake?"

"Benny's Lake?"

"You call it Lake in the Woods."

He nodded. "Well, like most things with my father, it was a serendipitous discovery. He wasn't at all looking to set up a campground."

"Really?"

"He had this idea that he'd promote another Woodstock, get all the big bands to perform."

Woodstock had just happened a couple of years earlier. Brenda and I were barely fourteen, but she tried to talk me into hitchhiking with her. She was going to tell her parents she was staying with me, and she'd wanted me to tell my father I was staying with her. I refused, and she didn't talk to me for about a week.

"He was looking for a nice piece of property to do it on, but once he found your lake and discovered how eager the farmers were to sell, well, he decided to give KOA a run for its money. Woodstock redux became history, all because my father likes to gamble with his investments."

"And now you want to cut more trees down," I said.

Vincent didn't respond immediately. He took a steady sip of his champagne before saying, "It's all talk right now."

Talk. I recalled the "talk" from a couple of years earlier and how that quickly had spawned a resort from what had been only trees and rocky terrain. I had a sinking feeling it could easily happen again. In my mind, I saw the Great White Pine falling, falling, falling, thrashing to the ground.

"So, your father is the one that decides if you're going to expand or not."

"Sort of. He sent Frank and me to check it out, to see what we thought. Believe it or not, your quaint little town is more a hobby for my father than anything. His money is locked up in so many other ventures. Bigger ventures."

"So," I said, with some hesitation, "what did you and Frank think?"

"We haven't really talked about it yet. We won't till we get back to the office. Frank's the one whose opinion my father really listens to, though. He may be an asshole in so many ways, but Frank's the one with the business savvy. That's okay, because not much else about his life impresses me. Well, I guess I'd like to have a wife and kids to go home to at night, even though *he* doesn't half the time."

My fork in midair, I said, "Frank's married?"

He straightened his tie, cleared his throat. "I can't cover for my brother or even apologize for him. His first love is money, but women are a close second. He craves the female gender."

"Brenda's going to be so crushed," I said, remembering how sullen she had been when she'd left work. She had asked if I minded her leaving early, since she was wiped out and thought she might be coming down with something. I had my bike, so I'd told her fine, but I knew all that she was coming down with was a heavy dose of disappointment.

"She's better off without him," Vincent said.

That I was certain, but I knew Brenda. She'd fallen hard for Frank. If she discovered I'd been out with Vincent doing all she was dying to do, it would kill her. I decided then not to tell her about my evening. Instead, I'd have to get her mind back on Montreal and hair salons.

We never got back to the topic of the lake's destiny during our dinner conversation. Vincent paid the bill then suggested we take a stroll. We ambled hand in hand up and down the steep inclines as night settled onto the city. I found myself talking to him about food the same way I used to talk to Kevin about certain recipes I wanted to try. I realized I must have been boring him.

"Not at all," Vincent said. "I wish I had that kind of passion for something."

Finally, we decided it was time to get me back home. The drive home was filled with conversation and laughter. Before I realized it, Vincent was walking me to the door.

Under a sky filled with stars and a full moon and a chorus of frogs croaking from across the road in the marshy woods, he held me. "I had a great time," he whispered.

"Me, too," I said, surprising myself, because it was true.

His kiss made me fluid in his arms, but then he broke away. "I don't think I want to see the barrel of a shotgun."

"They're asleep."

"Still, I think I'd better go." He kissed me on the forehead then went to his car. The white Mercedes whirred away in a flash.

I wanted to tell Grandpa thank you, but as I stood outside his bedroom door, I heard him snoring, so I made my way in the dark to my bedroom. I closed the door and stripped off my clothes. I didn't bother putting pajamas on before slipping under the covers. I began to think of the way Vincent had brought his lips to mine. I hugged my pillow, ready to burst with yearning. I began caressing my breasts, then let my hand wander further down, imagining it was Vincent touching me. I wanted to be filled, and before I realized what I was doing, I had the pillow between my legs, my thoughts on Vincent. I shifted myself, until it was no longer me making the effort but my body losing itself to the sensation. Never had I achieved such a glorious release—and I wanted more. I wanted the real thing.

I wanted Vincent.

CHAPTER 18

"Our Father who art in Heaven, hallowed be thy name…"

Like I'd done for as long as I could recall, I joined the congregation in prayer while resting my chin on the wobbly wooden pew in front of me. Grandpa and my father were on their knees to my right, both barely mumbling the words.

"…Thy will be done on earth as it is in heaven…"

Sunlight pressed through the stained glass windows, creating a subdued yellowish glow. A statue of some saint stood to the left of the altar, a toe broken off its marble foot.

"…and deliver us from evil."

How does a revered statue lose a toe?

On the other side of the church was the thicket of redheads, minus two. James and Charlie were on the altar assisting Father Richards, floating behind the priest in their black and white trappings. Recently, Daniel Hannigan had refused to serve as an altar boy any longer, believing he'd outgrown what he'd come to consider embarrassing servitude. He had even told his parents that he wanted to be in a rock group like the Who, so he didn't have time for church. Although Mr. and Mrs. Hannigan had never heard of the band, they sent Daniel to his room and instructed him not to come out until he was ready to ask both God and them for forgiveness. One would think that Daniel had learned from Brenda's experience some time ago.

At about the age of fourteen, Brenda had braved the announcement that she didn't believe in Jesus. "Come on, Mom. You think this man really came back to life?"

Following that train of thought, she didn't think it was necessary to attend church any longer. I'm not sure how Brenda thought her declaration would make her life any easier. Instead, her dramatic statement was what kept her from any sort of socializing, outside of school, mass, and catechism. She would also be forced to repeat the rosary daily, reciting the Ten Commandments, Lord's Prayer, Hail Mary, and Act of Contrition aloud for her parents' ears.

When she was about ready to snap with cabin fever, she apologized to her parents and announced she'd had such a change of heart—or "cathartic experience," as she called it—that maybe she'd become a nun. Bad thing to say because they knew what she was trying to do and added another week to the grounding.

Now she was still an atheist, or so she said, but she didn't let her parents know that, so there she and Daniel sat on the other side of the church, along with the rest of the Hannigans, rolling prayers off their tongues if for no other reason but to maintain their freedom.

I can't say for sure what I believe, but I gazed across the church and wondered what it would be like to sit between a father and mother who wanted to leave a legacy. I didn't recall much about my grandmother, but she was the one who taught me to say the rosary, to keep my legs together at all times, but especially during mass, and to keep my eyes on the altar instead of on the mural spanning the ceiling where a water stain marked one of the winged angel's cheeks. For as long as I could remember, that stain had been there.

We rarely spoke of God in the Finley household, whereas in the Hannigan home God was part of their everyday conversation: During lent they recited the rosary at the table before laying out the meal. At Christmas, they sang "Happy Birthday" to Jesus before tearing into their gifts. Good Friday was a time when the family had to remain on their knees in the quiet of their home from noon until three in the afternoon to recall the sacrifice Christ had made for them.

Brenda said God did nothing but cramp her lifestyle and that she couldn't wait to get away from all the religious mumbo jumbo.

I, on the other hand, found calm in the ancient house of worship. Mass was not drudgery for me. Of course, I rarely paid much attention while I was there. One thing I liked to do was hold my hand just the right way so that the light coming through the stained glass bounced off the peridot stone in a ring my grandmother had left for me. It made the tiniest colorful prism, my own kaleidoscope, and I would turn my hand ever so slightly, taking pleasure in the various color patterns. The only thing that distracted me was when someone would come in through the door. Churubusco was a small town where everyone knew everyone else, but I always watched the faces of those who came through that door in case one resembled the one in the Polaroid.

It was time to take Holy Communion. Grandpa and Dad did not budge. Neither did I, for no reason other than I did not like parading in front of my neighbors knowing they were seeing her when they looked at me. The Hannigan clan, including Brenda and Daniel, lined up for the host, their hands clasped, their expressions grim. One by one, they received the circular wafers on their tongues. They blessed themselves and shuffled back to their pew. Brenda paced by me, gulped down the body of Christ, and mouthed, "Meet me out front after."

I nodded, hoping she was in a better frame of mind than she had been yesterday.

After Father Richards told us to go in peace, my grandfather pulled me off to the side. "We're going to see Father for a few minutes. If you want, you can wait outside. Can't say for sure how long we'll be, though."

I glanced at Dad, who was talking to Ed Hogan. Actually, Ed was doing the talking, and my father appeared as though he were looking right through him.

"I'll get a ride," I said, wanting to kiss Grandpa on the cheek for caring so much. But I didn't.

"Where were you last night?" Brenda said, shuffling alongside me as we went with the tide of worshipers through the vestibule.

The question caught me off guard. I didn't tell her I'd had a date, thinking it would be too painful for her to hear. I figured she'd gone straight home to bed to cry herself to sleep.

Biding for time, I said, "Why? Did you come over?"

"I called. Your grandfather said you went out."

Someone pushed the door open and the glare of the sun whited out my vision for a moment, a blast of warmth rushing at me. Then, across the road, I saw Vincent leaning against his car, catching my attention with his casual stance and sweet smile.

Brenda obviously didn't see him. "So," she said, "where were you?"

I hesitated, then decided to go directly to him. He greeted me with a hug. When I turned, Brenda was standing next to me. She eyed Vincent with derision.

"Nice day for a picnic," he said.

Brenda said, "Sorry, but I was about to ask Vicky if she wanted to drive into Montreal to check out apartments."

I was in the middle and didn't know what to say. It didn't matter, though, because Vincent said, "Hey, tell her about that one building we saw near Notre Dame."

Brenda's mouth dropped. "We?"

Vincent nodded. "Last night, we strolled around, did some investigating."

I was at a loss for words, knowing what Brenda was thinking.

She said, "It makes sense you'd check it out with him and not me."

"It wasn't on purpose, Bren. We were there for dinner and just decided—"

"Whatever," she said, dashing down the road to where her car was parked.

My heart sank.

"Do you want to go talk to her?" he said.

I nodded and ran toward her, but just as I reached her car, she pulled out, swerving by me, refusing to look in my direction.

I went back to Vincent. "Maybe I'd better not go."

Evelyn Smith ambled by, studying Vincent and giving me the once over through squinty eyes. I tried to toss her an I-don't-give-a-damn-what-you're-thinking look, but failed miserably.

"Listen, I already have a basket filled with food and a blanket," Vincent said. "And you look like you're dressed for the occasion."

It was true. Mass no longed demanded the frilly dress and patent leather shoes Grandma used to make me wear. Now I was in a pair of jeans and pink blouse.

"I was hoping you'd tell me more about why you love this place so much."

That would be easy for me. Besides, the weather was perfect for a picnic. "Okay," I said. "I know just the spot."

We drove under a cloudless blue sky and I directed him to take one turn after the next until we were on a tight path that cut through a pasture. Vincent looked at me with uncertainty as the path became more and more narrow along the makeshift roadway.

"That looks like a pretty steep drop," he said, stretching to see the cliff on his side of the road. Soon the trail became so tight, with branches swiping at the car, that I wondered if I'd misdirected him. However, before I expressed my fear, we came to a familiar clearing.

"This is it!" I shouted, almost too joyfully.

"Where in God's name did you bring me?"

"We haven't even gotten there, yet," I said.

With the blanket draped across my arm, I led the way while Vincent held the basket. We pushed the underbrush aside and stumbled down a steep footpath. Eventually, we heard the whisperings of moving water, accompanied by the chirping of unseen birds. We passed a broken-down foundation of cement covered with ivy and overgrowth. Years ago, it had been a paper mill, but now it was nothing more than a hangout, the scattered beer bottles the evidence.

We lurched down the path until the rushing water drowned out the chirping and snapping of branches. Sure enough, the rocky clearing I recalled was where I was hoping it would be, and we found ourselves standing below a waterfall spilling in to a steep chasm, sprinkling a fine spray of wet diamonds over us, then charging by our feet in a rush.

"Holy Jesus," he said, this is incredible."

"I know."

We stood there for a few moments wondering at the magnificence. It was a place where Kevin had brought me every once in a while, but because it wasn't as accessible as Benny's Lake, we had saved it for special times. This was a special time.

"Who owns this?" Vincent said.

Fearful I'd brought another piece of heaven to the attention of Scoleri Enterprise, I said, "God."

"Can't improve on that then, can we?" Vincent smiled and wrapped an arm around me. "So, where do we set up our picnic?"

We were surrounded by a thick forest on one side, which refused to let in much sunlight, and a steep drop on the other leading to a moss-covered rocky shoreline. But it was private, and that's what I'd had in mind when I thought of this place. Our only possibility was a gigantic flat rock protruding from the water in the middle of the stream. "How about out there?" I said.

With his moccasins in his hand and my sandals in mine, our pants rolled above our knees, we waded through icy water. Its force tugged at me, threatening to knock me over. Pointed rocks and sharp stones dug into my heels, but eventually we landed on the rock. It was large enough for us to spread out the blanket and our picnic. Sun poured into the chasm, warming us.

"This is incredible," Vincent said, pulling a bottle of Chardonnay from the basket and nestling it between some rocks in the stream. He then took out finger sandwiches and deviled eggs.

"*This* is incredible," I said, biting into watercress on pumpernickel.

"Got in good with the chef at the hotel. He put it all together for me. Pretty nice, huh?"

"The hotel?"

"Yeah, I'm staying at the Ritz."

"Thought you were staying on the boat."

"Friday night three would've been a crowd, if you recall. So I decided to take the drive into Montreal."

"You went back and forth last night just for me?"

He nodded. "Couldn't very well expect you to spend the night, could I?"

"No," I said, unsure I meant it. Nobody had ever made me feel the way Vincent did. I leaned back on my elbows and closed my eyes, basking in the warmth and enjoying the cool spray from the plunging cataract. Vincent's mouth on mine was a welcome surprise. It was a gentle yet hasty kiss. Then he said, "Your brother used to bring you here, didn't he?"

"How'd you know?"

"Tell me about him, Vicky."

We situated ourselves so that I was leaning against him, his arms around me, and I began to talk. I told Vincent the story about how Kevin had seen our mother leave and how he had invented the detail about her kissing me. I also told him about how Kevin had helped me in the kitchen before I was allowed to use the stove, and then about his struggle to keep the farm. I went on for some time while Vincent caressed me, asking me an occasional question.

When I could talk no more, he said, "What a loss. You must miss him so much."

The sound of rushing falls filled the sudden quiet between us. Vincent brought my mouth to his. We kissed a long while and then he lay down on the blanket, bringing me to him, cushioning me from the rock. He unbuttoned my blouse and I helped him slip out of his shirt, then his pants. Soon, we were flesh against flesh, his touch cautious. Then he stopped and rooted around in the picnic basket until he found a small square package that crinkled in his hand.

He whispered, "That chef certainly thinks of everything."

He wrapped the blanket around us, not rushing me, even though I wanted to be rushed, to be taken. Still, I have to admit I was frightened. Not because it was my first time or because we might get caught. I was afraid of what I was feeling the moment I opened up to him: I felt myself become free from the child I'd been.

I was now a woman, and it scared me beyond reason.

CHAPTER 19

When nine o'clock came *and* went the following morning and there was no sign of Brenda, I called her house.

"She's not feeling quite herself this morning," her mother said. "Sorry, Vicky, thought she called you."

I said it was okay and to tell her I hoped she felt better, even though I knew the reason she wasn't quite herself was from Frank's hasty departure contrasted by Vincent's attentiveness toward me.

The one good thing about having to rely on my bike again was that it gave me a luxurious amount of time to replay my Sunday afternoon with Vincent in my mind. It wasn't so much the lovemaking, though that had been surprisingly wonderful; it had been liberating to talk about my brother, and Vincent had seemed genuinely interested.

I wheeled my bike into the back room of Snack Shack then immediately began the process of opening for business. When Mr. Collings approached, I was sure he was going to make a comment about my being late. Instead, he said, "What's got you all giddy?" He set the boxes of donuts and croissants on the counter.

"Huh?"

"Not used to seeing you smile," he said. "Hey, where's your friend?"

"Sick. That's why I'm late. I had to ride my bike here."

"Want me to call Kelly?"

I shrugged. "Think I'll be okay," I said, preferring to work alone and think of Vincent whenever I could while serving my continuous stream of patrons.

When Vincent had dropped me off early Sunday evening, he said he would see me the next day, but I wasn't sure when or where; however, in the middle of the afternoon, the Mercedes pulled up and he climbed out, carrying two grocery bags.

"Think it's time you got back on the horse," he said.

I didn't know what he meant until he came behind the counter and began unpacking eggplants and sweet potatoes.

"Vincent—"

"Hey, technically I'm your boss, and I'm telling you I want these items back on the menu."

"Well, not today. I'm here by myself and—"

He pulled out a large bottle of cooking oil. "I'll take care of the soda and ice cream; you do what you need to with these." He finished unloading the groceries and went to the front, where a young customer was waiting. When he came back, he found me where he'd left me.

"You don't know," I said. "I almost burned down this whole place. I...I...can't take the risk."

"So you learned your lesson, and now you'll be extra careful. Right?" He went to the back and returned with the large kettle, poured in the oil, and then turned to me. "Haven't got a clue what to do from here."

I sighed and washed the vegetables, and when I finally dared to turn on the gas burner, my hands trembled. Eventually, I was lowering the vegetable-filled strainer into the scalding oil.

A short time later, there was a gathering of people who had been drawn by the aroma.

"About time you made these again," Mrs. Ducharme said. Ralph the boxer was next to her on his leash. Vincent handed her a plate and she lumbered over to an open spot at the picnic table and began chowing down French-fried eggplant dipped in sauce. One customer after the next didn't want a burger or fries, but all wanted the day's special, and we served French-fried vegetables until we were sold out, which didn't take that long.

Vincent came over and brushed a wisp of hair from my face. "You're glowing."

"Thank you," I said.

"For what? You're the one who did it."

"But you're the one who made me."

Back home, the garden was barren; I hadn't had the desire to watch anything flourish. But now, I began to miss the thrill of seeing vibrant cucumbers sprouting from the ground and juicy tomatoes hanging on the vine. I spotted

Sandy approaching for the evening shift. I was stunned that it was already time to go home.

"Need a ride?" Vincent said.

"I have my bike."

"It'll be fine here."

"Well, I was going to stop by Brenda's and see how she's feeling."

"So, let's stop by Brenda's and see how she's feeling."

Not much later, we were pulling into the long dirt driveway, passing a knot of redheads of various sizes who were straddling bikes while three yapping mongrels snapped at the car's fender. The weathered clapboard farmhouse stood a short distance from the Hannigan sawmill. As we drew closer, the hum and whine of sawing logs could be heard. Mrs. H and Jane were sitting on the open porch.

"I'll be right back," I said, while Vincent waited in the purring car.

With the constant whine of sawing lumber in the background, Mrs. H. said hello. She never stopped peeling the potato in her hand, the curled skins falling into a flattened grocery bag. Jane was rocking Tommy, who was asleep in her arms.

"I didn't know you were here," I said to Jane.

"Tryin' to get her to move back to the area," Mrs. H. said. "Syracuse is just too far away."

Jane rolled her eyes and whispered, "That's some car."

"Whose is it, Vicky?" Mrs. H. said, her thick fingers rotating round the spud.

"A friend of mine."

"The one from the big city?" She searched me, scowling, as if disapproving.

I gave a slight nod then said, "Is Brenda home?"

"Up in her room. Was sound asleep last I checked."

With slack-jawed Tommy heavy in her arms, Jane struggled to get up off the chair. "I'll see if she's awake," she whispered. "I have to put him down anyway." She picked her way around plastic toys and blocks that were scattered along the porch. I ran ahead of her, opened the screen door, and eased it shut with barely a creak.

"I'm worried about you, Vicky," Mrs. H. said. "I saw that man outside church yesterday." She nodded toward the car, her double chin quivering with the movement. "He's not a boy, you know. He must be somewhere in his twenties."

Twenty-four to be exact, but I didn't forward the information.

"He's a man. Been around the world, so to speak. He's gonna 'spect you to be a woman, if you know what I mean."

"It's not like that—"

"If you need to talk, honey, I'd be glad to listen. Young girl like yourself without a mother to guide her—"

The screen door creaked open and Jane was back. Thankfully.

"Sleeping like a baby," she said. I thought she meant Tommy, until she added, "I didn't have the heart to wake her."

"What's wrong with her?" As if I didn't know.

Mrs. H. reached in the burlap bag for another potato and sighed. "Out of sorts is all. Should be better by tomorrow, the good Lord willing."

"Would you tell her I was by?"

"Absolutely, dear, but wouldn't you and your friend stay for supper? There's plenty."

"Oh, that would be nice," I said, scuffing my foot, "but we already have plans." It was a lie, but I couldn't imagine sitting at a chaotic Hannigan table while Mrs. H. grilled Vincent.

"Well, then," Mrs. H. said, standing, brushing her hands on her worn cotton sundress and tottering on her short, wobbly legs. Clearly, Brenda took after her father, who was as thin as a sapling. "I'd best be getting these on to boil. You sure you can't stay, dear?"

"No, no thanks," I said, running down the porch steps. "Please tell her I was by."

I climbed in the car. I looked up at the window directly over the porch and saw the curtain move. It could have been any one of the Hannigans, but I was willing to bet it was Brenda.

Grandpa had bought salmon, as I'd asked him to, so I invited Vincent to have supper with us. A risky undertaking, to be sure. Unfortunately, Grandpa had also bought a small jar of French's mustard, thinking it was what I had written on the list instead of dry mustard for the sauce I'd planned to make for the fish. I improvised and made a horseradish crust. For side dishes, I prepared freshly steamed carrots and wild rice. I knew the meal called for a nice white wine, and Vincent suggested he take the twenty-minute ride to the liquor store. I took advantage of his temporary disappearance and jumped into the shower then slipped into a summer dress. By the time he returned, supper was ready and the cheap wine glasses that had been collecting dust on the top shelf in the cabinet were now shiny and on the table. I had never had occasion to use them before.

"This looks incredible," Vincent said, taking the chair across from me.

"That's Kevin's place," Dad said, without looking at Vincent.

Vincent immediately stood, but Grandpa said, "Sit down, son. *Used* to be Kevin's place."

Since there was no other place for Vincent to sit, he eased himself back down.

Our dinner conversation was strained, with me trying to work up various topics for conversation. Dad didn't bother responding and Grandpa would either hum a reply or say, "That right?" Conroy sat at my feet, glancing up hopefully for a morsel. Finally, Dad got up and headed toward the garage.

"Don't you want your coffee?" I said. He hadn't touched his wine.

He didn't reply, letting the screen door shut behind him just as Conroy slipped through.

Grandpa said, "What did you say your line of work is, son?"

"Real estate," Vincent said, refreshing his glass and Grandpa's with more wine.

"Not much call for that line of work up in these parts, eh?"

Vincent said, "Well, we certainly did okay with Lake in the Woods, wouldn't you say?"

Grandpa stopped chewing, his expression deliberative. He looked at me as if he didn't recognize me. I hadn't told him just who Vincent was, and now it was becoming clear to me as to why. How could I rationalize dating the enemy? Granted, he wasn't at all like his avaricious brother, but he was still a Scoleri, the family that robbed Kevin of his ability to reason.

"Grandpa," I said, feeling like Judas at the last supper, "Vincent wasn't responsible for bringing the resort here."

"That right?"

"Yes, sir. That would be my father. I just work for him."

"Maybe you should think about getting into a more respectable line of work," Grandpa said. Even though there was a nice piece of salmon left on Grandpa's plate, he got up from the table and headed toward the porch.

My appetite was suddenly stifled, as was Vincent's. He said, "Maybe I should go."

I didn't reply, because I didn't want him to go. I didn't want him to stay either. I hastily cleared off the table and Vincent helped me by washing the dishes. It was a curious sight to see a man at the sink, suds up to his elbows, and on the dishes in the rack. I didn't correct his attempt, though; it didn't seem important. We worked rapidly in silence, and once we were finished I suggested we take a ride.

Vincent drove without any direction from me until we reached the dead end of Covington Road. There wasn't a house for miles, not a soul around. The sky was becoming thick with clouds, and the air was still. We climbed out of the car and sat on the hood.

"Sorry," I said. "I don't know what I was thinking inviting you to my house."

"Don't worry about it." He wrapped an arm around me. "That was some meal, Vicky. First today, with the vegetables, and then tonight. You really are talented."

I shrugged.

"You know, there are some really excellent cooking schools in Manhattan."

"Oh, I know."

Thunder rumbled in the distance and a breeze began to pick up.

He cleared his throat then said, "I have to leave tomorrow."

No. No. No.

"Senior, my father, says I've pushed it, and it's time to get back to work."

Vincent was leaving. I'd probably never see him again. I ached with the thought.

"Silent protest?" he said.

"Maybe you should think about getting into a more respectable line of work." I forced a smile. "Of course you have to get back to work. Back home."

"I was hoping I could convince you to come back with me and check out the schools down there."

I looked at him, which was a mistake. Those brown eyes were difficult to resist. I mentally set my sights on the future and said, "I can't. Everything's planned for Montreal."

"Plans can change."

A long, jagged yellow streak cut through the sky. *One. Two. Three. Four. Five. Six. Seven. Eight.* Finally, the deafening clap of thunder.

"Vicky, I like the way you make me feel when I'm around you. If you go to Montreal, I'll lose you."

"If I don't go to Montreal, *I'll lose me*," I said.

He slipped his hand beneath the V of my neckline, cupping my breast while droplets began to splash on us. I reached for his zipper and pulled it down in one hasty tug. He lifted the skirt to my thin summer dress, finding me.

The mantle of gray filled with a sudden flash of light, followed by another burst of thunder, shaking the foundation beneath us. With Vincent under me, I situated myself with his urgent guidance. The droplets grew to a drenching downpour and in leaping waves, I plunged on him, rivulets streaming down the tip of my nose and on to his face. I clawed at him, drove him into me, my hands in a locked grip on his shoulders. Unlike the gentleness of the first time, this was a reckless hunger, with me now pounding him with my fists, crying out. Protesting.

Eventually, the storm moved on. We lay across the hood of the car, soaked and breathless, my body feeling the pulse of his.

"I'm so sorry, Vicky," Vincent said, holding me close to him.

"It's okay. I didn't expect you to stay."

"That's not what I mean," he said, reaching for my hand, clasping it. "I didn't..." He cleared his throat. "We didn't use anything."

The storm had returned, except this time it was roaring in my head, quaking in my gut. How could I have forgotten that meticulous detail?

"If anything happens, I'll marry you."

I jumped off the car and picked my panties up from the ground, balling them into my hands.

"Vicky, did you hear me?"

"Nothing happened, Vincent." Right then I said a silent, desperate prayer to Mother Mary of God to make it so.

He slid off the hood and zipped his jeans. "You're shivering."

"So are you," I said, the two of us soaked from the rain.

"Let's get you home," he said.

We drove in silence until we reached my house.

"I guess we'd better make this quick," he said.

I nodded, not sure if I was trembling from my wet clothes, the possibility of him leaving, or the reckless game of Russian roulette we had just played.

He wrapped an arm around me. "Listen, I'll stay in touch, make sure you're okay."

I knew what he meant but trusted Mother of God to have already answered my prayer. I said," Don't let your Dad cut down any more trees, okay?"

"I'll see what I can do," he said, kissing me lightly on the cheek before I got out of the car.

I watched the Mercedes back out, then drive off. I'd never see Vincent Scoleri again. I was sure. With Montreal on the horizon, I refused to care.

CHAPTER 20

The car ride to work was quiet, except for the rumbling of Brenda's jalopy. I finally spoke up. "So, what was it? The flu or something?"

She shrugged. "Just sick of this place is all. Can't wait to get out of here."

"Me, too," I said. It was just the kind of distraction Brenda and I needed to forget about the Scoleri men.

It was another gloomy day, the threat of rain hanging over us, the air thick with humidity. We arrived at Snack Shack and opened the aluminum shutter. Brenda immediately spotted the additional items on the menu board.

"So, you decided to make the fried vegetables again? Even after last year's fiasco?"

I almost told her that it was Vincent who had convinced me but decided to spare her. I said, "Yeah, Mr. Collings is coming by with some green beans and sweet potatoes so I can—"

Ignoring me, she went to the back room to get more napkins. When she came out, she said, "What's your bike doing in there?"

"Oh, I ended up getting a ride home, so I—"

"Whatever." She ripped open the napkins, cramming them in the holders.

The morning passed at a snail's pace, with only a few campers coming over for coffee and donuts. Brenda and I spoke when we needed to, but it was obvious that the air was thick with more than just the humidity. Eventually, we were left with nothing to do but sit on stools. I longed to discuss one of her favorite topics, but I knew no matter how I brought it up, she'd guess that it had less to do with a young woman's curiosity about sex and more with a young woman's fear at having been caught.

"So," she said, playing with her straw, "I hear Vinny helped out."

"A little." I let the "Vinny" pass this time.

"Mr. Collings came by last night to see how I was feeling. Said you and your *boyfriend* were doing a fine job and that I shouldn't worry about anything." She drummed her fingers on the counter.

"He can't make a shake the way you can. No one can."

"Spare me." Her lips were pursed and her breathing heavy.

I tossed my hands in the air. "Bren, I don't know what to say. I'm sorry. Besides, he's gone. I'll never see him again."

"And you accept that? I mean, I can't stop thinking about Frank." Her eyes brimmed with tears. "He was so nice. He told me he'd be back." She gazed hopefully at me. "He didn't come back while I was gone, did he?"

I shook my head and rubbed her back. "Bren, forget about him. Before you know it, we'll be living in Montreal. Soon, you'll have your own salon and I'll be cooking in the best restaurant!"

She looked out toward the lake in silence for a moment. Then she blurted, "He said he'd be back. I gave him my phone number, but he probably couldn't get through. You know how my line's always busy."

"Bren, maybe not. Maybe he was just, you know, looking for a one-night thing. Maybe—"

"How would you know?" she snapped. "You weren't there."

A couple of older women I'd never seen before interrupted us, wanting iced tea. We served them, and they went to sit at the picnic table. Brenda then turned to me and said, "I've been thinking. We should take a quick trip down to Long Island to see the guys."

"Brenda, no. We can't just go and surprise them." In truth, I knew Brenda would be the one surprised.

"Why not? What are they going to do, turn us away?"

"Brenda, just kiss it goodbye." I tried to lighten the mood by singing our song. "Nahnahnahnah, nahnahnahnah, hey, hey, hey, goodbye."

"Why not? Risks should be taken in this life, otherwise—"

"Bren! Frank's married. He's got kids and everything."

She froze, and her face paled.

"I'm sorry. I didn't want you to be hurt, but—"

She lunged at me, coming within inches from my face. "You liar! You're just making that up."

"Why would I do that?"

"Because, because I couldn't possibly get someone like him, could I? You were so jealous when he asked me to dance. You couldn't believe it. I saw the way you looked."

"I was jealous that big goon asked you to dance?" I shrieked.

The two women at the picnic table turned their attention to us, but Brenda didn't bother lowering her voice.

"Yes, you were angry because I took off, leaving you with Vinny. It's time you grew up, Vicky."

"Frank used you, Brenda. He was nothing but a jerk. Vincent says he does things like that all the time."

She jumped off the stool. "Like you *weren't* being used?"

"At least I didn't behave like some desperate, pitiful slut!"

She grabbed her cup of soda and tossed it in my face. I sputtered, wiping Pepsi from my eyes. I deserved it, though. The comment was cruel, and I regretted it immediately.

"How...how long did you know about Frank?" she screamed. "You and Vincent talking about me like I'm some poor loser...how long did you know?"

"You're not a loser. I'm sorry. I didn't mean—"

"How long?" she shouted.

"Does it really matter? Let's just forget about it. Let's talk about Montreal."

"Oh, I want to go to Montreal with someone like *you*? Or should I say, someone like your mother?"

The accusation drained me, sucked all the life from me. I could barely budge.

"I don't need you here," she said. "I can handle this by myself, unlike some people, so go home." She went to the menu board and rubbed off "French-fried vegetables."

I grabbed a napkin and wiped my sticky face and hair. Others had gathered around the two women to watch the drama. I went to the storage room and wheeled out my bike. Once I was far enough away that Brenda couldn't see me, I went to the water's edge and splashed the soda from my face and rinsed out my hair. I sat down, the water cool on my neck. Perhaps a cooling-off period was all both of us needed. Tomorrow morning, like most mornings, she'd be sitting in my driveway honking that pathetic horn of hers.

If I had known how long it would be before I got to feel the cool water of Benny's Lake again, I probably wouldn't have left so quickly. I pedaled home at an easygoing pace, the sky overhead gray. Sweat ran down my back while my mind replayed the argument. It was one of our worst yet. I supposed as we got older, one fight would top the next, but with each one, we'd eventually reach a truce. Wasn't that what being an adult meant?

Heading home, though, meant facing Grandpa's inquiries about Vincent. Somehow, in his authoritative way, he would let me know I'd disappointed him by dating the man who was responsible, albeit in a roundabout way, for so much sadness in our lives. Still, I longed to hear Vincent's voice again, and I felt guilty for it.

I took the turn down my road and was alarmed by the most heart-stopping sound. I slowed down and listened, trying to make sense of it. To my left were the marshy woods. I veered the bike in that direction. There it was again, but it was not coming from the woods. It seemed to be coming from the barn, perhaps Conroy suffering from a porcupine's defense mechanism. It used to take Kevin the better part of a day to extract the quills from the mutt's face. As I drew closer, I realized the sound I was hearing from the barn wasn't a pained dog, but the panicked cry of a human.

I pedaled full force, cutting across the field, racing over the pebbled driveway toward the cries. As I got closer, I made out Grandpa's voice. "Please, Jesus. Please send help."

I shouted that I was coming, but the bike seemed to be hindering me more than giving me speed. I jumped off, dropping it, and attempted to run, feeling as though I were wading in slow motion through the overgrown grass and burdock. I reached the back of the barn. The cumbersome sliding door was opened wide enough that I could squeeze in. Once I did, I stopped to make sense of what I was seeing.

Except none of it made sense.

"I cain't let go," Grandpa said, his arms wrapped around my father's dangling legs. "Otherwise, the rope'll tighten."

My heart pounded so hard it hurt; sweat stung my eyes, blurred my vision.

"There's no time to get help," Grandpa said, the veins bulging in his arms while he fought to keep my father up so the rope around his neck wouldn't gain any more purchase than it had.

"Is he...?"

"You got to get it off him," Grandpa said, his voice weak.

"What do you mean?" Then I realized my father was slipping from Grandpa's shaky grasp. The other end of the rope was tied around a crossbeam. There was the ladder on the floor. I tripped over a milk can on its side to get to it and lifted the ladder, resting it against the crossbeam. I was in some horrid dream in which I couldn't move fast enough as I scrambled up and then lost my footing, scraping my shins on the rungs. Finally, I reached the beam.

Grandpa grunted and whispered pleas to Jesus, Mother Mary, and even the almighty Father for me to hurry. Crouching down, I crawled to the middle. Dad was suspended directly below me. I straddled the beam, causing it to creak with my every movement, and began to feel lightheaded. I tried not to look, but my father's arms were loose at his sides, his chin to his chest. I tugged on the knot, discovering I didn't have the strength to loosen it. Grandpa's breathing was growing louder. I swiped the tears from my face and shook the panic from my hands. Grandpa then gave one final heave, using every last bit of his strength, to raise Dad just enough so that I was able to poke my finger through the loop, widening it until it slipped from my grip. Down went the body, taking Grandpa with it, the two men sprawling on the barn floor.

Blood pumped through every vein in my body. I felt it, the pulse in my head, carrying with it an odd memory. There was Grandpa, taking the monstrous curved tines connected to the pulley from the loft and ramming them into a pile of hay.

"Go tell your father it's a go," he says.

I run through the milk station and to the front of the barn, where my father is sitting on the tractor waiting for me. Waiting for *me*!

I shout, "Grandpa says it's a go!"

For the briefest of moments, my father studies me with a slight smile, then backs the tractor with the pulley hitched to it away from the barn. That's when I run back to see the ominous forks clutched to the hay, carry the stack up into the loft to release it. Kevin is up there, scattering it, making room for the next pile.

"Vicky!"

Grandpa was on his knees, leaning over Dad's lifeless form.

"Call an ambulance."

Not again. Please, not again. Maybe I didn't call for an ambulance. I can't be sure. I don't remember going to the house or making any desperate phone call. Still, I don't remember Grandpa leaving me alone with the gray lump sprawled on the barn floor; and yet, an ambulance appeared. This time, though, it didn't stay long. While the medical technicians violated the body, coaxing life back into it, I watched Grandpa climb in before they closed the doors and whisked Dad away.

Grandma called the doctor and the doctor said, 'No more monkeys jumpin' on the bed.'

Somehow, I managed to drive Dad's car along the same path the ambulance traveled, except I was light-years behind it. When I got to the hospital, I found Grandpa in the waiting room, his eyes red and moist. Slumped in an orange plastic-molded chair, he gazed up at me.

"Doctor says he's gonna make it," he said. "He'll be here for a while, but he's gonna make it."

I sighed, grateful for the news.

"Gotta thank sweet Jesus for sending you. If you hadn't come when you did..."

That's when I realized if Brenda hadn't chased me from work, and if my bike hadn't been there, things could have turned out drastically different.

"I was there," Grandpa said in monotone. "Still couldn't stop him. Grabbed him so the rope couldn't...He must've been trying to hurry before I got to him, 'cause the knot was wrong. Still, they can't say for sure how much damage he's done to himself."

I took Grandpa's hand and sat with him for the rest of the afternoon. The doctor gave us updates between long periods of waiting. Dad's status didn't improve much that first day, but it didn't deteriorate either. By the time I thought Brenda should be home, I found a payphone to call her, hoping she'd come sit with me. One of her brothers answered. I couldn't tell which one, since all of their voices sounded identical.

"It's Vicky. Can I speak to Brenda?"

He was off the line for several minutes, while I fed the pay phone dimes. He finally came back on. "She says she doesn't want to talk to you."

"Please tell her it's really important. Please."

Again, he left the line; this time he was back within seconds. "She doesn't care. Says she doesn't want to speak to you ever again."

"Could you tell her I'm here at the hospital? My father's here and—"

The phone clunked, and there was a mess of intermingled voices, some angry, others chastising. Finally, Mrs. H. came on the line.

"Vicky?"

"Hi, Mrs. Hannigan. I really need to speak—"

"Listen, I think you two need a break from each other," Mrs. H. said.

"But—"

"Vicky, now let it be for a while." Then she hung up on me.

When I returned to the waiting room, Grandpa wasn't there. A nurse told me he had been given five minutes to see my father.

"May I see him?" I said.

"Only one family member at a time," she said. "Maybe next time."

I was waiting in the plastic chair when Grandpa shuffled in, the breathing fortress who was beginning to show defeat in battle. He dropped in the chair next to me.

"How is he?"

"He'll make it."

I knelt down by Grandpa, resting my head on his leg. "Thank you."

"Don't guarantee nothing for next time, though. Might not waste his time with a rope, either."

"I want to see him."

"Wouldn't do 'im much good right now."

In the movies, a loved one rushing to a victim's bedside is the universal remedy. But when I imagine standing at to my father's bedside, he doesn't open his eyes, not until it's Kevin standing there.

Movies. Brenda was the one who made me sit in front of the TV with her, a box of tissues between us while we sobbed over maudlin nonsense: Fathers were heroes, brothers outwitted death, and mothers never, ever ran away.

CHAPTER 21

Word must have gotten around what Dad had tried to do, because the next morning, Mr. Collings came by the house. He stood on the front steps and said, "Just wanted you to know with your dad and all, ain't no need to come back to work."

I remained at a distance standing on the porch, tightening the sash to my bathrobe. Grandpa had left awhile earlier to go back to the hospital. I was planning to meet him there after work, again, using my father's car.

"Here," Mr. Collings said, handing me my paycheck, refusing to make eye contact with me.

"But I was coming in today," I said.

Mr. Collings rubbed his pointy chin. "Nah, don't worry 'bout it. I'm sure you'll want to spend time with your dad and all."

"I'll visit him later. We called the hospital earlier, and he's doing much better. He's just resting." What I wasn't saying was that I didn't want to spend time with my father.

He looked up at the clouds. "Truth is, Brenda told me you two had a falling out. Figured it'd be best if you stayed away."

"We had a fight, but we have lots of fights. Once I see her, things'll be back to normal." Actually, I was in desperate need of a friend with a sympathetic ear, which would have to be Brenda, since she was the only friend I had.

"I don't think so, Vicky. Even the campers said it was pretty bad."

It took me a moment to digest what he was saying. "You're firing me?" I stared at him in disbelief.

"Let's not call it that."

"You *are* firing me."

He tossed his hands in the air and turned to walk away.

I called to him, and just before he got to his Jeep, I said, "Would you tell Brenda about my dad, please?"

Mr. Collings turned and said, "She's the one who told me." He climbed into the Jeep and drove away.

It was a long, tedious day at the hospital. Dad was no longer in ICU, which meant there was no limit to the amount of time Grandpa and I could spend with him. There was a television in his room and it blasted most of the time with tasteless talk or loud game shows. Every once in a while, a nurse came in to check Dad's vitals and then Grandpa would follow her out into the hallway to keep abreast of the latest developments. When my father and I were alone in the room, our eyes stayed focused on the television. I can't say for sure what my father felt, but I could feel a palpable uneasiness. Grandpa would then come back into the room and announce, "They say you're getting there, Jack."

Dad would gaze at Grandpa and nod, as if he hadn't been the one responsible for putting himself in the hospital in the first place.

Father Richards made an appearance, and Grandpa and I decided to give him time alone with Dad. We strolled down to the lounge.

"Want some candy?" Grandpa said, taking a dime out of his pocket.

"Sure," I said, watching Grandpa lean in, squinting to see the number of his selection on the candy machine. "You're going to need more than a dime, Grandpa," I said, handing him a quarter.

He shook his head. "Goddamn crooks."

"Why don't we share it?"

We sat in the lounge, breaking sections from a Hershey bar, Grandpa staring off. Finally, he said, "I don't want you taking it personally what your daddy did, Vicky. Sometimes, things happen that cloud up any reasonable thinking. Thought he was rolling with the punches by the way he just up and sold the farm."

When I was little and there was talk of selling the farm, I'd always thought it meant we'd have to leave. It wasn't until just a few months earlier, when I watched Dad haul away the cows, sell the tractor and wagon, and make an agreement with Don to hay the fields for us while he made the profit from it, that I realized selling the farm was the way we could stay put.

"Grandpa," I said, "was Dad always the way he is?"

Grandpa popped the last square of chocolate in his mouth and let it melt away before he spoke. "Nah. He was a lot like your brother when he was young.

Except his passion was for wrestling." He paused, before adding, "Then, of course, your mother came along. He was crazy about your mother." He shook his head. "She was a pretty little thing. Shame things got out of hand."

I don't know why I understood what he meant, but I did. I said, "They had to get married, didn't they?"

"Your Grandma wasn't too happy, until the first time she laid eyes on your brother. Then she forgot all about the rushed wedding and our moving from the big house to the little one so your father could have a bigger home for his family."

I rested my hand on my stomach, churning with unease. Again, I prayed a silent prayer to Mother Mary of God.

"Did you like my mother, Grandpa?"

"Up till the day she walked out on her husband and two kids." He crumpled the candy wrapper in the palm of his hand. "Should've seen it comin', though. You were supposed to keep her grounded. Least, that's what your father was shooting for." Grandpa stood. "Well, let's see if Father Richards is still here."

I didn't want the talk to end. It was the most I'd found out since the bit of information Kevin had given me all those years ago. Apparently, Grandpa wasn't willing to reveal much else. Or, perhaps time had dissolved the real truth. Or, maybe that was the story in a nutshell. Like everything with my mother, there were more questions than answers.

We returned to the room to find that Father Richards had left. Grandpa suggested I go home to feed Conroy and get supper ready for the two of us. I gave Dad a hasty kiss on his cheek and bolted out the door. Instead of driving home, though, I hoped Brenda had had enough time to miss me. I took the turn to go toward her house and was soon traveling up the Hannigan driveway. The sawmill was whining, the mongrels yapping at my fender as I pulled up to the house. I ascended the porch steps with hesitation and waited for a moment before I knocked on the screen door. The sounds of a soap opera were coming from the living room. A moment later, Brenda appeared, but she did not invite me in.

"What do you want?" she hissed.

"To talk."

"You can't be serious."

"Come on, Bren, it's not my fault he was married. Please, we've been friends too long. And I have news."

"I heard. And I heard he's getting better."

I nodded and then said, "Grandpa told me some stuff about my mother." I figured this would pique her interest, since Brenda had always loved playing detective when it came to why my mother left.

Your father beat her, Brenda would say. Or, *She went on tour with some big band*. Then, *She found out she was dying of some dreaded disease and didn't want to be a burden to her family*. And so it went, on and on. I was sure she'd eat up what little I discovered.

"Like I care," she said. "Would you please just leave?"

"Brenda, please," I said. There was desperation in my voice. "I was wondering when we could go to Montreal and check out the apartment situation."

"I'm not going to Montreal with you," she said, "so forget it."

"That's silly. We've been planning this for so long."

"Plans change. Now leave."

"You can't just throw it away," I said. "Come on, Bren, kiss it—" I had my hand on the door handle, but she stopped me from coming in.

"Shut up with that juvenile saying! I *have* thrown it away. Now leave me alone."

I stared at her, finally realizing she was serious. It made me feel almost dizzy, my gut empty.

"Look what you do to people, making them run away, making them hang themselves. You think I want a friend like that? I should have…"

I didn't hear any more of what she said; my mind shut out her words. But she was right. I stumbled down the porch steps.

She called me and I turned, hoping she couldn't keep up with the cruelty. "Just so you know, Scoleri Enterprise *is* going to expand Lake in the Woods."

I didn't answer, but jumped into the car and rammed it into drive and fled down the driveway, my entire body shaking. Place of Angels, Place of Angels, I needed to escape this Place of Angels. What did I have to keep me here anyway?

When I got to the house, I went to my room and collapsed on my bed. A short time later, the phone rang, pulling me out of my tearful contemplation. *Brenda calling to apologize? Or to curse me out again?* No longer did I consider it might be Brad, who had become little more than a bad memory. I was going to let it continue ringing, until it occurred to me that it could be the hospital. I ran downstairs and picked up.

"I miss you."

The sound of Vincent's calm voice brought me to the floor. I couldn't speak, too choked up with tears.

"You okay, hon? Vicky?"

I shook my head no as if he could see me.

"Vicky, what's wrong?"

Slowly, and in spurts, the phrases came out. I told him about my father, about Brenda and how we were no longer friends. Then I said, "Brenda says you *are* going to expand Lake in the Woods."

"I told you, that hasn't even been decided yet."

"Then why would she say it?"

"Vicky, she's hurt. She's going to say anything to hurt you."

I supposed he was right.

"Come stay with me," he said. "I'll take care of you."

"Why do you say things like that?"

"Because I'm crazy about you."

And Jack was crazy about Grace.

I said, "You don't even know me. I'm nothing like what you think I am."

"You're not what you think you are."

"Listen, I have to go," I said.

"Vicky—"

"Thanks for calling—"

"If anything happened, you know, when we—"

"Nothing happened," I said, and then I hung up. Seconds later, the phone rang. And I let it keep ringing.

I needed to be busy, so I began to make supper, preparing eggplant parmigiana and strawberry shortcake for dessert. I'd even splurged and made meatballs as a special treat for Conroy in my desire to cook, cook, cook.

Later, Grandpa shambled in, looking exhausted. "Vicky, you didn't have to go to all this trouble," he said. "A burger would've been good enough."

"No," I said, "it wouldn't have."

🍁   🍁   🍁

Two weeks had passed since Dad tried to check out of this world. Now he was back home. I spent most of my time in the kitchen, baking bread and casseroles then stocking them in the freezer. It had never been so full. I cooked because I had to and because it was a good excuse to make sure there was plenty of prepared meals for Dad and Grandpa when I finally left for Montreal.

While I concentrated on recipes, Grandpa concentrated on my father. When Dad went to bed, Grandpa stood at his slightly open door, peering in to make sure he was asleep before he himself turned in for the night. When it was time for Dad to take his prescription, Grandpa appeared with the bottle and dispensed the exact amount, then hid the bottle until it was time for another dosage. Before Dad was released from the hospital, Grandpa made sure to take the gun out of the rack and put it where Dad wouldn't find it.

"I'd cut every goddamn rope down to no more than a few feet if I could," Grandpa said to no one in particular as he shuffled by me, the gun in his hand.

When even I saw I was going overboard with all the cooking, I turned my energy to cleaning. It had been a long time since anyone had given the house a thorough cleaning, or a "spring cleaning" as Mrs. H. called it. So I dusted, swept cobwebs from the corners of each room, and cleaned out closets, discovering an old suitcase that I decided would be something I'd need in a couple of weeks for Montreal. I put it in the "to-be-saved" pile then pulled out the old Electrolux, placing it in the "to-be-tossed" pile.

One day, during this cleaning frenzy, I heard the slow shuffle of Grandpa's footsteps as he came upstairs. He stopped in the hallway and watched me for a while. I knew he was either bored or nervous, since he paced in both cases, as he was doing now. He might have been bored, since Dad, having gone back to work, was no longer under his charge, or he may have been nervous, because he couldn't be sure if Dad was going to return in one piece.

"You're keeping this old thing?" Grandpa said, pointing to the suitcase. Sure there were a couple of ripped seams, and the zipper needed to be put back on track, but it was all I had.

"Yup," I said. "I'll be leaving pretty soon, Grandpa." Actually, due to a change of plans, it was a little more than a week.

"I don't like the idea of you living alone," Grandpa said. "That little redhead said she'd go with you. She should keep her word."

"She's not going to change her mind. I'll be okay." I didn't mention how much the loft was going to cost me; I'd found it a few days earlier after taking the train from Plattsburgh into Montreal to secure a place to live. I needed to get a job and, as it happened, the restaurant where I was going to train needed a waitress. So, when I wasn't learning how to be a great chef, I would be waiting tables. However, the waitress position needed to be filled as soon as possible. I went home to break the news.

Grandpa took off his glasses, pulled out a handkerchief, and wiped his eyes. "Why you in such a hurry to get out of here?"

I didn't answer, but simply went to him and held on to him while tears rolled down his face.

Later, Dad said, "You still have something to do here before you go running off."

I knew what he meant, and it was something I'd been avoiding for months. Perhaps that's why I did so much baking and concentrated on cleaning the big house. Now it was time to deal with the little house.

The next morning, armed with cleaners, dust rags, and a box of garbage bags, I trekked across the field that Don had recently mowed. I passed Kevin's truck and went up the front steps. The door was unlocked and I walked in, not certain I was ready to do this.

I set the cleaners, rags, and bags on the kitchen table and wandered through the house. There was a reason we called it the little house. I went from the kitchen into the connecting living room then down a small, narrow hallway, the bathroom on the left, the bedroom at the end, on the right. As small as it was, the job was daunting. I had little idea where to begin. So I went back to the kitchen and began there. A plate, fork, knife, and glass were in the dish rack. Placing them back in the cabinet was the first brave step of many. I continued on, emptying the refrigerator of its nasty contents before unplugging it. The cabinets were rather empty, and soon I was ready to work on the living room.

Future Farmers of America medals were placed in a box, and I intended to keep them. I tossed a worn copy of *Walden* in a bag for garbage, but then pulled it back out once I spotted certain highlighted passages. Thoreau's work went into the box with the medals. There were yearbooks that I placed in that box, too.

Then, I came across a shoebox. I untied the twine that kept it closed and lifted the lid. I stopped and stared for a moment, digesting its contents. Inside were the dozen or so letters I'd sent years ago to Grace Finley. I leafed through them. All the envelopes were still sealed, but none bore the stamped message: Address Unknown. They weren't even postmarked. Funny, at such a young age, I'd thought all a letter needed to find its destination was a name. All these years later, though, I didn't have much more information to go on. Apparently, Kevin had tried to protect me from the disappointment until I was old enough to send out and receive mail on my own. But he'd kept my unsent letters, and I wondered why. Maybe he was holding them to show her when she returned.

I put the shoebox in with the medals and other collectables.

I then began emptying his closet and drawers, keeping a shirt or two for myself and tossing the rest in a bag to give to Goodwill. Kevin hadn't been a large man, but I couldn't imagine anyone being able to fill his clothes properly.

Hours later, sweaty and grimy, I crossed the field and headed back to the house. I stored the boxes in the little house's bedroom closet. I'd kept my promise, but the task had drained me. When I walked into the kitchen, I discovered two brand-new black leather suitcases sitting in the middle of the floor. Grandpa appeared.

"Don't want you going off looking like a pauper," he said.

Overwhelmed, I couldn't speak at first.

"Just be sure they come passin' through these doors every once in a while, okay?"

I nodded. It was really happening. Not the way Brenda and I planned it, but I was going to Montreal to learn how to become the next Julia Child. Nothing was going to stop me, especially since Mother Mary of God, had answered my prayers.

CHAPTER 22

Living in Montreal was culture shock for me. I quickly discovered that it was not the same city I had seen the evening Vincent had wined and dined me. I missed the uncomplicated pace of 'Busco, yearning for the quiet. Instead, I had to depend on rattling subways and roaring buses to get myself from my loft in Old Montréal to Le Palais for work and training, and then back to the loft for four long, luxurious hours of sleep before beginning the cycle again. Most days I couldn't fathom why I'd put myself in such chaos.

Fortunately, I didn't have to live alone. I ended up sharing the loft with a young woman named Monique. She also was a waitress at Le Palais, when she wasn't taking classes at McGill University in hopes of becoming a doctor. Unlike me, she had little interest in the culinary world, only in the tips she made waitressing. We rarely saw each other when we weren't at work, and then it was only in passing, when we ferried dishes out to the dining room. During the day, her classes involved dissecting and exploring diseases, while mine involved Chef Dupuis screaming in my face that I would never make it in the culinary world.

I kept trying to remember what Mrs. Fitz had said in her recommendation on my behalf, but whatever it was, Chef Dupuis was out to prove her wrong.

"Have you any idea how long Le Palais has been a four-star restaurant?" he shouted at me on my first day. Before I could answer, he shouted, "Long before you were even a *pétiller* in *les yeux de ta mere*. And I'm not about to let some inexperienced *enfant* ruin the reputation I've worked so hard to maintain!"

Most days were filled with chopping scallions, stirring sauces, measuring, cleaning, cutting, peeling, and grinding. Other days, I was the *garde manger* for special receptions we hosted, which meant I was responsible for preparing the variety of salads and the arrangement of carved fruits on platters.

"*Présentation!*" Chef would shout. "It's all about *présentation!* Charles, come make a miracle out of this *désastre.*" Charles was the sous chef. He rarely said a word, and I would watch to see what he could do that I had not been able to manage. Every day, I was sure I'd been beaten enough so that I would go back to the loft, pack up, and head home. However, I knew that there wasn't much waiting for me there, so I would fight through the doubts and harassment and remind myself that Chef screamed at everyone. I wasn't even sure if he knew how to talk with a civil tongue.

Then, when my tutelage under Chef's watchful eye was over, my night of waitressing would begin. There were occasions when I could barely keep my eyes from filling with tears and my chin from quivering, for example, when serving a patron disgruntled for a less-than-stellar dining experience. Monique would be the one to breeze by me and tell me to hang in there. It wasn't the same as Brenda telling me to kiss it goodbye, but she would remind me that I was on the path to a long-desired goal and had to simply "hang in there."

Still, for the most part, I was resilient and would begin each day optimistically. Monday was my day off, since the restaurant was closed, and I would use it by calling as many Finleys in the Montreal phonebook as possible. One day, when dialing a G. Finley from the list, I had to dial several times before I punched in the correct number. Then, when a woman answered, I could barely speak. In my mind, I saw that she had long blonde hair and was smiling as she'd picked up the receiver. However, she had a very strong French accent and said there was no Grace Finley there. I found out that the "G" stood for her husband, "George."

"You're driving yourself crazy," Monique said, looking up from her biology book. It was early Monday evening, and she was sprawled across her bed on the other side of the room. She had long, jet black hair and big brown eyes set in a full round face. "She obviously doesn't want to be found."

That was not news. But I needed *her* to find *me*.

One good thing about having only Mondays off was that I didn't have much time to think about Vincent. Besides, when I did have time to fill my mind with thoughts, they were usually worried thoughts about how Dad and Grandpa were doing. I would have gone home on the occasional Monday if the train ride hadn't been so expensive, but I was using all my tips to pay my share of the rent and the hefty phone bill that was mostly my responsibility. Finally, Chef gave me his blessing to go home for Thanksgiving. I think he needed a break from me as much as I needed to go home, even if it was just for a brief visit.

Late Wednesday evening, as the train pulled into the Plattsburgh station, I could see Grandpa standing on the platform. His saggy neck stretched, first to the right then the left, as he attempted to find me behind the moving squares of glass. I banged the window as I sailed by his hunched figure, but he didn't see me. Then the train came to a lurching stop, and I jumped from my seat and pulled down my suitcase from the overhead rack. It was going to be a quick trip home, and my suitcase was filled mostly with dirty laundry.

"Grandpa!" I called as I stepped onto the platform. There was panic in his squinting eyes. Once again, I called him, shouting even louder, causing several heads to turn and look. A passerby tugged on his sleeve and pointed him in my direction. He shot a hand in the air, as if he were the one who had spotted me first. Hindered by my suitcase, I slogged toward him. Hindered by his creaky bones, he shuffled toward me. We reached each other and I dropped my suitcase as he pulled me into a hug.

"My sweet angel," he said. "God, I missed you." He backed away, took off his glasses, and wiped them with a red handkerchief he'd pulled from his pants pocket.

"I missed you, too," I said, acknowledging how much I really did for the first time.

He reached for my suitcase.

"I got it, Grandpa."

"I may be old, but I ain't useless. Now let your old Grandpa help you."

I didn't argue, but saw his arm tremble in his chivalrous effort as he put the bag in the back seat of his Buick. Before long, we were coasting at a steady pace along Military Turnpike, heading home.

"How's Dad?" I said. I'd made a habit of calling the house on Sunday mornings to see how the Finley men were doing. Each time, Grandpa's response would be the same. "Can't complain," he'd say about himself. Regarding Dad, he'd say, "Long as he takes his medicine, he'll be all right."

Now, he said, "He quit the cheese plant."

The very idea was shocking, a signal that the end was near. But not according to my grandfather. He said, "I think he's seeing some light at the end of the tunnel, Vicky. Just wish it was without those blasted pills."

"If they help—" I started to say, but Grandpa kept talking.

"It's so gosh darn hard to keep track of. He won't let me give them to him anymore, but I watch that he doesn't do anything crazy."

I knew by "crazy" he meant something like hanging himself from a rope. I reached over and patted Grandpa's leg. "You're a good man."

We pulled into the driveway and I noticed there were some horses in the pasture near the barn. "Whose are those?" I said.

"Oh, we're boarding them for the Mitchells. Keepin' your father busy, which is a good thing."

I spotted Dad in the garage polishing the hood of a red Thunderbird. "Wow," I said, "looks like that's been keeping him busy, too. He should make a nice amount of money when he sells it." Over the years, I'd learned about cars and their value simply by watching my father turn useless jalopies into smooth-running machines.

"Why don't you go say hello to him. I'll get your suitcase."

Conroy, tongue lolling, tail wagging, swaggered toward me as I climbed out of the car. I greeted him with a scratch behind his ear, purposely passing time so that I wouldn't have to go directly to my father. He hadn't stopped swirling the rag across the hood. Finally, after some hesitation, I went over to him. I was going to try to kiss him on the cheek, but he spoke before I had the chance.

"Can't keep spending money on the train."

His not-so-subtle way of telling me not to come home hadn't escaped me. I didn't know how to respond, or if I even should.

"She's not brand new," he went on, "but the engine purrs like a kitten."

Grandpa shuffled by, carrying my suitcase. "Jack," he said, "just tell her what you're tryin' to say."

First he hesitated, and then Dad said, "Want you to have this." He patted the hood.

I looked from Dad to Grandpa and then back to Dad. "You're giving me this car?"

"This way you don't have to worry 'bout train schedules. You wanna come home, you get in the car and come home."

At first I was stunned, then I began to cry. I went to him and hugged his stiffened body. He patted me lightly on the shoulder, as if uncertain where to touch me.

"I bought a bushel of Granny Smith apples," Grandpa said, heading into the house. "S'pose we can make a pie or two?"

I rolled out the crust while Grandpa tried to peel the apples, but his curled fingers fought against his attempt. "Damn blast it," he said, dropping the knife for the third time.

"Grandpa, I'll do it," I said. "Just stay and chat with me; tell me what's going on in 'Busco these days."

He drove the knife into the apple and let it rest there. "Hear Miss Smith got herself a boyfriend."

"About time."

"Well, your Dad's breathing a hell of a lot easier."

We both laughed, and then I said, "Shame he never met anyone else."

Grandpa looked up at me. "You don't know your father very well, do you?"

I stopped the rolling pin. "What do you mean?"

"He'll carry a torch for Grace Finley till the day he dies."

"But he hates her."

"Vicky, there's a fine line between love and hate. And he's been walking that line a long, long time."

I folded the piecrust in quarters, rested it in the dish, and then unfolded it, pressing it into place.

"Got some other news, too."

Intuitively, I knew what it would be.

"Somethin' more's going on with Benny's Lake."

"What do you mean?"

"Can't say for sure. Just gossip going round that those sonsofbitches want to expand. *Improve* on what's there."

The last time I'd spoken to Vincent, he'd said nothing had been decided, but that had been some time ago.

"Funny," Grandpa said, "but the town's not as thrilled this time round. Pretty soon, there'll be none of us left here. I think they regret not listening to Kevin."

Later that night, with apple and pumpkin pies cooling on the counter and Dad and Grandpa in bed, I dialed long distance to Long Island. The phone rang several times. I sat down on a chair in the kitchen. A night light was all that lit my surroundings. Then I heard his voice as he said hello.

"Vincent?" I said.

"Vicky! Happy Thanks—"

"You lied to me."

"—giving. What do you mean, I lied to you?"

"You *are* expanding the campground."

He sighed, but didn't say anything.

"Is it true?"

"Fine and you? Oh, I'm fine. Haven't talked to you in a while. You miss me? Hey—"

"This may be funny to you, but I can't do the small talk."

There was silence on his end. Then, finally, he spoke. "Here's the deal. Since my father sold the resort to Frank and me, with him having enough percentage to maintain an interest, it's now up to Frank and me to do what we want to with it."

"And what do you want to do with it?"

"Me? I'd like to keep it as it is."

"And your brother?"

"Vicky, it's all talk now, and I doubt—"

"Vincent, what does Frank want to do?"

After some hesitation, he said, "He wants to expand. He thinks it needs some tennis courts. A gym. You know—options. But I've been vetoing him tooth and nail, Vicky."

"So your father has the final vote then?"

"Yeah, but for him it's more a game, watching his sons duke it out. He really doesn't care either way about the lake."

"Then it's up to you to get him to care," I said before hanging up.

It was barely dusk when I arose. Grandpa was sitting at the kitchen table with a cup of coffee in front of him. I pulled the turkey from the refrigerator and filled its cavity with stuffing I'd prepared the night before.

"Dad up yet?" I said.

"Out in the barn with the horses. Find anything out last night?"

I told him what Vincent had told me. "He said he's going to give it his biggest fight," I said. "He wants it to stay the same."

"And you believe him?"

I did up till that moment. Perhaps Vincent was as dishonest as Frank. Or maybe he was more sinister, since he didn't wear the trait like a badge. I had little idea how I could find out. I needed to think it through, so once the bird was in the oven, I told Grandpa I was itching to test drive the Thunderbird. I bundled up more than was necessary for a car ride, with a certain destination in mind.

I went outside and stood next to the car. My car. The sun was breaking through the clear morning sky. I stopped long enough to watch my father, who was some distance away in the pasture with the horses. It was comforting seeing life on the farm again. It was difficult to imagine that a few short miles away was a resort that had no appreciation of what had been and what could be again.

The car ran smoothly over the tarred road and handled the back road to Benny's Lake just as easily. I pulled up to the lowered gates. Even without the gates, there would be no easy access due to the half-foot of snow that had accumulated from a recent snowfall. I slipped between the posts and trudged in. There were rabbit tracks, but no sign of human footsteps. I was surrounded by silence. A piece of heaven was what Kevin had called it.

    I walked on, my breath visible, my hands pushing snow-laden branches aside. Finally, I reached the Great White Pine and saw Kevin huddled beneath the branches. Perhaps I saw him the same way he'd seen Benny, but I saw him. He was there. And where would he go if the Great White Pine were cut down? For a moment, I closed my eyes and listened the way Kevin had taught me to listen, then I walked down to the frozen lake's edge. I tested the snow-covered ice then took sliding steps to the boulder and climbed atop it. From that vantage point, Lake in the Woods looked like Benny's Lake without a hint of man's invasion. Moonshadows was out of view, and the resort area was a good distance away. But that was going to change thanks to the lust for profit.

    Just then, the silence was broken by a rustling. I immediately looked over at the Great White Pine. I stopped—my entire being stopped—as I made out the eyes, wide and cautious, gazing back at me. Just beyond those big brown eyes were another set. Then doe and fawn dashed away, leaping into the thick of woods.

    It was then that I knew I had to fight my brother's fight.

Three and a half miles later, I pulled off the back road in front of the trailer. Mr. Collings' Jeep was parked in front. As far as I knew, he lived alone. I picked my way across a frozen, rutted path to get to the front door. I could hear the blast of the television. I knocked and knocked again before he opened the door. He took a moment before he seemed to recognize me.

    "Vicky! It's you." He was wearing a white T-shirt and jeans, and not budging from the entranceway.

    "Sorry to bother you." I said. "Happy Thanksgiving."

    "Thanks. Turkey won't be having one, though." He laughed then stretched to see over my head. "That yours?"

    I glanced back at the Thunderbird. "Dad gave it to me."

    "Hmm. How's he doing, anyway?"

"Better," I said. "Mr. Collings, I wonder if you know what's going on with the resort."

"There's been talk. Can't say I love the idea," he said. "I've got enough to keep me busy as it is."

"What kind of talk?"

He sighed. "Seems they ain't satisfied. Want bigger things. Damn fools, I say."

"I wish we could change their minds."

"You see how they move, Vicky. Once they make up their minds, nothin' we can do. The town gave it up to them; now it seems they're giving up on the town."

"What do you mean?"

"People 'round here know farming and little else. Tennis courts and gyms? What the hell. Even heard some folks say they should've listened to your brother."

"Vincent says he's trying to keep it from happening."

"I've seen those two brothers at it. Doesn't seem like the younger one's got a prayer." He shifted nervously. "Listen, I'd invite you in, but I got to get ready to go over to the Hannigans for dinner."

I had a sudden yearning, imagining the warmth around the harried Hannigan table. I said, "How are they doing?"

"Fine. Fine. Everyone's growin' up."

"And Brenda?"

He coughed, reaching for the door handle. "She's fine, too. Living with Jane in Syracuse, going to some hair-cutting school."

I smiled. "Good…good for her. I'm glad." And I was.

"Well," he said, indicating I was wearing out my welcome.

I said goodbye and went to the car, sidestepping ice patches as best I could. There was something Mr. Collings had said that nagged at me, and it wasn't until I walked into the kitchen, to the aroma of roasting turkey, that it occurred to me. Dad was sitting at the table with Grandpa, the two of them appearing to be waiting for their meal.

"It won't be ready for a while," I said, tugging off my coat.

"We know," Dad said. "We were waiting to hear how it runs." He had his prescription bottle in his hand.

It took me a moment to realize he was talking about the Thunderbird. "Great," I said. "Think it can make a long trip?"

"Where to?"

"Long Island."

"What's on Long Island?" my father said, opening up his bottle and popping a pill into his mouth.

"She's going to try 'n talk some sense into some hard-headed fools, is all," Grandpa said.

I nodded. "Just have to see when I can get off from work first."

Early Friday morning I was sitting in my car in the driveway, preparing to head back to Montreal. Grandpa had packed a turkey leg, some stuffing, and a wedge of pumpkin pie for me to take back to the loft. I tossed my suitcase, now filled with clean clothes, in the back seat.

"Be sure to get your money back from that round-trip ticket," Grandpa said as I began to back out of the driveway. Dad was standing next to him. I could tell by his expression that he was listening to the engine. Once his hand shot up in the air, I knew he was satisfied it would be smooth sailing for me. From my rearview mirror, I saw him head out toward the barn, his walk eager and alive.

CHAPTER 23

The next three weeks were filled with long hours, little sleep, and lots of frustration, since Chef wouldn't give me any time off to take a quick trip to Long Island. I'd been hired as the *sauté* cook, which meant I not only had a title and was lead cook on the hot line, but it would also be more difficult to get away for any stretch of time. It also meant that my days of waitressing were over. I was happy for the chance to prove myself, but I did miss the tips. However, Chef told me if I continued making the grievous mistakes I'd been making, I would soon be a full-time waitress and could flip burgers at MacDonald's. He was right to be angry. I was distracted. While envisioning hundreds of beer cans washing up along the shore of Benny's Lake and the Great White Pine being felled by none other than Brad Hunt, I would burn the onions or curdle the cheese sauce. Chef would go through dramatic fanfare of tossing the onions, cheese sauce, or whatever else I'd ruined in the garbage while grumbling about overhead and wastefulness and my inability to cook.

I was grateful that Le Palais wasn't opened on Christmas Day, which meant I could escape back home, even if it were for just a day. I sat at the table with Grandpa while Dad was in the garage giving the Thunderbird a tune-up.

"And all you do is stir?" Grandpa said when I told him about my promotion.

"Well, it's not all I do," I said, while sorting through the small stack of Christmas cards, still hoping, foolishly hoping, for that long-awaited one. "But it's a step in the right direction."

"That right?" Grandpa said. He didn't seem to hear what I'd been saying.

"You okay?" I said.

He took his handkerchief from his pocket and wiped his eyes. "A year's comin' up since we lost your brother. Still doesn't seem right."

The guilt washed over me again. If it had been me they had put into the ground, the farm would be flourishing, and 'Busco would have a resolute advocate on its side.

Dad walked into the kitchen and took in the scene. "Father Richards is saying a special mass for him on New Year's Eve," he said.

I cast my eyes downward.

"I imagine the whole town'll be there," Dad said, clomping to the sink and washing the grease from his hands. "They're beginning to look at your brother as some kind of hero."

I wanted to be at that mass—yet another part of me did not. Either way, I knew it wouldn't matter, since Chef expected me to work. New Year's Eve was one of Le Palais' biggest nights. Besides, I was waiting for just the right time to ask for a couple days off to make my trip to Long Island.

A week later, I climbed out of the shower, grabbed a towel, dried off, and wrapped myself in it. In just a few short hours, the celebration for the New Year would begin, but I wasn't thinking about sautéing or the pandemonium the kitchen would be in. Instead, I kept thinking of Dad and Grandpa at the special Mass. I hoped my father was taking his medicine. He'd been making steady gains, but he could easily slip into depression remembering what had occurred a year earlier. I longed to be with those from 'Busco who were participating while Father Richards brought Kevin's memory before the altar.

"Are you almost done?" Monique called from outside the bathroom.

I grabbed the blow dryer and brush and blasted on the heat. How could I greet the New Year without recalling the horror of the previous one?

I couldn't.

I slumped to the bathroom floor and began to sob.

"Vicky?" Monique edged the door open and peeked in. "You okay?" She crouched in front of me. "Listen, we'll go in together today." She picked up the blow dryer, lifted strands of my hair, and began drying them. Once she was finished, she suggested I get dressed while she took a shower. Some time later, in our respective uniforms, we walked into Le Palais, Monique giving my hand an encouraging squeeze before I went into the kitchen.

Le Palais was more than a restaurant that night. The guests made reservations months in advance so that they could nibble on caviar, sip on champagne, and dance to the music of a live orchestra. Trays laden with all sorts of hors d'oeuvres were served to the guests before they took their seats and dined on surf and turf. I was responsible for the presentation of the entrée, making sure to garnish each plate with a sprig of this and a dash of that. I tried to remain focused but kept thinking about how Kevin had been safe in his bed until I'd made that desperate albeit erroneous phone call.

I prepared one plate after the next with filet mignon and lobster tail. Drawn butter, fresh parsley, and a wedge of lemon were the finishing details. Occasionally, I'd glance at the clock and recall what I'd been doing a year ago:

This was when I tucked Jonathan and Jamie in bed.
Now Brenda and I were gabbing on the phone.
The electricity went out.
Life as I knew it came to a halt.

Eventually, I was finished with the entrées and began to help line up the desserts that would go out once the New Year had rolled in. Moments before midnight, Monique whizzed in. "Vicky, there's some man at the bar asking for you."

"Who?"

"He didn't say." Someone handed her a tray of cookies and told her to bring it out to one of her tables.

I hadn't taken a break all night, so I gave myself permission to do so just then. I weaved around tables, the confusion of party blowers, music, and raucous laughter filling up the room with charged anticipation. The bar was directly off the dining room, and I went in to see who could be waiting for me. Part of me was hoping it would be Vincent, but I immediately spotted the one man out of his element.

"Dad? What are you doing here?"

He was in a suit and was rotating his cap, with the cheese plant logo, in his hand. "What time you get off?" he said.

"Why?"

"Someplace I want to bring you."

"Tonight?"

He nodded, but then the orchestra began the countdown to midnight. "Ten, nine..." There would be no getting back to the kitchen just now, as bodies filled up every space. Dad had a bottle of beer in his hand and he shouted for the bartender to give me something. I was handed a Coke in haste.

"six...five..."

Monique stretched her neck to see me from across the bar. I mouthed, "My father." She smiled.

I felt Dad's arm around my shoulder and heard him join the countdown. I wondered about Kevin's Mass, but my question would have been drowned out.

"three...two..."

I didn't want it to be said. For some reason, the beginning of a new year, one that did not begin or end with Kevin or his dreams, should not happen as far as I was concerned.

"one!" Corks popping and shouts of "Happy New Year!" exploded throughout the room. Dad planted a kiss on my cheek.

"Let me get my coat," I said, hiding my face, my tears. I wasn't sure how I was going to get off before I was supposed to, but since my father had driven through uncharted territory to see me, I would risk the punishment. But when I found Chef, it was he who told me I was done for the night. I had no proof, but I believed Monique had said something to him about my father waiting for me.

When I got back to the bar with my coat on, Dad was nowhere to be seen. I ran outside and found him sitting in his car at the front door, arguing with the valet, who was insisting he move his car out of the way.

"See, she's right here," Dad said, as I ran around to the passenger side and climbed in.

"What's the surprise?" I said.

"You'll see, but we have to hurry."

Some time later, we were on the outskirts of Montreal, when he pulled in front of a small church. He jumped out and raced around, opening my door and taking my hand. He led us in a run up the steep walkway and pushed open a heavy oak door and called to a small figure standing near the altar, "Here we are! We're here!"

"Dad?" I said.

"We missed you tonight, but I got Brother André here to hold a special Mass for your brother right now—for you."

I stared at him. "How...when..."

"Took me five churches, and he doesn't speak English too good, but I was able to tell him what I wanted."

Brother André was standing at the front of the altar in his vestments. "*Bonsoir*," he said. He pointed to the pew. "*S'il vous plaît.*" A young man, dressed to serve the Brother, came from the back and stood off to the side.

My father and I dropped to our knees and the Brother approached the altar. The church was spare of adornment and stained glass, a simple cross hanging alone at the altar. It was the perfect atmosphere for a man as humble as Kevin.

Brother André began speaking, mostly in French with an occasional word of English thrown in for what I assumed was for our benefit. Then, he said, "*Laisser nous priers*," and bowed his head. I did as well.

Kevin! Kevin! Can you hear me? Brad's trying to break in!

"*Paix pour…Kevin Finley.*"

The loud whir of the snowmobile roars in my head. There is determination on his face in his attempt to reach me before Brad does.

Brother André walked toward the back of the altar, the young man following him.

It wasn't Brad after all, but a poor defenseless mute left out in the cold.

Brother André held up chalice and blessed it.

Watch out for the fence, Kevin!

He raised the host toward the heavens.

If I hadn't called you, you'd still be in bed, asleep, your alarm set to nudge you awake to milk the cows…

The roar has died.

Then silence.

Brother André walked down the few steps and offered us communion. I lifted my head and felt my father's gentle touch as he wiped the tears from my face. I took communion and then fell into my father's shoulder, remaining still for some time.

"*Allez en paix*," the Brother eventually said, nodding to us. He and the young man disappeared to the back, and then the young man came back, no longer garbed to serve. "*Bonne nuit*," he said.

My father gave an appreciative nod and guided me back to the car. "I'll drive you home," he said.

"You can stay over. I'll bunk with Monique."

"Nah. Grandpa'll worry 'bout me." When we got to the loft, he leaned over, kissed me on the forehead, and said, "That blame you been carrying, I hope you left it back there in that church."

Speechless, I climbed out of the car and walked to my doorway. I turned and watched him drive off, wondering what kind of medicine made a man who had once invited death, of sound mind again. Even though he was out of hearing range, I shouted, "Love you!"

CHAPTER 24

According to Dad and Grandpa, after the special mass had been said for Kevin, 'Busco began to rally around his cause in earnest. *Plattsburgh Press* did another article, and this time, each of the residents who were interviewed praised Kevin's insight and regretted not having listened to him. Mr. Scott was quoted as saying, "What the hell they need a gym for? They can come toss some bales for me if they want exercise." The article also stated that Scoleri Enterprise could not be reached for comment, adding that they were within their rights to expand.

Could not be reached for comment? Did that include Vincent?

I couldn't put it off any longer. I called him and told him I needed to come down, to talk to his father.

"Senior doesn't like to be told what he can and cannot do, Vicky."

"I just want to talk to him, Vincent. Maybe get him to listen to reason."

Vincent chuckled. "Hey, if it means I get to see you, please come down, but I don't want you to be disappointed."

So, it was settled. Chef gave me the time off, Dad checked under the hood of the Thunderbird to make sure it would make the trip, and on early Monday morning, mid-January, I was set to go.

"Just not too thrilled with you going off like this all alone," Dad said.

"Specially this time of year," Grandpa said, standing next to my father in the driveway.

"I listened to the forecast," I said. "It's supposed to be clear the next few days." I started the engine, rolled up my window, and backed out. It seemed I was no longer representing just Kevin, but all of Churubusco. With the roadmap on the seat next to me, I used the time heading south on the Northway, then the Thruway, to figure out exactly how I would approach Vincent's father. Vincent's mother, on the other hand, sounded reasonable enough. Once she found out I was coming down, she had insisted I have dinner with the Scoleris that very evening.

Several hours later, I pulled into a hotel on the North Shore of Long Island, where Vincent had made reservations for me. There were flowers in the room with a note stating: "Be strong. Love, Vincent."

I had a couple of hours before I was expected for dinner. In that time, I took a shower, and then, wrapped in my bathrobe, I sat on the bed and went through the phone book. There were thirty-three Finleys. Most had answering machines, and those who did not hung up after saying that no one by that name lived there, and I had only gotten about halfway through the list before it was time to get ready to leave.

I wore a red pantsuit that Monique had helped me select just for the occasion. The directions were a bit tricky, and I had to veer from the main highway and travel along a more secluded tree-lined road. The houses—when I could even see them through thick foliage—were becoming larger than any I'd seen so far, and they were set farther back from the road the farther I traveled, with longer stretches between one house and the next as well. One residence, set quite a distance back from the road, had a corral with two horses. Then I spotted the sign warning me that there was a private driveway just ahead, which Vincent had told me to look for. I took the turn.

The graveled path cut through what appeared to be a small forest, and it took some time before it began to widen and the trees thinned out. That's when a house—actually, a mansion—came into view. When I saw the prodigious white structure at the center of the circular driveway, I knew I was approaching power and privilege. At that moment, I didn't know how I could have possibly thought I could meet Mr. Scoleri on reasonable terms.

I slowed, looking in awe at the front yard's shrubbery, shaped like a pride of lions. Besides a fire-red Jaguar sitting in the driveway, I spotted Vincent's white Mercedes. I wanted to keep driving, to head out of the circle and back onto the path that would take me home, but Vincent appeared on the verandah and waved to me. I pulled off to the side, sucked up some air, and climbed out.

"God, you look beautiful," Vincent said, coming up to me and grasping the collar of my sheepskin coat. He kissed me on the mouth.

"I shouldn't have come," I said. "Nothing I'm going to say will matter."

"I'm just glad you're here," Vincent said.

"I've never seen anything like this before," I said, motioning toward the shrubbery.

"It's Senior's not-so-subtle way of letting people know he's king and will forever hold court. Come on inside."

The entrance was grand with a cathedral ceiling and a spiral staircase covered with a floral woolly runner. While Vincent was taking my coat and putting it in the front closet, I couldn't help but think how impressed Brenda would have been to be surrounded by such wealth. He then led me down a hallway past a room with opened double doors. Filled bookshelves lined the walls from ceiling to floor.

"Has anyone actually read all those?" I whispered over the click-clack of our footsteps.

Vincent laughed. "No one who lives here," he said, bringing me into another imposing room.

"Hey, Vicky!" Frank rose from one of the many scattered couches curiously situated. "Long time no see." He swooped in on me, wrapping those gorilla arms around me as if we were friends. The thought of kneeing him in the groin came to mind, but instead I pushed myself free.

"I see you haven't changed," he said.

My mouth was dry. Reasoning with Mr. Scoleri was going to be all the more difficult with Frank there.

Vincent said, "I want you to meet my mother." He led me across the room toward a woman sitting in a wingchair next to a fireplace. The room was arranged into various sitting areas for intimate gatherings, but it could have been converted to fit one large assembly at any given moment. The fireplace was blazing, and the woman had a sweater draped over a gray linen pantsuit. Her watery-blue eyes locked on me as we were introduced.

She shifted her globe, which contained an ounce or so of an amber-colored liquid, from her right hand to her left. I took her outstretched hand, startled by how bony it felt as her chilled fingers rested in my gentle grasp.

"Very nice to meet you, Mrs. Scoleri," I said.

She nodded, her thin lips stretching across an ashen-colored face similar in color to the outfit hanging over her reed-like frame. I struggled not to stare at her hair, cut so short it was nothing more than silver-white bristles cropped on her head.

"Could we get you a drink?" she said, the words coming out breathy.

"Already taken care of," Frank said, handing me a glass of red wine. "You do like Merlot, right?" He winked at me then immediately looked to Vincent, as if trying to get a rise out of him.

"Is not!" cried a voice from the corner of the room. I looked over and saw a gaggle of little girls sitting on the floor, surrounded by dolls and toys. It was a most welcome sight.

"Frank's children," Mrs. Scoleri stated with a warm smile. "Girls, we have a guest. Let's be on our best behavior."

"Come on, I'll introduce you," Vincent said, leading me to the other side of the room. I felt the cool gaze of his mother following me while I navigated around different arrangements of furniture, all having the appearance of precious heirlooms.

"Hey, girls, I want you to meet someone special. This is Vicky. Vicky," Vincent said, pointing to the oldest of the group, "this is Theresa. She's eighteen."

"Am not, Uncle Vincent," Theresa said. She giggled, showing a big gap in her mouth where teeth were missing. "I'm seven."

"I'm six," said another girl, having the same curly black hair as her sisters.

I crouched to her level. "And what's your name?"

"Maria." She pointed to a younger girl sitting on the floor, combing out the hair on a Barbie doll. "She's Andrea and she's four. Flori's just a baby."

Frank had been busy.

"Hey!" Theresa said, "You're wearing the same outfit Barbie has on."

It was true. The doll Andrea was holding was wearing a red pantsuit similar to the one I was wearing. When Monique saw the outfit in the store window, she said, "You have to look as classy as they are. That is classy." I'd spent a chunk of my own money for what I had thought was classy, and now it suddenly seemed cheap, nothing more than a Barbie knock-off.

Frank strolled over, took the doll from Andrea, and said, "I'll be, she sure does." Using his thumb, he began caressing Barbie's breasts, until Vincent grabbed the doll and tossed it to the floor. "Do you always have to be such an asshole?"

"Hey!" Andrea picked the doll up and straightened her outfit.

Frank chuckled, sauntering back to the couch. "Can't figure out who has more life in her, Barbie or Vicky."

"Ohmygawd," a voice said from across the room. I turned to see a short woman staring at me with brown beady eyes lost in a round, full face. She lurched into the room, a tunic draped over her lumpy body, her stubby hands wrapped around a glass, the edges stained with bright red lipstick.

"Camille, I'd like you to meet Vicky," Vincent said. To me, he said, "Camille is Frank's wife."

"Get that?" she said as I took her limp, chubby hand in mine and attempted to shake it. "Frank's *wife*." Her fingernails were polished a bright red, and in spite of it being the middle of January, she was wearing sandals, her matching red toenails straining against the leather straps. She looked me up and down, appearing to be contemplating something.

"I used to have a body," she said. "Not tall and thin like yours, but it was a body. Frank always said I looked like Sophia Loren." She glanced toward her husband, who had a dish of nuts cradled in his hand. "But he's so damned intent on getting a son, I'll never get my body back." She swayed then added, "Now I got you to compete with."

"There's *no* competition, *Sophia*," Frank said, stirring the nuts until he found what he was looking for and tossed it in his mouth.

"Bastard," she said, stumbling toward the bar.

Suddenly, an atmospheric change came into the room.

Camille immediately put the bottle of liquor down.

Frank stopped chewing.

The girls, hunkered in the corner, lowered their voices.

Vincent shoved his hands in his pockets and cleared his throat.

And I followed Mrs. Scoleri's gaze toward the entranceway.

"We have a guest," said a man who filled the room with his presence. "Certainly, Frank, you could restrain your wife for such occasions." He immediately came to me, taking my hand and bringing it to his lips. "You must be Miss Finley, Churubusco's ambassador. How wonderful to have the opportunity to meet you."

Vincent came alongside of me. "Vicky, this is my father, Senior Scoleri."

"And do call me Senior," he said, as he glided across the room toward his wife, straightening her sweater. "Wouldn't want you to catch cold, dear."

Mrs. Scoleri emitted a chilly reserve and undid what her husband had just done to her sweater. Camille was now slouched in a brocaded chair, clutching an empty glass. Thankfully, the girls were changing Barbie's outfit.

"So," he said, turning his attention back to me, "I understand you're here to plead for your little town's cause."

I glanced at Vincent, but I wasn't sure if his eyes were encouraging or warning me to be careful in my approach. His father stood ramrod straight, his eyes locked on me. His suit was flawless, his shoes shined to a gleam.

I cleared my throat. "Well, Mr. Scol—"

"Tut, tut. Senior. The name's Senior."

I sucked up some air. "Senior. I really don't know what I can say to make you understand. It's just that—"

"To be honest, Vicky—or is it Victoria?"

"Vicky."

"Okay, then, Vicky. First, let me tell you I don't care either way about this resort. It's really between my sons. Vincent has been vehemently against this expansion, and now that I've met you I believe it may have less to do with environment and land development and more with my son's desire to win you over."

"Please don't," Vincent said, his voice low.

I decided then to take advantage of Frank's presence. Looking pointedly at him, I said, "And what's your reason for wanting to expand?"

Still cradling the bowl of nuts with one hand, Frank used his free hand to rub his fingers together, indicating money.

Just then, a young woman appeared, her skin dark, her black hair long and shiny. She gathered the children and began to herd them out of the room.

"Hey!" Frank shouted, causing the children and woman to stop. "Where you going?"

"To feed the children," the young woman said with a strong Jamaican accent.

Frank stretched out his arms and the woman's eyes widened. She backed away, looking downward.

"Not you, Aggie," Camille said. "He wants a hug from his kids." She stood and murmured, "Ah, to hell with it," and thumped to the bar.

Aggie forced a nervous laugh and told the girls to go to their father. Frank scooped them up then bopped each one on the behind, keeping his eyes on the young woman the whole time.

"They're not going to eat with us?" I said to Vincent. Their cheerful chatter would have been welcoming.

"No," he said. "They live across the way, just beyond the stand of trees."

Another woman, this one robust, with graying hair pulled in a tight bun, appeared and announced that dinner was ready.

Senior said, "Thank you, Blanche." He then turned to me. "We will continue this dialogue after dinner. Talking business while dining gives me indigestion."

We all followed Blanche into the dining room, yet I would have preferred to keep going beyond the swinging door where the kitchen had to be. Certainly,

I'd be more at home chopping and stirring instead of sitting at a table where the silverware shined but the conversation dulled, especially since I'd been temporarily reined in on my topic of choice.

Blanche placed plates of salads on chargers in front of us, and it wasn't until Senior picked up his fork and took a bite that the rest of the Scoleris followed suit.

"So, Vicky," Mrs. Scoleri said, barely above a whisper, "I understand you live on a farm."

I thought of what had it been when Kevin was alive—the number of livestock increasing, the fields rototilled and planted with corn, and the chickens yielding more eggs than we'd ever seen before Kevin committed his life to farming.

I said, "Well, no, not really. I mean, we used to have cows and chickens, but that was before—"

"So," Frank said, "if it had cows and chickens but wasn't a farm, what did you call it?" He popped a cherry tomato into his mouth.

Looking him in the eye, I said, "Home."

Senior chuckled while Camille swilled the last bit of her wine and waved the drained glass at Blanche. "Would you mind freshning thish up a bit?"

Blanche picked up the bottle, refilling Camille's glass until Senior said, "Don't you think you've had quite enough, Camille?" Without hesitation, Blanche stopped pouring and gave the partially filled glass back to Camille. She gathered up the salad plates and moments later was placing Cornish hens, wild rice, and creamed spinach before us.

"So," Mrs. Scoleri said, "I understand you want to be a chef."

This was not the conversation I wanted to be having, but I knew I'd have to wait until Senior gave the go ahead before I could talk about the resort. Until then, I was left little choice but to make small talk. I said, "Yes. I've always enjoyed cooking."

Mrs. Scoleri smiled and nodded. "Did your mother teach you?"

"Mom," Vincent said, "could we change the subject?"

I could take it no longer. I said, "Mr. Scoleri, if the expansion doesn't matter either way to you, I am begging you, please let 'Busco stay as it is." I could feel the tension at the table. Camille was watching me with curiosity.

Senior's eyes hardened and he stared at me without saying a word. I refused to let him intimidate me.

"If any more trees are cut down," I continued, "it'll destroy so much more than just the lake. It used to be a wide stretch of heaven, but if you come in and put up buildings and tennis courts, it'll be nothing but ordinary."

After an uncomfortable stretch of silence, Frank began applauding loudly, sarcastically, until Senior turned his glare toward him. He said, "It's my understanding that you worked at Lake in the Woods. It's how you met my sons."

"Yup," Frank said, "you made me a Michelin."

In unison, Vincent and I corrected him: "Michigan." I added, "Actually, Brenda helped. You do remember Brenda, right, Frank?"

I was hoping I'd embarrass him into silence, but instead he said, "Yeah, the redhead who couldn't keep her hands off me."

Camille raised her glass. "To all the women who want to fuck Frank Scoleri." She was alone in her toast.

Senior turned to Vincent. "Why don't you show Vicky around, then we'll regroup for dessert."

I had barely touched my meal but was grateful for the reprieve. We slipped on our coats, after Vincent retrieved mine from the front closet, and went outside through French doors that opened onto a patio. Vincent took my hand and we walked down a path, passing a built-in pool and fountain.

"I don't think I made much headway," I said.

"He likes you," Vincent said.

"How can you tell?"

"He didn't dismiss you."

"Then what was that back there?"

"Oh, when he told me to show you around the grounds?"

I nodded.

"That's so he can remind Frank that he needs to restrain his wife, yet again."

"Your mother's nice." We kept walking, passing what appeared to be a guest house.

"She is. Things were pretty tense with her awhile ago, but she's in remission now."

"Oh, Vincent, why didn't you tell me?"

"It's something we don't discuss. Senior doesn't want people to know. He doesn't like any kind of attention brought to the Scoleri name. He's still trying to get everyone to forget what Camille did to herself a couple years back."

"What'd she do?" We'd arrived at the end of the path and stood on the edge of a stand of trees.

"Used a hanger to end a pregnancy."

I gasped. "Someone like her must have had options."

Vincent sniffed. "When you're a Scoleri, you don't go out in public without someone noticing. And she couldn't very well have asked her doctor, since he's a close friend of the family. In her muddled mind, she didn't have an option."

"Did people find out what she tried to do?"

Vincent shrugged. "Senior insisted to anyone who asked that it had been a miscarriage and had us all pretend to be devastated in front of anyone who might be watching. He then made sure Frank got her pregnant shortly after so that it would look like a baby was what she wanted. Naturally, she had another girl."

"What an awful way to live," I said.

"We all learn to deal with Senior one way or another. Camille uses the bottle."

"What about you?" I said. "What do you use?"

"You wouldn't believe me if I told you," he said, looking away.

"Try me."

His expression was thoughtful. "Up till a few months ago, I just played the game, did what Senior expected. I didn't know anything better, until I discovered something more powerful."

"What?"

"Passion," he said. "Well, not my own, but yours, to be honest."

Perhaps it was unwise, but I believed him. What he said seemed to make sense, and I thought it was sincere.

"I want to know what that feels like to feel so strongly about something that everything else loses its importance."

I thought of Kevin just then. "Then you know why I'm here."

He nodded, his eyes glistening. "I'd like to think it was for me, but I know better."

He grasped my hand and led me back to the house, where we found the Scoleris in the sitting room. Camille was nowhere to be found, but Frank was there, looking somewhat somber.

Senior said, "Vicky, I've heard what you said, and you don't really have a sound argument. So, why don't we put this debate behind us and have some dessert?"

At that moment, I recalled a day from several seasons earlier, sitting with Kevin in his pickup and the way he had stared into the woods, believing his neighbors had sold out. And then there was that horrible moment when he'd discovered that I'd betrayed him.

I took a step closer to Senior and said, "Maybe to someone like you, it isn't a sound argument. When I got here today and saw all you own, I realized that you have an appreciation for the good things and value what you have. I can't imagine you standing by if someone were to try and take it all away from you."

He studied me for a moment. "For the right price, I wouldn't be too sure," he said. "Everything has a price, Vicky." He breezed by me then said, "I believe there are strawberries in Grand Marnier and biscotti awaiting us."

"I have to go," I said.

Vincent didn't argue with me but walked me outside to my car. He wanted to come back to the hotel with me, but I discouraged the idea, and he didn't pressure me. When I drove out of the driveway, I veered off the path ever so slightly, the Thunderbird scraping the pride of lions.

CHAPTER 25

I got back to Churubusco late in the afternoon the following day. I found Grandpa snoozing on the couch when I walked in. I watched him for a moment, looking at the deep lines in his face, each representing one sorrow after the next. Then his eyes opened and he saw me standing there, and the evidence of his suffering vanished in a smile.

"Well, look who's home," he said, his creaky bones struggling to get him off the couch. We hugged, and he wanted to know how it went.

"Not very good, Grandpa. Mr. Scoleri doesn't care what happens with the lake. Vincent was right. His father just enjoys the contest of wills."

"One mean sonofabitch, ain't he?"

I thought of the way Senior had been with his ailing wife and what he'd done to poor Camille and nodded at Grandpa's accurate assessment.

"Well, we'll just have to see," Grandpa said, heading into the kitchen with me trailing after him. "How about old Grandpa makes us some hot cocoa?" He went to the refrigerator and pulled out a container of milk. I still hadn't gotten used to the store-bought containers. When the farm was running, we'd had fresh milk and cream at our disposal.

Even so, I said, "Sounds good."

Later, after having supper with Dad and Grandpa, I was preparing to head back to Montreal when Mr. Scott pulled into the driveway. It had been some time since I'd seen him. Jonathan was with him and looked to have grown a good inch or two since the night I babysat for him and Jamie. Standing in our kitchen, he averted his eyes when I said hello.

"Hey, Vicky," Mr. Scott said, "heard you went down state. Was wonderin' how it went."

I glanced at Dad. During supper, he'd mentioned how everyone was up in arms about the expansion, but there'd been no town meeting this time, since they had no legal recourse. He hadn't told me my trip to Long Island was general knowledge.

Taking a step forward, Dad said, "Not very good. Those bastards don't give a shit about us. Never did."

I wanted to jump in, to tell them that Vincent was fighting it and that until he relented we had a chance to keep things from changing drastically. Instead, I asked how Jamie was doing.

It was Jonathan who said, "Annoying."

Mr. Scott ruffled his son's hair and said, "That's what sisters are for." He then said, "Well, come on, then. Just wish we could do something to stop 'em. Pretty soon this'll be all built up, pushing us few farmers out."

They shambled out of the kitchen and Dad walked them to their car, and I felt I'd failed yet again.

The months passed without any word from Vincent—or any Scoleri, for that matter. I kept busy at Le Palais. My red velvet cake was on the special Valentine's Day menu and a lamb dish I'd created was one of the entrées for Easter dinner. Then, late one night at the end of April, when I was sound asleep, the phone rang. Monique answered it, since she was still up studying.

"For you," she said, tapping me on the shoulder.

"Did I wake you?" a voice said from the other end.

"Vincent?" I said. "How are you?"

"I have some news."

I steeled myself, felt the pounding of my heart.

"Don't ask me why or how," he said, "but Frank withdrew his motion to expand."

"What?" I said, catching my breath, feeling the tears of relief come to my eyes.

"You heard me."

"I don't believe it."

"To be honest," he said, "neither do I."

"Oh my God. But he can change his mind, right?"

"Not after tomorrow. He's selling his share to me."

"Vincent, I really don't understand any of this." I wanted to believe it, but felt it was too easy. He was holding something back. "You think your father has anything to do with it?"

"Oh, I'm sure. But I'll never know why. Frank said after going over all the figures, the bit of profit wouldn't be worth it. Then he said he didn't want to be bothered with it anymore. He's actually signing over his share to me."

My alarm clock said it was well past eleven. Dad and Grandpa would be in bed asleep. Otherwise, I would have called them with the news.

"Vicky."

"Yes?"

"I'm glad for you. I really am. It killed me to see how much this was upsetting you."

"But *you* didn't give up the fight."

He cleared his throat. "Thing is, I did. A couple of weeks ago. It was getting out of hand."

"What?" I said.

"That's why you haven't heard from me. I felt like a piece of shit and thought you'd never want to see me again. The thing is—"

He was still trying to explain himself as I placed the phone down in the cradle.

The following day was Monday, and the restaurant was closed. I decided it would be fun to see Dad and Grandpa's faces when I told them the news. I went home with two bags of groceries and began to prepare a special supper for them.

"It's like you're celebratin'," Grandpa said.

"Maybe," I said, cubing the fresh beef and tossing it in a huge pot with pearl onions, potatoes, and carrots, along with herbs and beef stock.

With a twinkle in his eye, Grandpa said, "You got another promotion."

I laughed. "I can't say till Dad comes in." My father was feeding the horses, having taken in several more since the last time I'd been home.

I made a batch of biscuits, and by the time Dad walked in, everything was ready. Dad traipsed toward the bathroom to wash. Grandpa called, "Don't forget your medicine, Jack."

"Hell, you don't give me a chance," Dad returned.

Once they sat down, I ceremoniously placed the crock of beef stew in front of Dad. I watched him, waiting for his reaction. Immediately, he ladled out a generous amount into his bowl, then reached for a biscuit and buttered it.

There was no plate of cheese on the table, but since he no longer worked at the factory, it didn't seem as important any longer. Nor did he seem to remember my promise never to make beef stew again. I alone knew how significant the meal was.

Then, I made Dad raise his cup of coffee and Grandpa his water while I held my glass of Coke high. They looked at me expectantly.

"Scoleri Enterprise has dropped any plans to expand."

Their drinks went immediately back to the table. Dad said, "How do you know?"

"Vincent called. He told me Frank gave up the whole thing. He even sold his share to Vincent."

"I'll be," Grandpa said. "Looks like you had some pull after all, Vicky."

"No, Grandpa. Sounds like Frank was into it more for the fight; once Vincent gave up, he didn't care any more."

"That right?" Grandpa said, his chin quivering.

Just then, the phone rang. Dad got up and answered it. "How ya doing?" he said. "Yup, just heard." There was a pause. "Vicky. She's here right now. She found out last night." He looked over to see Grandpa and me looking back at him. "He sure would be. Yup, I'm sure he's smiling down, too."

Once he hung up, Grandpa said, "Who was that?"

"Mr. Collings. Seems word is spreading already. Scoleri's attorney called him today."

I took a bite of the beef stew and felt almost giddy. I could see there was a spirit of jubilation in my father and Grandpa's faces, as well. The phone rang again, and this time it was Mr. Hamilton, calling to see if we'd heard the news. By the time the meal was over, several more people had called, including a reporter from the *Plattsburgh Press*.

Finally, after cleaning up the kitchen and the phone calls had stopped, I went out to the porch to sit with Grandpa. Dad was out in the garage tinkering. From the porch window, the moon was nothing but a sliver in the sky. Grandpa reached over and placed my hand in his.

"Oh, you're so cold," I said, rubbing his hands.

"Blood doesn't move the way it used to."

"I can't believe the battle was won," I said, still afraid this would be some cruel joke on Frank's part.

"Ah, there'll be more," Grandpa said. "You're young yet." He squeezed my hand. "Don't be too hard on him, Vicky."

"We're doing better, don't you think?"

"Who?"

"Dad and me."

"I'm talking about that Long Island fella."

I looked down at my hand in his. "You didn't seem too impressed with him."

"S'pose not. Still, I can be wrong 'bout some things."

We sat quietly for a while, staring out at the sky as it grew darker and darker then filled up with one star after the next. I heard Dad come into the kitchen and wash, and then wander through the house. He stopped at the entranceway to the porch.

"See you in the morning," he said, heading off to bed.

"Got to make sure he takes his medicine, Vicky. Don't forget that." Grandpa patted me on the leg then pushed himself up. "Guess I'm goin' to call it a night, too. You stayin'?"

I nodded. I didn't have to be at work the following day until three in the afternoon.

He bent down and kissed me on the forehead. "The stew was good. Glad you decided to give it another go round."

I smiled. "I made enough so there'd be leftovers."

He said goodnight then shuffled off the porch and went up to bed.

The following morning, I woke up to find Dad sitting at the kitchen table, his cup of coffee in front of him, his eyes red and watery. I was certain that Frank had indeed changed his mind and somehow Dad had found out. I approached him with uncertainty.

"Dad?"

"Coroner's coming."

I stood there stunned, taken back to the last time the coroner had come.

He sniffled. "Found him lying there. Still as anything. Must've went some time in the night."

I began to tremble. I shook my head. "Are you sure? He was really tired last night. Maybe...maybe he's just sleeping really hard."

I ran upstairs and pushed the door open to Grandpa's bedroom. His eyes were closed, his body motionless. I wanted to believe it was simply the deepest of sleeps and he would suddenly open his eyes and be happy to see me.

There's my sweet angel.

As usual for such an event, my mind was obsessed with images of Grace Finley finally making her long-awaited appearance. I sat in the funeral home, watching each familiar face walk in to offer their condolences while hoping only for the woman in the three-by-five Polaroid. For a brief moment, I did stop looking for her when the group of redheads walked in. I searched for Brenda in the mix, but she was the one redhead missing.

Pointless platitudes were offered:
He lived a long life.
God needed another angel.
Now he's with Kevin.

I stood shoulder to shoulder with Dad at the cemetery. I surveyed Grandma and Kevin's headstones while the priest talked about ashes and dust. Perhaps Grandma was ash and dust and Grandpa would be content to mingle with her, but I couldn't believe someone as vibrant as Kevin had been to have succumbed to such useless means. We tossed dirt on the coffin then headed back to Mr. Scott's car. He had been our chauffeur. I looked up to see the white Mercedes parked across the street. Vincent started toward me, his eyes soft on me. I wanted to go over to him, yet another part of me wanted to pretend I did not see him.

"Who told you?" I said.

"No one. I didn't know till I got up here."

"There's a ton of food back at the house," I said. "You're welcome to come over."

"I don't want to intrude."

"I wouldn't have invited you if I felt you were." I climbed in the back seat of Mr. Scott's car with my father and told Vincent to follow us.

Miss Smith was now Mrs. Robare, and she took it upon herself to make sure all the salads, cold cuts, and rolls our neighbors had generously supplied were on the table, along with plastic utensils and paper plates. Seems all of 'Busco came to our house to grieve. Or eat. It was difficult to tell which.

I didn't have the desire to put a thing in my mouth, nor did I want to make small talk with anyone. But I did introduce Vincent, and once the locals found out who he was, they crowded around him, shaking his hand, patting him on the back, and thanking him for making the right decision. He didn't explain how he'd given up to Frank and I didn't offer the information. It didn't seem important any longer.

The mood gradually shifted from sorrow to acceptance. Grandpa's memory created an atmosphere of warmth. Mr. Robare, the portly, jovial man now married to Miss Smith, was encouraged to bring his guitar into the house, and soon people were singing songs I didn't recognize. Dad's voice rose above the rest. It was the first time I recall hearing him sing. I hadn't asked him whether he had taken his medicine for few hours, but he appeared to be okay.

> *From this valley they say you are leaving.*
> *We shall miss your bright eyes and sweet smile.*
> *For you take with you all of the sunshine*
> *That has brightened our path for a while.*
>
> *Then come sit by my side if you love me.*
> *Do not hasten to bid me adieu.*
> *Just remember the Red River Valley*
> *And the cowboy that's loved you through.*

Overwhelmed with sadness, I told Vincent I needed to escape for a while. We climbed in his car and he seemed to sense where I needed to be. Soon we were slogging through the damp path that led to the lake. I hesitated at the Great White Pine, touching its needles, before wandering down to the boulder. I climbed on it and sat down, feeling the sun wash over me.

"You okay?" Vincent said.

I rested my head on my knees. "Just numb." I looked across the smooth surface of the water.

Vincent wrapped an arm around me. "You've lost some pretty important people in your life."

I remembered the advice Grandpa had given me about Vincent. I shifted, resting my head against his shoulder.

"When I drove up here," Vincent said, "I had no idea this was going on."

"So, why did you come up?"

"To bring you a peace offering."

"For what?"

"I knew I'd disappointed you. I went to the loft and your roommate told me you wouldn't be back for a few days and why."

"You weren't afraid I'd slam the door in your face?"

"I was willing to take the risk." He squeezed me with a hug. "So, don't you want to know what the peace offering is?"

"Since you drove all the way," I said, "I suppose."

He cleared his throat before saying, "I was hoping you'd consider working at Moonshadows for the summer as the sous chef."

I studied him. A year earlier, I had only dreamed of such things. Now I could barely absorb what he was saying.

"It'd be a great opportunity," he said. "Only thing is you'd have to work under Chef Bresette."

"If I can work with Chef Dupuis, I can work with anybody."

"So, this is a yes?" He held me with his gaze.

I hesitated. "What will I do once summer's over?"

"I don't think that will be problem."

He was right. There were many restaurants in Montreal that I was sure would hire me, but I didn't want to think about that. Working at Moonshadows meant I would be able to keep an eye on Dad.

I nodded a yes, and Vincent pulled me into him and kissed me a long, long while.

And I didn't stop him.

CHAPTER 26

Chef Dupuis was not eager to see me go. At first he said I was giving him no time to find a replacement. I countered by telling him I'd give him an entire month.

"But you're not ready for such *responsibilité*," Chef Dupuis said.

"I think I am," I replied. What I didn't say was that Chef Bresette had planned to put me through his culinary hoops well before opening day.

"It's only a summer job. What will you do after?"

"You're telling me you wouldn't take me back?"

"There can be no guarantee. You're making a very big mistake."

I went over to the stove, turned on the burner to heat the pan for crepes, and said, "My father needs me right now."

Pushing through the double doors, he grumbled, "Your papa, your papa. It's time you cut the apron strings."

As promised, I tried to help him find a replacement for me, but all of the candidates were either too "*paresseux*," which I'd discovered long ago meant lazy, or too inexperienced. One young man whom I thought would be perfect was dismissed with a wave of the hand and the comment, "I don't trust him. He'll come in, suck all my *information* from me, then go open his own restaurant."

By the time I was due to leave, there was no replacement for me, and Chef tried to force me to stay. I surprised him with a hug and promised I'd stay in touch, then I walked out, feeling an unexpected sadness. For all his curmudgeonly ways, he'd become the grumpy uncle I'd never had, and I was grateful for all he had taught me.

Monique promised to stay in touch with me, and I with her, but leaving Montreal was not very difficult.

When I got back home, Dad told me to meet him down at the little house. I couldn't imagine why, but when I walked in, I was greeted with the smell of fresh paint. Other than the familiar kitchen set and worn-out couch, all remnants of Kevin were gone, except for the boxes, which Dad had left alone in the closet. He had even transferred my bedroom furniture to the little house.

"Thought you needed your own place," Dad said.

I looked out the back window where the Datsun had been parked. It was gone.

"Sold it," Dad said, without my saying another word.

I didn't know if I was ready to live in the little house, but I didn't think I had a choice. It wasn't too long before I was settled in. Sometimes, after a long night at Moonshadows of preparing and garnishing a variety of dishes, I'd return home and sit in the quiet of my kitchen and sip on a cold glass of iced tea. From my window, I could see the small figure of Dad bumping around in his kitchen. There was still so much space between us, and I wanted to fill it. But I wasn't sure with what.

I had been apprehensive about starting over under a new chef. However, Chef Bresette treated me with a curious amount of respect. Or perhaps I was confusing respect with an inordinate amount of responsibility. I soon learned I was to train the new hires, order supplies, pick up the slack during the rush, and plan the menu. When Chef Bresette was out of earshot, I asked one of the staff what it was that Chef did, and he mimed the act of tossing back a drink. Once we were open for business, I discovered that was indeed the case. Each night, Chef Bresette sat in the back office downing a bottle of scotch. By closing time, his eyes were bloodshot, his gait tipsy. For whatever reason, I didn't mention it to Vincent when he came every couple of weeks to check on Lake in the Woods. Chef Bresette couldn't understand why he needed to do any such thing.

"Why?" Chef Bresette would say. "Why does he need to come when I can tell him over the phone that all is okay?"

I knew why, and I was grateful for the chance to alleviate my loneliness, spending long afternoons at the chasm or sharing my bed until the early-morning hours, before Vincent had to head back to Long Island. I wanted to ask him to stay, but I didn't dare, feeling I didn't have the right. Besides, there was nothing for him in Churubusco.

Cooking, planning the menu, keeping an eye on my father, and staying in close contact with an organization called People Finders kept me so busy that when August came, I was stunned. It seemed I'd just started at Moonshadows, and now I would have to close up the kitchen for the season. My temper became short, so short that I ended up telling Chef Bresette he was nothing but a useless drunk one day when he complained that my roasted duck was too greasy. He was right, it was, but I didn't want to hear it. Not from him, anyway. Each day, I promised myself I'd call Chef Dupuis to see if he'd take me back once Moonshadows closed, and each day I failed. Montreal was not home to me. I had no roots there, no window to look out of to keep an eye on my father. But 'Busco provided no means of support once Lake in the Woods closed for the season. To make it worse, I was expected to throw a grand finale on closing night.

One camper after the next questioned me, wanting to know just what the theme would be. It had been a summer of themed menus for Moonshadows. On the Fourth of July we had prepared dishes at tableside, using gallons of brandy, Jamaican rum, and bourbon to cause the flames to rise in celebration of the holiday. The following week we'd had a luau on the beach, complete with a pig rotating on a spit and dancers flown in from Hawaii to give hula lessons. Word spread quickly that besides the placid lake and thick woods, Moonshadows was one of the main draws for tourists. Now the closing act had to be something memorable. However, my mind was elsewhere, and I wasn't sure I was up to the task. One night I called Vincent to tell him as much. I forgot it was almost one in the morning and woke him out of a stupor.

"What's wrong, hon?" he mumbled.

"I don't want this to end."

"If you recall, if Frank had his way, it wouldn't."

"It wouldn't have been like this," I said.

"I know, but don't worry; next summer will be here before you know it, and you'll be back."

"Seems like eons away."

"Vicky," he said.

"Yes?"

"What's the finale going to be?"

I sighed. "Haven't a clue."

"You'll come up with something. I know you."

"Any ideas?" I said.

"Not at this hour."

"I want it to be something really special."

There was silence on the other end. Then: "I'm sure it will be. Either way, I'll be there."

There was only a week to go before closing. I'd yet to come up with anything original for a send off, and I hadn't called Chef Dupuis to ask for my job back.

But none of that mattered at the moment.

I sat at one of the tables in the restaurant, surrounded by silence. It was almost two in the morning. The patrons were across the lake playing cards, watching their portable televisions, or sleeping soundly. The exhausted staff had long gone.

I took the envelope out of my pocket. It had arrived earlier in the day's mail at home, but I could not leave it there, fearing it would somehow disappear. It had been a weight on me all day. The envelope held a slim newspaper clipping. No letter, no note inside, and no return address on the envelope, except for the telling postmark from Syracuse. I'd written Brenda some time ago, asking for a reunion, and I had opened the envelope expecting her reply. Instead, I had found a clipping from the *Syracuse News*. At first, I didn't understand why she would send me a clipping of ads for a sale at a furniture store, and then I flipped the paper over and saw a sidebar with the heading "Goings On About Town." There was going to be an auction for the Chesterton Farm, which was calling it quits. Then the town library was hosting a reading with local author Steven Davis, who had published his novel *Weeping Willow*. Also, the Syracuse Field Day was to take place that Saturday, rain or shine. There would be rides for the kids, a variety of foods, and a special performance by singer Grace.

Grace?

Directly below the minuscule photo of author Steven Davis was an equally minuscule one of Grace. There was no mistaking the woman I was looking at was my mother. It wasn't exactly the same face as the one in the three-by-five Polaroid, but it was without a doubt Grace Finley. And she'd be performing at Syracuse Field Day on Saturday night, scheduled to go onstage at seven o'clock. Brenda had been able to do what People Finders had not.

Saturday was always one of Moonshadows busiest days, but I gave Chef Bresette a couple days' notice that he was going to have to be in charge, since I had someplace important to go.

"Impossible!" he'd said. "You cannot run off on a whim."

"I can and I am. You'll just have to stay sober and do your job."

"You're an impertinent little thing, aren't you?" he said. "I don't care if Mr. Scoleri finds you sumptuous; I will not allow you to abandon me on our busiest night."

"You don't have a choice," I said. As far as I was concerned, I didn't either.

"Well, then, I'm taking tonight off," he said, stumbling into the back, as though his disappearance was something new.

I looked over at assistants Gerry and Paulie and said, "Remind me to look up impertinent."

Early Saturday morning, I tossed an overnight bag in the car, having little idea what the present day's outcome would be. Just as I was about to leave, I jumped back out of the car, ran into the house, and went to my closet. After digging around, I grabbed the box with my unsent letters and ran back out to the car, putting it on the passenger seat. I didn't tell my father about the clipping, and as I passed his house, I wondered what my curious departure would stir in him.

During the five-hour ride, I kept the radio off, enacting one scenario after the next. At a quarter to twelve, I walked bleary-eyed into a small, dingy diner on the outskirts of Syracuse. The smell of grease filled the room. I passed a couple of tables occupied by truckers, their eyes locked on me, and sat at a booth where the yellow vinyl had been covered with masking tape. A tired-looking waitress approached with a coffee pot in hand and poured me a cup. I ordered a cheese sandwich and asked if she had a telephone book I could borrow.

"See if I can find one," she said.

Moments later, while sipping on coffee, I tried to appear grateful for the outdated phone book, which was yellow with age. After eating my sandwich and finishing my coffee, I paid the bill and found a payphone near the restrooms. I dropped the change in and dialed the operator, asking for Brenda Hannigan. After a moment or two, the operator came up with nothing. Then she said, "I have a Hannigan's Hairdos."

"Hannigan's Hairdos?"

"It's listed under beauty salons."

Could it be? Brenda certainly had moved fast, opening her own salon! I thought it must be a coincidence but scribbled down the address and phone number just the same. After I hung up, I asked the waitress for directions. She was familiar with the street but had never heard of Hannigan's Hairdos.

"I understand there's a field day today," I said, handing the phone book back to the waitress.

"Happens every year this time," she said. "Lots of folks prefer it over the state fair. Not as expensive, for one thing. That why you're here?"

I nodded. "I'm looking forward to hearing Grace sing." For some reason, my heart did double time and my face grew warm.

"Never heard of her," she said, returning to the counter to get the coffee pot. "Have a good time," she shouted, refilling cups as I walked out.

Fifteen minutes later, I was sitting in the Thunderbird in front of a small, run-down building with a sign swinging on a post letting me know I was at the right place. It didn't guarantee it was Brenda's place, though. When we used to talk about our dreams, Brenda imagined owning a salon that rose high above city streets, the expansive windows looking out over the St. Lawrence River. And there'd always be a line of customers trying desperately to get an appointment.

I climbed out and walked up a cracked cement walkway. Someone had started to paint the house's shingles a dark brown but had stopped about midway. A sign on the front door invited walk-ins, and a bell jingled when I opened it. There was no foyer, no waiting area with a receptionist. Instead, I'd walked directly into a tiny salon to find Brenda snipping away at some woman's nest of curls. The plank floor creaked beneath my feet, and the scissors came to a standstill. Brenda stopped and stared at me. The woman, making goo-goo sounds at a baby in its infant seat next to her, barely glanced in my direction.

"Hi," I said, with as much enthusiasm as I could manage.

Brenda stiffened, and I could see the rise and fall of her chest.

"Say something," I said.

She cleared her throat, straightened her back, and said, "I can't take any walk-ins today. I'm booked."

"Oh," I said, playing the impromptu game, "that's too bad. I was hoping for a new look." I brushed my hair from my shoulder.

She placed the scissors on the counter, went to the desk jammed in the corner of the room, and flipped the pages of an appointment book. Her long, frizzy red hair was now short, and it looked as though she had used an entire bottle of gel to flatten it.

"Well," she said, still flipping the pages, all of which looked empty from my vantage point, "Guess I could squeeze you in once I'm done with Mrs. O'Connell here."

Looking over at me, Mrs. O'Connell said, "You're cutting that beautiful long blond hair?"

I took a seat near the baby. "Probably just a trim."

"So much for the new look," Brenda said, picking up the scissors and snipping more curls.

From the mirror, Mrs. O'Connell glanced at Brenda then looked at me. For a few minutes, the only sounds were the hasty clipping of scissors and the gurgling of a contented baby. Garbed in blue, it was a safe bet the baby was a boy. To fill up the uncomfortable silence in the room, I told his mother how cute he was.

Mrs. O'Connell smiled. "He sure is."

"What's his name?"

The woman hesitated then said, "Josh. Wait, no. Jere...Brenda, you gonna let me struggle here?"

Brenda's face was bright red. "Jason," she said.

"He's not yours?" I said to Mrs. O'Connell. A silly question to be sure, but the truth was having a difficult time sinking in.

"Heaven's no." She laughed. "My baby's in high school. This little one belongs to Brenda."

Brenda wouldn't look at me, and I didn't say a word. I couldn't, really, and while she blow-dried Mrs. O'Connell's hair, I surveyed the surroundings. Posters of women and men with perfectly coifed hair covered the canary-yellow walls. There was only one station, Brenda's. The small space could hardly be considered a salon. Still, I saw accomplishment. She'd had a baby, and during that time she had been able to get not only her license but her own shop.

After Mrs. O'Connell paid and left, Brenda wordlessly swept the curls into a dustpan, tossed them into a garbage can, and patted the chair for me to come over.

"Brenda, you don't have to—"

"What, you chickening out?"

I edged past the baby, who was now sleeping, and took the chair. "Why didn't you tell me?"

"So, what do you want?"

"To see you," I said. "To thank you—"

She tossed the strands of my hair. "I meant with these golden locks."

I shrugged. "It's up to you."

She raised her eyebrows and took a spray bottle, squirting my hair until it was soaked, the water dripping all over my blouse. Then she repeatedly raced a comb from my scalp to the ends. I saw her look of determination reflected in the mirror.

"He's the best thing that's happened to me," she sputtered. "I don't ever want him to think he was a mistake."

"Does Frank know?"

She twirled the chair around so that my back was facing the mirror. "Who says he's the father?"

Then the scissors began to click at a rapid rate, moving longer and faster than I liked. When it was clear she wasn't going to initiate any more conversation, I said, "You've done well, Bren."

The scissors came to a stop. "Maybe you didn't notice, but this isn't some state-of-the-art salon in Montreal, and I don't have a line of people waiting for me." The clicking began again.

"So," I said, "how's Jane?"

She sucked up some air then said, "You really have no idea what I've been through, have you? While you're off cooking in that fancy restaurant and dating Vincent Scoleri, I'm struggling week to week to get by. You even get to move back to 'Busco without any shame."

Finally, the scissors came to a stop, and Brenda picked up the blow dryer, blasting my head with intense heat. She then turned the chair back to face the mirror. I gasped, reaching for hair that was no longer there. Long, blond strands that moments ago had touched my shoulders was now as short as a schoolboy's and swept back in the same schoolboy style.

But it was Brenda who was crying, sputtering apologies. "I'm sorry. I shouldn't have done that."

I stared at my reflection.

"You were always just so perfect. It made me so mad."

When I could finally say something, I said, "It's...it's different."

"I don't blame you if you never want to talk to me again." She took out a tissue from her pocket and blew her nose. "I've just been so angry all these months."

"Frank *is* the father, isn't he?" When she didn't deny it, I said, "He needs to help out, Bren. He's got to pay child support."

"I ended up getting what I wanted from him."

"So, he does know." I thought of the cavalier way he'd spoken about Brenda in front of Camille. I wished I'd known then what I knew now.

"He knows," she said. "He knew right away, but said he wasn't going to do anything about it."

"And you let him get away with that?"

"Don't worry," she said. "He's paid."

Yes, she'd accomplished quite a lot in such a short time, but with Scoleri money she could easily be in a high-rise overlooking the St. Lawrence River. I tried to tell her as much, but she cut me off and said, "Damn, you still look beautiful."

It was odd, but I now had little trouble looking in the mirror. Eventually it dawned on me why: No longer was it *her* reflection gazing back at me. I studied the image—me—hardly recognizing the woman looking back.

Brenda wiped the tears from her face and lunged at me, hugging me. "I missed you so much. I wanted to tell you about Jason, about my salon." She shrugged. "To apologize for how wicked I was to you that day."

I hugged her back. "How did you do all this with a baby?"

"Wasn't easy. No place would hire me because I couldn't do the hours they wanted," she said. "I didn't have a babysitter, so I gathered up all my resources and rented this place out. We live in the back."

Just then, Jason began to cry. Brenda picked him up, sat down, and lifted her shirt. He began to suck at an easy-going pace then drifted back to sleep. I watched in disbelief. Brenda was a mother? As the thought hit me, I remembered why I'd sought her out.

"I got the clipping," I said.

She glanced up at me. "Hmm?"

"The clipping. From the paper."

She shook her head. "Sorry, I don't know what you're talking about."

I pulled the paper from my purse and showed it to her, pointing to my mother. She gasped. "Oh my gosh. It's her."

"You didn't send this to me?"

"I don't have time to read the paper, Vicky. It wasn't me."

I stared at it, at the postmark. I looked up at Brenda. "You think… maybe…she sent it to me? Her way of trying to get in touch?"

"It's possible. You going to go see her?"

I recalled all the times Brenda and I had played out one scene after the next, how my mother would come back into my life. This had not been one of the possibilities. I reached over and grasped Jason's tiny finger. "Yeah," I said.

"Where you staying tonight?"

I shrugged. I was actually hoping to spend the night with my mother, the two of us talking until early morning, getting acquainted. I didn't want to say it aloud, though.

"Well, I'm going to die waiting to hear how everything goes. Why don't you come back here? I have a couch you're welcomed to."

"I'll see," I said.

"I'd even go with you, but I don't have anyone to watch him." She looked down at Jason. "Jane is about ready to pop."

"Again?"

"Yeah, it's that Hannigan blood." She rolled her eyes.

"I'll be fine," I said.

"I know, but I'd like to be there rootin' you on when you tell her off."

Tell her off?

We talked away the afternoon, and I noticed not another soul came in for a haircut and that the phone rang only twice. As early evening approached, Brenda gave me directions to the field day, and I promised to stay in touch after heading back to 'Busco. I shook with nervous anticipation as I walked to the car.

With the shoebox in my hand, I arrived at the field day a good hour before Grace was scheduled to appear onstage. The grounds were crowded, the aroma of popcorn and cotton candy commingling with grease and sweat. A Ferris wheel circled high in the sky, and another ride, named THE CLAW, jutted in and out at a whipping pace, inspiring non-stop screaming. The ticket vendor had told me the stage was across the grounds, so I headed in that direction, my stomach churning. When I reached the seating area, not a soul was there. The concert was to begin in about twenty minutes. A stagehand was setting up a small amp and microphone, and it didn't appear there would be much else. He tested the mike by inviting passersby to come on over.

"Show's gonna start in a few minutes, folks!"

I took one of the chairs in the back row, resting the shoebox on my lap, and waited. Eventually, a group of people came over carrying cups of what I supposed was beer. They slumped into the first row, nudging each other, laughing loudly and cursing each other out. If they saw me, they didn't let on. I began to doubt that the Grace who was about to perform in front of empty seats at a field day was the same Grace who'd been willing to walk out on her family almost twenty years earlier. But I wouldn't have to wonder much longer. A man with a large beer gut walked on stage, tipping his cowboy hat to the few of us in the audience. He approached the microphone and invited people to come on over.

"Just like Cher," he said, "she goes by one name only. She's toured the world and has agreed to perform for us tonight."

The people in the front row, still roughhousing with each other, were oblivious that the show was about to begin.

"Ladies and gentlemen, please give a warm welcome for Grace!"

I leaned in, searching the recesses waiting for her to enter, part of me doubting that she would. I imagined him repeating her name again, looking back, and discovering that she wouldn't be there. Then, a woman appeared in the stage, a guitar slung around her bosom. She adjusted her mike and said something about it being good to be in Syracuse before breaking into song:

"*Busted flat in Baton Rouge...*"

A few stragglers came over and sat down.

"*...waitin' for a train...*"

I studied her, in awe at how she was able to transcend that she was performing at some pathetic field day, and not somewhere more grand. She was still beautiful, unless I looked with the eyes of a stranger and not of a longing daughter. Then, she looked a bit harder around the edges, something the dated Polaroid picture did not reveal, something that possibly happens after you've walked out on your family.

She ended her song and there was a light smattering of applause. Her focus shifted to where I was standing. I didn't remember having gravitated to the front of the stage. But there I was.

"Hello," she said.

I turned to see who she was speaking to. My throat was dry and my heart pounded.

"Yeah, I'm talking to you."

I couldn't speak.

She looked out at the few who'd gathered and said, "Looks like I got a fan." A couple of chuckles came from the audience.

"You got a request?" She tuned her guitar.

I shook my head then confirmed it with a very weak "no." A little louder, I finally blurted, "I got the clipping."

"*I got the clipping?*" Never heard of that one.

"From the *Syracuse News*. Didn't you send me the clipping?"

She studied me, and I believed recognition was beginning to set in. "Can't say I know what you're talking about, but I have to get back to performing or I'll lose these folks." She began to strum her guitar.

"I'm Vicky," I said, my voice shaky.

The tiniest wave of shock crossed her face. She looked over her shoulder toward backstage and said, "How do you do?" She strummed louder and said into the microphone, "This next number—"

"I'm your daughter!" I shouted.

She stopped strumming and said, "Back in a few" before running offstage.

The cowboy seemed confused, first running up to the mike to tell the few people to stay, some of whom were booing, then dashing offstage calling out to Grace to come on back. I was uncertain what to make of her rush to get away from me, but I'd waited too long and come too far just to turn around and head back to my car. I walked around to the back of the stage, where a trailer was parked. I could hear shouting coming from inside. I went up to it and knocked on the thin metal door. The shouting stopped, but no one answered. I knocked again. Eventually, the door opened, and Grace was standing there, a cigarette in her hand. The cowboy was standing directly behind her.

"Come in," she said, her tone resigned.

I stepped into the small, dingy space, which reeked of cigarettes and fried foods. She introduced me to the cowboy, whose name was Billy. Billy didn't appear to have any intention of leaving, so I made the suggestion.

He glanced at Grace, and after a moment of hesitation she said she'd be fine.

"Well, she's only got a minute," he said to me. "She's got to get back onstage." He then brushed past me, going out the door.

Grace shoved some magazines off a metal chair and motioned for me to sit. I did, placing the box on the table, not knowing what to say. Each question I wanted to ask knocked another away while I kept hoping she would begin.

"Care for one?" she said, pointing to her cigarette.

I shook my head.

"Good. Glad you never picked up the dirty habit." She inhaled. As smoke billowed out, she said, "Always pictured you with long hair."

I brought my hand to my head. Her hair hadn't changed much from how it looked in the photograph. I reached into my purse, pulled out a yellow envelope, and slipped out the Polaroid, handing it to her.

"Would you know where this was taken?" I said.

She grasped it by the edges, the crease down the middle visible. She studied it for a moment then handed it back. "Haven't a clue. Not even sure who took it."

"There more in that box?" she said.

I shook my head. "It was the only one Kevin was able to save. Grandma threw out the rest."

"Not surprised. She was a tough old bird," Grace said.

"You seem so happy here," I said, pointing to the photograph.

"Certainly looks that way, doesn't it?" she said. "I couldn't have been more than sixteen at the time."

She began picking up the clothes that were piled on the floor and tossing them on the bed. "How'd you find me?" she said.

"The clipping. You sent it, right?"

"I never sent you any clipping." She went to the table and crushed the stub in an overfilled ashtray.

It occurred to me then that I was nothing more than an intruder. I wanted to get up and run away. Instead, I said, "I've been wondering about you." I felt like I was twelve again.

She nodded, then coughed.

I thought my throat might close up. I wanted to lunge at her, but I wasn't sure if it would be to give her the hug I'd dreamt about for years or to punch her over and over again. "Have you, you know, ever wondered about me?"

She cast her eyes downward. After a long pause, she said, "Every day. You *and* Kevin." She seemed to be mellowing, letting her guard down. "How is he?"

I didn't like hearing myself say the words. Because she was making me say them now, I felt a geyser of anger rising in me. "Kev...Kevin died."

Her hand went to her mouth, her eyes filling with tears. She turned her back and began emptying a dish rack, putting dishes in a cabinet. A moment or so passed before she rasped, "He was always such a good little boy."

"He was an incredible brother." It took all my strength not to cry. "He tried to protect you."

She picked up a pack of cigarettes from the table, tamped one out, and lit it. "Protect me?"

I nodded. "He tried to make me believe you loved me."

She leaned against the counter, letting the smoke puff all around her. "I didn't want that kind of life for him." Her hand was trembling.

"What kind?"

She looked away. "Farming. Night and day. It's such a rough life, and he was such a gentle little boy."

"He loved it. He gave up everything to try and make it work."

"Your father and grandfather tried, too. It was a cycle I wanted no part of."

"Maybe if you had stayed," I said, "things would have been different."

She seemed to mull this over and then said, "I was going to come back. I had every intention of coming back, after I made it in this business." She looked at her shabby surroundings, and I didn't need to guess what she was thinking. She then looked at me as if studying me for the first time. "Look at you," she said. "You grew up to be so beautiful. You have your father's eyes."

No one had ever told me I had anything of my father's.

"That's a compliment, by the way," she said. "Your father was a very handsome man. He's the one who bought me my very first guitar."

"The same guitar you had when you left?"

"Huh?"

"That's what Kevin remembered. You walking out with a suitcase and guitar. And Dad crying."

Grace rested her chin in the palm of her hand. There was a faraway look in her eyes. "Your father seemed to know I wasn't coming back even before I did."

I thought of Brenda and the dreams she'd had all her life, how she had been able to adjust those dreams for her baby.

There was a quick knock on the door, and without waiting for an invitation to come in, Billy flung it open. "Grace, we're not gonna get paid you don't get back out there."

"Okay," she said.

"Grace—"

"I'll be right out!" she said. Billy shut the door.

"Is he your boyfriend?" I said.

She shrugged. "What about you? You must have a long line of boyfriends. You remind me of me."

"We're nothing alike." The words surprised me, but it was at that moment that I knew they were true.

Grace looked over at her guitar, which was lying on the bed. "Funny, I forgot about that first guitar till now," she said. "This one's a beauty, though, don't you think?"

I didn't know one guitar from the next. Nor did I care to know. I said, "Didn't seem to impress anyone tonight."

She didn't say anything more, and neither did I. When I had imagined our reunion, time and time again, I had fantasized the two of us catching up, me finishing her sentences and her finishing mine. She'd tell me about the places she had traveled to and I'd see a framed photograph of me on her dresser near her bed. Near her heart. But now, I realized there was nothing to catch up on. We were strangers who knew nothing about each other.

She grabbed a scrap of paper and a pen from the mess on the table. "Here's where you can reach me. I'm not always on the road. I really want to stay in touch." She handed me the note. "I'm glad you looked me up. Really."

It was her way of ending both of our misery. I couldn't imagine walking away from the woman I'd been searching for all my life, but that's exactly what I was about to do, standing up and reaching for the door handle.

"Vicky," she said.

I turned, perhaps still hoping for an answer that would make more sense of why she had left and never returned. Perhaps she was trying to come up with one.

She said, "You stopped answering the phone."

"What?"

"Awhile back, I had this real strong need to hear your voice, hear who you'd become. I'd call and…and…" Her voice began to strain. "…and you'd answer, and I wanted to say something, ask if maybe we could meet. But I wasn't even sure what you'd been told about me. And then you stopped answering. So I just stopped calling."

I felt a tear escape. I brushed it away quickly. So, the breathing I'd heard on the other end of the line hadn't been Brad's at all.

She took a step closer and leaned in, as if to give me a kiss on the cheek, but I backed away. A mother's kiss, a longing I'd yearned for, for as long as I could recall, I was now refusing. "Please don't," I said.

She nodded as if understanding and swiped at a tear rolling down her face. I started out the door, but then stopped and turned to her. "The guitar was nothing more than an excuse."

"What?"

"You didn't want to be a mother, but you couldn't just walk out without some sort of justification." I made sure she saw me looking at the filth she was living in, at the unmade bed, the dirty dishes stacked in the sink. "I'm glad you left," I said. "It's made me who I am today." My bottom lip began to quiver. "Kevin made me who I am today." I then turned and walked out, leaving behind not only the note with her phone number but the Polaroid and shoebox, as well.

I kept walking until I found my car. I was fine until Brenda opened her door and saw me standing there. That's when I broke down.

Later, sharing a bottle of beer and the intermittent breeze of her fan as it oscillated, we lay sprawled on the couch in our T-shirts and shorts, Jason asleep between us. I didn't think I had any tears left.

"Maybe Jane should've minded her own business," Brenda said. As it turned out, when Brenda had called Jane to tell her I'd been by, Jane had revealed she was the one who had sent me the clipping. She hadn't told Brenda earlier, because she was sure Brenda would have been furious.

Lifting a tousle of the baby's soft, down-like hair, Brenda said, "I can't imagine ever leaving him. I just wouldn't be able to do it."

"But it can't be easy," I said. "Doing this by yourself."

"It's not, but we're getting by."

Mothers had to reliable, but so did fathers. I said, "Frank has a responsibility to him."

She rested her hand on mine, to silence me. "Vicky," she said, "kiss it goodbye. Trust me, it worked out for everybody."

That's when it finally dawned on me what she was saying. I stared at her, mentally putting the pieces together.

"Oh, don't look at me that way," she said. "I didn't want anything more to happen to Benny's Lake, either." She placed the empty bottle on the floor. "We're not rich, but Jason's taken care of, and I got my own salon—even if it's not much. Now Frank can't keep threatening to knock any more trees down, and his wife will never find out what an asshole she's married to."

"Oh, I think she knows," I said.

"What about you and Vincent? When you going to tie the knot?"

"I'm not the marrying type," I said.

"Oh, I think you are. You know you're not the Grace type." She got up, scooping Jason from the couch. "Well, I'm beat. I'll see you in the morning."

Later, I lay on the couch, exhausted but unable to sleep. The room was stuffy, and I couldn't stop running the day's events over in my mind. I wasn't sure if I'd broken into new territory or simply buried the past. I did feel that if I wanted to find Grace again, it would be a whole lot easier. I just wasn't sure I would want to. However, there was someone I had an inexplicable need to see just then.

I tossed the sheet off myself, slipped back into my shorts and sandals, wrote a hasty note to Brenda telling her I'd call, and then left to go back home.

CHAPTER 27

I'd pulled into my driveway at about five o'clock Sunday morning. My plan was to sit in my kitchen and wait until I saw Dad moving about his before I would visit him, but he was already up. From across the field, he shouted my name as I climbed out of the Thunderbird.

"Where the hell you been?" he said, marching toward me, Conroy gamboling at his side. As he drew closer, I could see that his eyes were red and his face pale. "I was up all night," he said, "wondering if you were okay."

He gave me the strangest look as he reached me. "What?" I said.

"What the hell happened to your hair?"

Again, I found myself reaching up and feeling the short cut. "Long story."

"I've been sick worried about you. Called all over. The restaurant said you took the day off."

"I did," I said.

"I even called your fella. He didn't know where you could be."

"You called Vincent?"

Sheepishly, Dad said, "Yeah. You'd better call him, let him know you're okay. He's pretty frantic."

"I need coffee," I said. "Wanna cup?"

"No more for me," he said, following me into the house. Conroy took his place beneath the table.

While the coffee was brewing, I called Vincent. I told him I was okay and that I'd explain where I'd been later. Afterwards, I took my cup and sat next to Dad at the table.

"Dad," I said, "I found her."

He dropped his sights to his folded hands, hands that just then reminded me of Grandpa's.

"She was singing at some field day in Syracuse."

He nodded. "Good. Good for her." He stopped and had a distant look in his eyes. "She had a pretty voice."

"She ever sing for you, Dad?"

"When we were younger, when she thought she'd married the state champion wrestler and not some poor farmer."

I placed my hand over his. "I'm sorry it didn't work out the way you wanted it to."

"I know it's been hard for you, my baby girl."

A memory came to me, one that had been in the recesses of my mind for years. I recalled it now as if it had happened just yesterday. There I am, tiny, unable to form sentences, cradled in my father's strong arms. He is walking me from room to room, and in a quivering singsong voice, he tells me I'm his baby girl.

It dawned on me then that the reason my father would never look at me was that I had refused to let him do so. I was too busy blaming him for my mother leaving.

"Dad, I don't want to leave here, to leave you."

"I'll be fine," he said, but I didn't believe him.

I nudged him. "Who's going to remind you to take your pills?"

He expelled a loud sigh. "Your grandpa," he said, leaning forward, "doesn't know everything." He shoved his hand into his shirt pocket and set the bottle on the table. "Vicky, 'bout time you realize that those pills are nothin' more 'en Tic Tacs."

"What?"

"Pops was so sure they were what kept me from doing anything stupid that I just kept filling the bottle up with Tic Tacs."

I started to laugh. Then I laughed harder. Dad joined in, and we laughed for a while until exhaustion won out.

"Think it's time we call it a night, eh?"

I smiled, agreeing. Dad got up and Conroy followed him.

"You know," Dad said, stopping at the door, "even with that haircut, you're one beautiful woman."

Chef Bresette greeted me with thunderous, if not slurred, complaints. "You're late and irresponsible." Then, after actually looking at me, he said, "You take off just to get a new hairdo?"

I dashed into the kitchen and slipped on my apron. I had slept longer than I'd intended to, but didn't regret it. It was the first sleep I'd had in years where I didn't wonder where she was before drifting off. I said, "About time *you* did something around here, anyway." I checked the menu for what we'd be preparing that night and began instructing the staff, who'd been waiting for me. The fresh kill from a farm in Vermont had just arrived, and free-range chickens were the special of the evening.

"Mr. Scoleri called," Chef Bresette said. "He wants to know what we have planned for closing night."

I opened the refrigerator door, not really knowing why. "What did you tell him?"

"The truth. He wants you to call him."

I slammed the refrigerator door and shouted, "Does anyone here have any ideas?" Everyone shook their heads and continued chopping and stirring.

I sighed and threw myself into preparing for the dinner guests, taking on more kitchen duties than necessary. Chef Bresette once again disappeared. While I sautéed, garnished, and blended, I wracked my mind, attempting to think of a theme that would eclipse all past themes. But I came up empty. Worse, the guests were becoming more and more curious, wondering why the fast-approaching evening wasn't on the board of activities posted at the main office. The longer I waited, the bigger the night would have to be to fulfill their anticipation.

Around nine o'clock, Ben, one of the staff, told me that Vincent was on the phone. "He wants to speak to you."

"Tell him I'll call later. I'm very busy."

Ben gave me a curious look, since the job I was so involved with was watching green beans steam. He said, "I can watch those, if you want—"

"It's okay. Just tell him I'll call him later."

By the end of the evening, I went home not having returned Vincent's call. I poured myself a glass of iced tea and went outside, where I pulled out a lawn chair and sat in front of the little house beneath the full moon. It appeared larger that night, like a harvest moon. Across the field, I was able to make out the shadows of the horses grazing in the fenced-in area near the barn.

"Can't sleep?"

I jumped, startled by my father.

"Sorry. Didn't mean to scare you. Can I join you?"

"Sure," I said. "I'll get you some iced tea." I started to get up, but he stopped me.

"I'm good." He dragged one of the lawn chairs leaning against the house next to me and sat down.

"You look like you have the weight of the world on your shoulders."

I sighed, combating tears. "Just can't seem to come up with anything for closing night."

"Maybe it's because you don't want it to be closing night," he said.

He was right, but that still didn't mean I could avoid it. The campers, staff, and Vincent were depending on me.

"What are you going to do, Dad? I mean, I know the horses keep you busy, but what will you do the rest of the time?"

He leaned back. "Well, I've been thinking about cranking this place up a bit. You know, Kevin was starting to make a difference. He didn't get a chance to make a profit, but he was holding his own."

I thought of the free-range chickens Moonshadows had brought in from the farm in Vermont. Some nights we had fresh beef; other times, lamb. Something about what my father said stirred a notion in me, one that began to grow into an overwhelming thought. My mind raced with thoughts that closing night could be more than a farewell to the season, but a campaign to keep Moonshadows open year round.

I jumped from my chair. "I have to go."

"Go? Where?"

Where? "To make a list. I began walking in circles, the wheels turning. "Oh my God, this...yes, this could work." I leaned over, kissed Dad on the forehead, and started to run into the house, but then stopped. "Dad, are you free Friday night?"

"Sure. Why?"

"I'll need your help."

"You got it."

I ran inside and found a notepad and pen, and began to make notes, menu plans, and a to-do list. It was late, but I called Vincent to tell him that closing night was going to be no less than amazing.

Groggily, he said, "Chef B. thought otherwise."

"Chef B. is a drunk."

"Yeah, that's pretty much what I thought. So, you going to tell me what you've planned?"

"No. You'd just better be here."
"Wouldn't miss it, babe. But I should at least have a hint."
"Just be here."

The next few days were filled with nervous energy. My message posted at the main office was cryptic, telling the guests that they were forbidden to boat over to Moonshadows; instead, they would be transported in from the main entrance. I incorporated not only the staff's help, but Dad's and many of the townspeople's. I barely slept, and when I tried, I'd lie in bed thinking about how I could make sure my plan was a success. Failure was not an option, because leaving 'Busco was not an option.

While I was in the midst of planning, ordering fresh kill from the Vermont farm and making sure each person knew what his or her responsibility would be on the big night, Chef Dupuis called and asked when was I planning to let him know when I'd be coming back.

"If I have my way," I said, "I won't be."
"Who hired you? You're going with that *ivre bâtard*, aren't you?"
I said, "Give me more credit than that."
"Then where? Where are you going?"
"If things work out the way I plan, nowhere."

Finally, Friday night came, and I was both exhausted and exhilarated. During the week, I had thought I would never have enough time to pull off what I intended; yet, at the same time, I'd thought the night would never come. Now that it had, I didn't have time to be nervous. Low-braised lamb was rotating on the spit, while seasoned brook trout and perch were on the grill. Fresh corn on the cob and buttered baby carrots were ready to be served. Dad and Mr. Scott were conveying the guests in on horse-drawn wagons. Earlier, hay had been strewn along the way, and bales were scattered for seating. A camper or two tried to break the rules by boating over, but Jonathan Scott, who was waiting for them at the dock, sent them back, insisting they experience the night the way it was meant to be.

The guests arrived all aglow, most never having taken a hayride before. They gasped at what was called a "harvester's delight." I'd invited the locals to participate, ignoring the "members-only" clause. Mr. Robare brought his guitar, and the townspeople their stories of the days when the lake belonged to Benny.

Vincent kept shaking his head and saying he didn't know how I had managed to pull it off.

"Easy," I said, "I had help from my family and friends. People who come to Lake in the Woods are being cheated out of a unique experience if they never get to see what makes it special."

He said, "What do you mean?"

"Go get to know them."

I let the night take over. When I could, I strolled among the guests, making certain all was well.

"Yup," Mr. Hannigan was saying to a small gathering, "Old Man LeMieux refused to use a tractor for the longest time. His horses were what he'd depended on."

Mrs. Scott, who seemed to have forgotten what I'd done to her brother, smiled at me as I walked by. "It was a difficult time for him," she said to the Ducharmes, nodding toward Mr. Hannigan. "His sawmill was struck by lightning and burnt to the ground. Course, no insurance company would cover it, but they managed to rebuild somehow."

Mr. Miller had heard about the night we were planning and traveled the sixty miles from his new home to attend. He was regaling a group that surrounded him. "He was something special," he was saying. "Nobody loved this place more 'en he did. Had a heart of gold." He spotted me and said, "This is his sister. She's pretty special, too."

Someone from the group said, "One hellava cook, that's for sure." There was a smattering of applause.

I smiled and distanced myself from everyone. I gazed out across the lake to the other side, to the Great White Pine cutting into the skyline, standing tall above the other trees. I was home. Brenda, no doubt, didn't feel the same way. I hadn't been able to convince her to join us for the night. But that was okay. Some people are able to pick themselves up and set roots wherever they land. I discovered I could not.

Dad came up next to me and slung an arm across my shoulder. "So, is he getting it?"

I looked over at Vincent, who appeared to be enjoying the evening. "I doubt it," I said. "But he will."

Mr. Robare began to lead everyone in song, drawing Dad toward the music.

I went over to Vincent, slipping my hand in his.

"Well, you did it," he said. "This is just incredible." He ran his free hand through my short hair, something he had done time and time again since he had arrived.

I pulled him away from the singing, away from everyone. He wrapped his arms around me, ready to kiss me. I stepped back.

"Vincent, I don't want this to be closing night."

"I know, babe."

"No, I'm serious. Tonight was a preview of sorts."

"Preview?" he said.

"Use your imagination. Instead of hay lining the path into here, imagine snow. And instead of the hay wagon, imagine an old-fashioned buggy or sleigh."

He gave me a dubious look.

"We don't need to keep the campsite open, but why not the restaurant? It could be a dining experience that would rival any four-star restaurant. People from Montreal will come *here* to eat."

He nodded, deep in thought. "We could even cater affairs," he said, scratching his head. "Don't know why I didn't think of this."

"And Dad said he'd raise the livestock. We wouldn't need to get it from Vermont."

Vincent nodded, lost in thought again.

"We'd invite people to go back in time. Forget tennis courts and gyms. We could even have day trips, where people could come in and see how maple syrup is tapped."

He took a deep breath. "It's a pretty big undertaking. I won't be hiring Bresette again. I'd need a head chef."

I put my face in his, grinning.

"You do know how to cook, but who's going to manage the place? The finances?"

"I'm sure we can find someone, Vincent."

"We'd have to do a major ad campaign, which wouldn't be cheap."

"I'll forfeit my salary," I said.

"Then there's going to be the work of preparing for the summer crowd while keeping things running—"

"Yes, but we could figure all that out." His line of reasoning was daunting, and I saw he was beginning to see the impossibility of it all.

He shrugged. "Guess that will have to be me."

"What?"

"Guess I'd have to move up here to protect my investment."

"You'd move up here?"

"Why is that so unbelievable?" he said. "Your passion is catching. Besides, how else am I going to woo you?"

"Woo?"

"I thought it was an old-fashioned enough word for tonight." He pulled me into him, and while we kissed the entire campsite broke into song.

From this valley they say you are leaving.

We shall miss your bright eyes and sweet smile.

"Hey, I know this song," I said, leading Vincent closer to the gathering.

For you take with you all of the sunshine...

I never did find my mother—well, the idea of the mother I'd yearned for. All the casseroles, roast chickens, baked hams, chocolate cakes, cookies, and other creations I'd made—I'd always placed them on the table imagining her there, sitting across from my father, a twinkle in her eye, approving of what I'd brought to the family table. I had thought she was the missing ingredient, but now I realize that if she had stayed, chances are, Kevin and I would have lost our ability to make the best out of what we had.

Dad caught my eye, his scowl a question for the outcome. Vincent, not I, shot him the thumbs up. He smiled a jubilant smile and continued singing. I looked out over Benny's Lake, distracted by a moving shadow. I stepped away from the crowd and went to the water's edge, and for the briefest of moments, there he was, gliding by in a row boat. His paddle in mid-air, he glanced my way, waved a friendly wave, and then continued on.

I know now that I must do the same.

Printed in the United States
83641LV00008B/154-162/A